An Expected End

AMANDA SUE CREASEY

An Expected End

Amanda Sue Creasey

First Edition

ISBN 978-1-953278-45-6 Hard Back
ISBN 978-1-953278-46-3 Soft Back
ISBN 978-1-953278-47-0 E-Book

This is a work of fiction. The characters are both actual and fictitious. With the exception of verified historical events and persons, all incidents, descriptions, dialogue and opinions expressed are the products of the author's imagination and are not to be construed as real.

Published by

Chesapeake, VA 23322
www.indignorhouse.com

Cover Design: Mike Zaweski

"Amanda has conjured an all-too-believable world where death is no longer a surprise, yet few have the courage to reckon with their fate. *An Expected End* is a heart-piercing meditation on what it means to be mortal, threaded with literary allusion and tender melancholy."

- Melissa Scott Sinclair,
author of *It is not night*

"*An Expected End* asks and answers some of the most important questions of contemporary life and introduces emotional and unforgettable characters. Amanda has crafted a timely, thought-provoking and touching debut novel."

- Lesley St. James,
author of *The Sweet Scent of Death*

"Sorrow is knowledge: they who know the most must mourn the deepest o'er the fatal truth, the Tree of Knowledge is not that of Life."

-- Lord Byron

"… of the tree of the knowledge of good and evil, thou shalt not eat of it: for in the day that thou eatest thereof thou shalt surely die."

-- Genesis 2:17

Prologue

Marshall, 21 December 2034, Age 18, T-minus Unknown

"It's no different than a mother knowing the due date of her baby. Except perhaps more exact." The woman behind the large, white desk at the *Enrollment Office* grinned. She blinked once before glancing down at a small, flat device that rested flush on her desk. "Think of it as your due date in heaven."

Marshall shrugged. "How do I enroll?"

"Age?" she asked, without looking at him.

"Eighteen."

"Birth date and year?"

"December 21, 2016."

"Ah …" She hummed. "You're right on time."

Marshall knew some participants kept countdowns. He hoped he wouldn't be one of them.

The woman tapped on the small device before folding her hands. She sat still, staring at the little screen.

The device chirped.

"You've been assigned to Experimental Group B." She held up the tablet. "Please look right here." She pointed to the screen.

Marshall stared at his reflection and frowned.

"Good," she said, handing him the device. "Now it recognizes your face." She held eye contact and smiled briefly before looking away. "Have a seat and follow the directions."

Marshall sat in a chair and answered the questions. After swiping through the last screen, he stood and walked over to the woman.

She didn't look up.

"I'm done." He handed her the device.

She took it, opened a drawer, and without saying a word, dropped it inside.

Marshall tapped his foot. "Experimental Group B, you said?"

"Yes."

"What does that mean?"

Her eyes remained glued to her computer screen. "You'll get your Date of Departure after you download our app. It's called *DoD Experiment* and … call the hotline number."

Marshall nodded.

"Thank you for your enrollment in the *Experiment*." The woman smiled. "Heaven is waiting."

Marshall walked toward the doors. As they opened, he took a step.

"And Marshall …" the woman yelled, "happy birthday!"

Chapter 1

Marshall, 10 October 2044, Age 27, T-minus 49

Marshall dropped his phone in his pocket and turned to leave but muffled voices in the hallway grabbed his attention. Toby's ears perked. Marshall knew his dog's signal for company. Disappointed, he glanced at the clock and sighed. It was time to leave for dinner and sleep.

Why did these things always happen after hours? He hated the tradition no matter what the time, but maybe he'd hate it less if it didn't happen on *his* time. Marshall had prayed they would forget all about it, hoping he'd get away without one this year. Or maybe they'd just leave the cake in the office cafeteria for everyone to pick at throughout the day. That would be fine with him too. Marshall could definitely tolerate that. But this? This was embarrassing and uncomfortable, and he just wanted to go home.

The door flew open and several of his colleagues bustled in. Two dragged in a hovering cloud of black balloons, and another carried a large, black cake shaped like a tombstone, '*Heaven is Waiting*' scrawled across the top in white icing.

"Happy Deathday!" the man who worked in the next office over said with a huge smile. He placed several plastic goblets on the table.

A short, blonde woman held up a bottle of sparkling juice and laughed.

"To Marshall!" a voice echoed from across the room. "Heaven is waiting!"

Plastic goblets clicked as his colleagues toasted Marshall's crawl toward October 10, 2093.

Marshall tried to smile. It was what people did. He'd been to enough office deathday parties to know that everyone smiled. Inwardly though, he cringed. They weren't exactly celebrating him or his life. They just needed a reason to eat cake and drink sparkling juice and socialize. Here he was, aware of exactly how much time he had left, and he was stuck spending some of it like this, with them.

None of these people liked him that much, and he didn't like any of them. He wanted to. He really did, but he just – didn't. Marshall was merely indifferent. No matter how hard he tried to cultivate an interest in others, he couldn't. Connecting with people had always been a problem. The desire was there, but the ability seemed to elude him. That was why he enrolled in the first place. To feel like he had something in common with others.

Things were easier with his dog, Toby, than they were with humans. Much easier. His relationship with his black German shepherd was simple. Marshall only had to feed and walk and play with him. Toby was easy to please, and Marshall liked simplicity.

And Toby didn't know anything about deathdays.

"So, Marshall ..." – Ken, his supervisor, held up his goblet – "... how will you celebrate? Doing anything special?" He took a sip.

"To celebrate that I know I'm going to die in forty-nine years?" Marshall shrugged and stared into his cup. "I'll visit the grocery store and pick something up for dinner."

Ken scowled. "That's not a celebration."

"That's the point."

"What's the point?"

"Why would I celebrate?"

"Because heaven is waiting, Marshall. *Heaven* is waiting."

Heaven was definitely waiting – in the form of his quiet apartment high above the rapids of the James River, the roar from the water just a whisper when he opened his windows on the eleventh floor. Ken was obviously baiting him. The man liked to do that.

"Just a normal day, Ken." Marshall frowned.

Toby leaned against Marshall's leg. It was what Toby always did when Marshall felt anxious. Marshall reached down and rubbed Toby's soft, warm ears. His dog's silky coat felt soothing. Toby reciprocated with a calm, toffee-color stare.

You're right, boy. I can do this. I do this and then we can go home.

"Marshall! Come on. Just another day? Really?" Ken's tone sounded patronizing as he wrapped an arm around Marshall's shoulders. He guided him to a corner of the office.

Marshall stiffened at the touch, and Toby wedged himself between the two men. Marshall shrugged from under Ken's arm and stepped away. "Yeah, it *is* just another day. I get up. I walk Toby. I come to work. I eat food. Sometimes, I visit the grocery store."

Ken tossed up his arms.

Marshall felt relieved to have his space back, at least some of it.

"You're not doing anything to mark this special occasion? Nothing? T-minus forty-nine years as of today? What about him?" He pointed at Toby. "Does he get to celebrate? Here, boy." Ken offered a morsel of cake.

Toby turned away.

"Dogs can't eat chocolate," Marshall said. "Come here, Toby."

"What kind of dog doesn't like table scraps?"

"He's on the clock."

"The workday's over. It's after five."

"And yet we're still at work … anyway, Toby's workday is never over. I don't hop off the spectrum at five."

Ken raised his brows and nudged Marshall with his elbow. "You're a tough boss."

Marshall took a few steps back and replied, "He likes his job."

"Yeah, sure … so do I."

Marshall couldn't tell if Ken's tone was sincere or sarcastic. He decided it was probably sarcastic.

Ken took another sip. "Seriously, no plans to celebrate?"

"I'll write my Annual Deathday Diary Entry, but that's a given." Marshall had planned to read a little after dinner. But he didn't feel the need to share that bit of information. The familiar ridicule was becoming mundane.

Books, Marshall? Books? Why waste your time? Augmented Reality is the new book. That's what Ken always said.

AR wasn't real to Marshall.

"Marshall, writing in your deathday diary *is* a given." Ken huffed. "Last month on my deathday, my wife surprised me with bungee jumping." Ken leaned in a little closer. "Bungee … fucking … jumping! And I'm terrified of heights. Yah know what she said to me? She said, 'Ken, you know when you're gonna die, and it's not today. Why are you so afraid?' And you know what? She was right. I didn't die."

"You didn't go bungee jumping either, Ken."

"Fucking yeah I did, man."

"AR doesn't count."

"It's A ... *R* ... Marshall. A ... *R* ... you know what the R stands for?"

Of course Marshall knew. "What a stupid question, Ken, reality."

Ken slapped him on the back. "That's right! Reality. In reality I went bungee jumping. I could've died ... except I couldn't because it wasn't my deathday."

Marshall didn't want to extend the ridiculous conversation by pointing the absurdity of his boss's reasoning. He didn't want to remind him that his Date of Departure wasn't a sure thing since it didn't account for accidents. Ken knew that. Everyone knew that. But it was an easy fact to ignore. Experiencing an accident of any kind was similar to winning the lottery. It just wasn't going to happen, so it wasn't worth worrying about. Society had essentially eliminated every risk. Accidental deaths were all but impossible. Driverless cars and AR infiltrated every sector of existence, rendering life as a mere dull ride.

Marshall shrugged. "Some fates are worse than death," he replied, taking a bite of cake.

Chapter 2

Penelope, 10 October 2044, Age 25, T-minus Unknown

Penelope Hope stood on the corner of Broad and 21st as the traffic whizzed by. A few strands of her shoulder-length, blonde hair blew across her face with a gentle breeze. The drivers' faces were obscured by either AR devices or sleeping masks. Those with their seats reclined were completely out of view.

She waited, though waiting for the light to change was a waste of time. The traffic would stop if she darted across. A driverless car always detected the presence of a person. Then again, stepping into traffic could result in a hefty fine from the Traffic Control Commission. She had a choice – time or money. People generally chose money.

A few more pedestrians walked up, and when the sensor noted enough of them were waiting, the light changed and the cars slowed to a stop, buzzing like bees trapped in a jar.

An elderly woman stepped off the curb and stumbled. She grabbed Penelope's arm and frowned. "I'm so sorry."

"Oh, no problem." Penelope took the woman's hand, and they walked into the street. Her touch felt frail, the skin papery and cool. The woman glanced up with a grateful, closed-mouth smile. The corners of her eyes crinkled. How much time did this gentle, old soul have left? The things this woman must've seen during her life. Penelope smiled warmly, allowing the woman to step a few paces ahead.

As she watched the woman hobble into the intersection, a familiar but unplaceable sound grabbed Penelope's attention. It was a gas engine. She turned and stared at the speeding car – and not a driverless one either. The red blur filled her vision.

The old woman froze. The driverless vehicles parted like the Red Sea for Moses. Without thinking, Penelope ran and shoved the old woman aside. Air slammed against her face as something hard clipped her legs as her feet flew out from under her. She held her breath. Her face slapped against the curb, but there was no pain, not yet. Instead, the pavement felt warm and solid and rough like sandpaper. She opened her eyes and stared at a man kneeling beside her. Something wet and warm gently nuzzled her arm. Her head throbbed. She reached up to her forehead and felt something sticky. The pain exploded, forcing her to close her eyes.

"I lost control!" a masculine voice stated.

"Ma'am," the kneeling stranger asked, "are you okay?"

Penelope again felt the warm wetness on her arm.

"Toby, stop," the kneeling man said.

"TCC isn't gonna like this!" another voice yelled. "Probably the last time your car sees the road."

Penelope felt almost weightless as the paramedics placed her on the stretcher. With a loud bang, the doors to the ambulance slammed shut.

Penelope woke in a bright room. The fluorescent lights stung her eyes as she explored the white walls and ceiling. Sunlight danced between shadows along the floor. Tubes and cords were stuck in her arms, attached to various machines huddled around her bed like little attendants. With all the white and quiet, were it not for the garish lights and humming machines, she could almost mistake this place for a kind of heaven. A knock replaced her thoughts with an inexplicable sense of dread. She watched as the door inched open. *What if this was heaven? What if she was …?* She held her breath.

"Ah, you're awake," a man wearing a black shirt and white jacket stepped inside. "Penelope Hope?"

Penelope nodded.

"I'm Dr. Zeit. You're in the hospital. But you're okay. Just a little banged up."

"Hospital?" Penelope whispered.

"VCU Medical Center," the doctor replied. "Follow my finger."

Penelope looked right, left, up, and down, happy her eyes obeyed her directives. She shifted her hips, and a sharp pain shot down her leg. This definitely wasn't heaven. There wouldn't be this much pain. She winced. "What's today? How long have I been here?"

"You arrived several hours ago. Just a few cuts and bruises. The gash over your eye took a little extra glue."

She lifted her hand and gently touched the bandage. The shifting shadows on the floor reminded her of dusk when the world prepared for sleep. It struck her that early dawn looked no different. The world woke up much the same way it went to sleep. If it weren't for the forward movement of time, one might not be able to differentiate the start of day from the end. It was all a cycle. Who was to say when it started or ended? Penelope stared at the doctor's shirt, black like the night that separated dusk from dawn. It seemed to jump out from behind the stark, white coat. Even his nametag was white on black. The hands on the clock above the door were black against the white clockface. Black night. White daylight.

"Might be some scarring on your leg, but nothing laser therapy won't correct. You hit your head, but your scans are clean. We called your emergency contact. An Everett … Flach?" the doctor read from his device.

"Yes. My fiancé."

"I need you to answer a few more questions."

Penelope nodded.

"Birthday and age?" the doctor asked.

"January 2nd, 2019. I'm twenty-five."

"Date of last menstrual cycle?"

"September 15-ish?" Penelope couldn't imagine what that had to do with anything.

"Date of Departure and T-minus age?"

Penelope hesitated. "I … I don't know. I'm not enrolled." She waited for his response. "But I guess it's not today." She chuckled and shrugged, trying to make light of things.

What good would knowing have done? No DoD would've predicted a rogue car speeding down Broad Street. What an unusual headline her death would've made: *Unenrolled Woman Dies in Freak Car Accident.* Unenrolled women hardly existed and car accidents hardly happened. It would've been a sensation.

"Addre …" Dr. Zeit looked up. "I'm sorry?"

"I'm not enrolled," she repeated. "I don't have a deathday or T-minus age."

Penelope stared at his black shirt. The longer she studied it, the darker it seemed to grow. The stark difference between the white lab coat and the black shirt sent chills up her spine. And the mere mention of a deathday inside a hospital was disconcerting. There were some within these walls who would die today. Perhaps were dying right now. And they had known – many of them – for years that today would be their deathday. Did knowing help them prepare? Were they ready to die simply because they knew when death would find them? Were they letting the reaper take their hand and lead them into that *good night*?

The doctor's eyes widened and he frowned. "Antique cars don't have accident prevention."

"How would knowing have made a difference?"

The doctor shrugged. "Today was that old woman's deathday." He typed something on his device. "If not the red car, then something else. Perhaps natural causes. An aneurism or heart attack or …" He shrugged.

Penelope glared at him. How could someone who signed up to save lives feel such cold indifference toward death? But that was just how people were these days, including medical professionals. Cavalier attitudes regarding life and death. Today wasn't Penelope's deathday. That was what the doctor was thinking. Then again, the day wasn't over yet, so they couldn't exactly say for sure, could they? She had almost made sure it was her deathday, enrollment or not, and for what?

Someone who was going to die today anyway? Well … we're all gonna die … someday.

The doctor looked up from his device. He set it on the counter and folded his arms. He studied Penelope for what seemed like a very long time. "You know," he finally said, "I've never met anyone who wasn't enrolled." He softened his tone and grinned. "You could have died trying to save that old woman. But you ran out there anyway."

"I guess so." Penelope nodded. "Even if I were enrolled, it wouldn't have changed anything."

Would it? If she'd known how long she was supposed to live, would she have thought twice about risking her life, sacrificing her time? If she'd known she was allotted fifty more years or sixty or seventy, would she have hesitated to give them up for someone else? Would she have traded the time she knew she was entitled to, gambling it against an accident? And if she'd known she had mere months left to live, would she be more or less likely to risk her life? She closed her eyes and shook the question out of her head. These types of dilemmas were exactly why she *didn't* want to enroll. The thought irritated her, for this was the inescapable blight of a society empowered with knowledge. *Empowered? What a joke.*

"Why did you risk your life?"

"I don't know. I didn't think about it." *But would I have?*

It was pure instinct, an unconscious decision to help that old woman. In that moment, Penelope didn't have time to think about her death. Her irresistible impulse had been to prevent suffering, to cheat death. Only now, hours after the split-second decision, she was wondering if that knowledge would have made her reconsider. Would have made her the witness to an old woman's violent death and a driver's manslaughter charge. Today might be the old woman's deathday, but she didn't have to die like that, and her death didn't have to mean a lifetime of guilt for her accidental killer. Maybe she hadn't saved the woman's life, but in a way, she had saved the driver's. He was probably troubled enough about the accident without having killed someone. She was sure he felt guilty about her injuries and the penalties TCC would apply.

And even now, wondering if enrollment might've changed her mind, Penelope felt a sense of victory at having given the woman a little more time, just a little. Maybe minutes. Maybe hours. Maybe she had been on her way to spend her last day with her children or grandchildren. Maybe she was heading to her favorite spot along the river to feel the sunshine on her face and listen to the water sing her to sleep. Maybe she was going to finalize her will. There were a hundred things Penelope could imagine that woman might've wanted to experience or accomplish today – her last day, and Penelope felt like she'd played a part in giving that to her.

Penelope watched as the doctor worked on his tablet. She sighed and wondered why she'd pushed that old lady out of the way. Was it her way of frustrating death, making death wait? The thought of the Grim Reaper tapping his foot and drumming his fingers made her smile.

The old woman would still die today, and no one could do a thing about that. Perhaps death wanted to grab the woman a few hours early. But now, death would have to wait just a little longer. Penelope hoped she had at least helped the woman die on her terms. No unfinished business. To enroll and still fall victim to a fatal accident seemed to be the greatest injustice Penelope could imagine. To allegedly *know* that one was entitled to a set amount of time just to have it cut unexpectedly short. Of course, there were those who would say that was exactly Penelope's situation, given her unenrolled status, and that accidents were so uncommon, most considered them a waste of time. Would her death sneak up on her, catch her unprepared, unaware? Did it have to?

Penelope concentrated on the doctor's dark shirt. Her eyes traced along the white stitching and how they disappeared behind the white coat. Those thin, broken lines reminded her of a slithering snake searching – but for what?

"Really? You didn't think about it at all?"

Penelope's gaze returned to the doctor's eyes. After a pause, she answered, "Some fates are worse than death."

Chapter 3

Marshall's Annual Deathday Diary Entry

Date: October 10, 2044

Entry No. 10

The thing is, your birthday is always your birthday. The day has always been your birthday. You don't think about it. You take it for granted. You have never, ever approached or passed your birthday without knowing it's your birthday. It always has been. The day has had its significance since your arrival on Earth. It has always been special, always stood out.

It's not the same with your deathday. Suddenly, a day that has no particular meaning takes on a whole new significance. My whole life, December 21 has been significant, my birthday. But until ten years ago, October 10 blended in with all the other dates on the calendar. It had no particular significance tied to it. It does now. It has for the last ten years, and it will for the rest of my life, which consists of 17,898 more days, plus a few bonuses for leap years.

What I have noticed today: expiration dates on groceries. Someday, those expiration dates will reach beyond my own. That's a harrowing thought. I wonder when I will see the first one, the first expiration date, I mean, that outlasts me. The first gallon of milk that will outlast me, or the first box of cereal or package of dried pasta. I could encounter a can of beans with more longevity than I have a year and a half out. Unless I'm in a home. Or blind. Maybe by the time a can of beans will outlast me, I won't be healthy enough to do my own shopping. No telling. Maybe grocery stores won't even exist anymore. Aside from the Felix at checkout, I was the only moving thing in the store tonight. To be honest, though, I kind of like it that way. No one trying to talk to me. No one asking if I need help finding anything. Just peace and quiet and groceries.

No one has time for grocery shopping when they know how little time they have left. No one but me, it seems. To them, it's a chore. To me, a small pleasure. I want to spend time hand-selecting the freshest produce, savoring the smell in my kitchen while dinner bakes or boils, cleaning up the dishes after. It's not a chore; it's therapy.

Those were my day's thoughts, more or less. No doubt inspired by a conversation I had with Ken at the office today. Ken wouldn't be such a bad boss if he weren't, well, Ken. Not to mention the deathday cake that my coworkers so enthusiastically presented me with just when I thought I had avoided it. Here are my day's actions:

I awoke at 6:10 and listened to the morning broadcast with Toby while I drank my coffee and Toby ate. While Toby and I walked to work, I considered when I could stop working. It used to be people worked as long as they could, only to retire and die a few years later, never having done what they wanted to do -- whatever that was. Now, enrollment guarantees us all partial benefits at T-minus 20, or full at T-minus 10. We can know how many years we have left after retirement, barring an accident. We all, most of us, have an expected end. My choices: ten years or twenty to do all the things I would rather be doing than work. Read. Cook. Spend more time with Toby and less time with people. Though Toby is not likely to see my retirement. Not likely at all. Impossible, if I'm honest with myself. That's a sad thought. Life without Toby. I don't really want to think about it. It never occurred to me before. "One thing certain in an uncertain world," I guess. Not always a good thing.

I've digressed. I do that. I imagine it would be worse if I didn't know how limited my time was.

So, I awoke at 6:10, ate, fed Toby, and walked to work. At work I managed not to think about the fact that today was my DoD. I tried not to let it affect me; I tried to have a normal day. *But* what's *normal* anyway? Normal got difficult when my coworkers showed up with the cake. Deathday cake. Anyway, it was quite good. The cake, not the party. I could've done without the party and without Ken. Toby got me through it.

After work, I walked home. I helped a young lady today. She was actually hit by a real car, not a driverless one. Things like that are not supposed to happen, but it did. I hope she will be okay. Then, I stopped at the grocery store for a few things (that's when I started thinking about expiration dates), and now I am here. After this, I will eat something for dinner. Something I picked up at the store. I'll cook a recipe from my hardcover copy of *Joy of Cooking*. That's my celebration. I didn't tell Ken. He wouldn't understand. Few would anymore. Toby understands. Or at least he understands that he gets the broccoli stems and carrot ends and broth and whatever else would otherwise go to waste. He understands that.

So, today I thought about expiration dates and retirement, worked, and ate deathday cake. And exactly forty-nine years from now, I will be dead. Or dying. It is 7:12 PM, so depending on what time I die, forty-nine years from now, I could have as many as four hours and forty-eight minutes left. Or I could have died nineteen hours and twelve minutes ago.

One thing -- I know I'm better at simple, mental math. Better than I would have been had I never enrolled. But then again, maybe not. My mother always said I had a special mind for math. And a good memory. I may not understand people. But my brain is a calculator, and my memory is impeccable. "Math and memory," she would say. "Your mind is all math and memory."

Signed: Marshall Milton, Participant No. MM10102093

Chapter 4

Penelope, 14 October 2044, Age 25, T-minus Unknown

"When are you doing it?" Bea asked, sitting on her yellow, living room couch with a glass of water in one hand and a plate of apple slices in the other. Her chestnut brown hair was pulled back in a loose, graceful bun, and she wore an oversized, gray sweatshirt and skin-tight, lilac leggings that showed off the curvy shape of her legs. To Penelope, Bea was petite and beautiful.

"The wedding? I don't know … we haven't set a date. He's only just asked."

"Not the *wedding* … enrollment. Aren't you going to enroll together?"

"Enroll? Enroll in what?" Penelope raised her hands and scrunched her shoulders.

"Listen to you … *enroll in what*. You know perfectly well, what … the *Experiment*." Bea bit into an apple slice and chewed a little too loudly.

"We haven't talked about it. I hadn't even thought of –"

"He didn't enroll without you, did he?" Bea leaned forward, taking another bite of apple.

"No. But I wouldn't care if he did."

Bea tossed a pillow at her friend's head. Penelope ducked, and the pillow landed on top of the coffee table. She picked it up and sat it on the floor.

Bea leaned over, blinked twice, and laughed. "You're reading all this wedding stuff, but you're not concerned about enrollment?"

Penelope shrugged. "No."

Bea huffed and sat back. "You *have* to know. You'll regret it if you don't. It'll be special if you and Everett enroll together. It's not uncommon nowadays. I mean … it's not *weird.* At first, everyone thought it was morbid. But not anymore."

"It is morbid." Penelope frowned.

"It's a *thing* now … enrolling *together.* It's just like taking engagement photos or throwing a bridal shower. You only have one chance to enroll together."

Penelope ignored her friend who sat waiting for a reaction.

Bea took a deep breath. "You could have a DoD reveal party. It would be fun."

Again, Penelope ignored her friend's suggestion. Bea bit into another apple slice and tossed another pillow. Only this time, it hit Penelope in the face. She glanced over and sighed.

Bea laughed. "You like to plan things. Do you know how much *easier* end-of-life stuff is when you plan ahead?"

Penelope returned her attention to the tablet and pulled up her bridal holographs. The room filled with ribbons, lace, gloves, and jewelry.

Bea scooted off the sofa and joined her friend on the floor. "Important things like wills and funerals and burial plots –"

"Belinda!"

"Don't call me Belinda!"

"I'm trying to plan my wedding, not my funeral. You're my maid of honor not a pallbearer. Can we just focus on the wedding? My funeral can wait."

"I'm not so sure it can."

"Belinda Kaaliya!"

"What?" Bea shrugged. "You could die tomorrow, yah know."

"Not likely."

"You don't *know*." Bea held out the plate of apple slices. "Want one?"

"You're right. I don't know. And I like it that way." Penelope pushed the apple slices away.

Bea remained quiet for a few seconds. "I can't imagine not knowing."

Penelope softened. "I know."

Bea's parents had enrolled her before she graduated. Before she really understood. Therefore, Belinda Kaaliya Adams, who preferred to be called Bea, had acquired a second age, T-minus 56, early in life. Penelope resisted the urge to remind her friend that she too once had the option of not knowing. Rule number one of the *Experiment*: Legal guardians may enroll dependents. In such cases, guardians must withhold the dependent's Date of Departure until they reach legal age, at which time they may opt out of learning their DoD.

Bea had made her choice, and Penelope had made hers. Not that anyone respected her choice. The two people she loved most seemed hell-bent on knowing when she was going to die. And she seemed to be the only one who found it disturbing.

Bea shrugged. "I'm just saying. It makes things a lot easier. If you and Everett enroll together, you can buy your plots at the cemetery ahead of time. And the dates can be engraved on the tombstone. You'll see the finished product ... your names, your epitaphs, your birthdays, and … your deathdays. Your lifespans, right there on the stone. That wasn't even possible, what? Twenty … thirty years ago?" Bea counted on her fingers, seeming to recuperate her energy.

Penelope frowned. At what point had living become nothing more than planning for dying? It was as if black was a part of white, the black bleeding overtop, suffocating it. Or as if the sky were a part of the ground. They used to contrast each other, one never depending on the other. Enrollment somehow tied life and death together where life became a tangled mess. If someone spent a lifetime planning for its end, then what was the purpose of beginning at all?

Penelope rubbed her hand along the edge of the yellow cushion and frowned. The contrast between the dark, faux hardwood floor and the bright couch was definitive. There was a clear line between couch and floor. But who could say where living ended and dying began? Was planning your funeral decades in advance living or actively dying? Penelope didn't want to know when there was more life behind her than in front of her. She was afraid. Afraid that the moment she knew she'd crossed the halfway point, she'd feel like she was dying. Or worse, live as if she had already died. She'd stop planning for a future beyond her funeral, knowing there wasn't one. Not for her, anyway.

"Belinda –"

"Stop calling me that!"

Penelope grinned. "Would you be even half as morbid if you hadn't been enrolled?"

Bea stood. She grabbed another pillow from the couch and tossed it in Penelope's direction. "We'll never know, will we?"

An advertisement for enrollment materialized on the holograph.

"One thing certain in an uncertain world," Penelope said aloud, mimicking the ad.

"Exactly," Bea replied, raising her hand. "I've been trying to tell you." She sat and leaned her head on her friend's shoulder. "Doesn't it bother you that for the last twenty-some years, you've crossed each day not knowing if it will be the one engraved on your tombstone?"

"You sound like Thomas Hardy."

"Who?"

"Thomas Hardy. You know, *Tess of the d'Urbervilles*? 'When was it? Why did she not feel the chill of each yearly encounter with such a cold relation?'"

Bea blinked several times. "What are you talking about?"

"We read it in high school."

"Maybe *you* read it in high school. I just pretended to. Anyway, doesn't it bother you?"

The grass always seemed greener. Tess, from the story, wished she could know. Penelope, however, could know and didn't want to. She looked at her friend and frowned. "No, Bea. It doesn't bother me. And even if I did enroll, I could still die from an accident." Penelope touched the bandage above her eye. "Nothing is ever for certain."

Bea rolled her eyes. "Sure you don't want some?" She held up the plate again.

The slices were already turning brown. Penelope stared at the aging fruit. "I'm sure."

"Suit yourself." Bea took a final bite, stood, and walked into the kitchen.

Penelope watched as her friend's form diminished in the shadows. She shivered.

Chapter 5

Bea's Annual Deathday Diary Entry

Date: October 15, 2044

Entry No. 7

So if you're like my friend, Penelope, a normal person like she says, as in not enrolled, you know you'll die, but you don't know when. I just can't imagine that. Just knowing you're gonna die without knowing when, now that's way too abstract. It gives the illusion of having forever. I've heard the phrase "delusions of grandeur." Maybe it's like that, a delusion of eternity. I couldn't wait to turn 18 and find out my deathday. Knowing that date is like having a deadline. Imagine if you didn't have a deadline at work and the project was just due someday. Who would have the motivation to get it done? I like having my DoD. I know exactly how much time I have left to get things done. I have no delusion of eternity. I can't just get around to it someday. My deadline is October 15, 2075. I have no idea what it might be, the thing that will get me. But you certainly don't die of old age at 56.

Anyway, Penelope just got engaged to Everett. I'm going to be her maid of honor. Of course, I've known that since forever, but it's still exciting that it's all official and stuff. I told her she and Everett should enroll together. She told me I was being morbid.

Signed: Belinda Adams, Participant No. BA10152075

Chapter 6

Marshall, 18 October 2044, Age 27, T-minus 49

Marshall glanced out the window. His booth at the Hill Cafè usually offered a bustling view of people walking their dogs or jogging. Maybe a couple meandering down the sidewalk, or a mother pushing a stroller. Tonight, however, the cloudy chill that dampened the city kept most indoors. His only entertainment was cars pulling in and out of parking spots. The booth was situated near the front, and he was facing the door. Absentmindedly, he stirred the ice in his water with his reusable straw and stared blankly out the window. The gravy on his meatloaf had congealed into a gelatinous, brown mound that vibrated slightly with each rotation. The meatloaf reminded him of his mother's. Though hers was better, Marshall wouldn't admit that to himself or anyone else. He was still too angry with her.

He liked this restaurant. It was one of the few places that had real, paper menus and fried chicken. Very few patronized places like this – places that served comfort food. Most had fallen out of fashion after the *Experiment* revealed that people with the highest T-minus ages typically avoided fried foods and high levels of sodium – and pretty much anything else that made food taste good. Since his T-minus age was high, Marshall figured the opposite. He could eat what he wanted. It wouldn't kill him – or maybe it would – but not for a while. Tonight, though, he just wasn't hungry, and neither meatloaf nor fried chicken sounded appetizing. But he had to eat and they knew him here and never looked at him twice – at least not anymore. He always brought Toby with him. Toby would lay down and wait. Marshall glanced at his dog and smiled. Toby looked quite handsome wearing his service vest, maybe even a little official.

"Sir?" A waiter stood at Marshall's side. "Everything taste good?"

Marshall turned his head toward the waiter, but his eyes never left his plate. He frowned. He hadn't touched his food. He picked up his fork and took a bite.

"Yes," Marshall said. "Everything tastes just fine."

It really didn't matter if it tasted fine or not. And it didn't – taste fine – but Marshall couldn't blame the café for that. It might have tasted fine ten minutes ago if Marshall had eaten while it was still hot. Either way, it was food and it would keep him alive until his deathday. Therefore, he was obligated to eat it.

"Fine, sir," the waiter said. "More water?"

Marshall and the waiter looked at the glass sweating on the table. Marshall hadn't taken the first sip.

"Uh, no," Marshall said. "It's still full."

"Right then." The waiter nodded and hesitated just an instant longer, as if expecting Marshall to ask for something.

Marshall looked down at his plate. He shrugged before taking another bite of the lukewarm meatloaf. The bell on the café door dinged, and he glanced up. He stopped chewing as a woman with long, blonde hair, looking more vibrant, more alive, than anyone he'd ever seen, glance around. She stood firm with her shoulders pulled back. Her black jacket slightly covered a yellow blouse that complemented her rosy lips. Together they provided a striking contrast to the golden sheen of her hair.

A small, white bandage above her left eye gave Marshall reason to pause. Was she the same woman who'd been hit by the car the other day? Perhaps so. Various abrasions darkened her left cheek.

As he reached for his water, Marshall's sleeve dragged across his plate, soaking up gravy. He gasped and jerked away his arm. His glass tipped and water ran over the table. Jumping up, he sent gravy splattering across his seat.

"Damn!"

A waiter ran to his side with a dishcloth.

Marshall glanced over at the woman who smiled. Her eyes were beautiful when she smiled. A sudden rush fluttered in his stomach, bursting with a flush of adrenaline. A thrill he'd never experienced. The few times he dared to ride a virtual roller coaster had never been this invigorating.

He grinned. Wanting to laugh, he held it back. She would surely misconstrue, and therefore he made an effort to control himself.

She had made it through the accident without much damage and was more than alright. Now she was even more alluring, the bandage and bruises lending her an air of mystery. She was the most beautiful woman in the world.

Again, the woman slightly glanced his way and smiled.

Marshall sat and nodded as the waiter took his plate. The woman must have a very high T-minus age to be so confident as to eat here.

When he next looked at her, her gray eyes seemed to glance right through him. She was obviously looking for someone, and her focus was not on Marshall. She shrugged and relaxed, and Marshall watched her lips move as she spoke to the host. He couldn't take his eyes off those lips. The host handed the woman a menu and led her to a seat at the bar. She sat on the second chair from the left, and the shadows accentuated the beautiful curve of her high cheekbones.

What if he walked over and introduced himself? Not only would it be impulsive but totally out of character. Born of irresistible compulsion, Marshall couldn't stop the urge that was coursing through his body.

Calm down, Marshall!

Marshall picked up the check and pulled out his phone to pay. He thought of the first time Nick saw Myrtle in F. Scott Fitzgerald's *The Great Gatsby* and understood a line he'd never understood before. He knew now what it felt like to have the nerves of his body smolder, and he felt a sudden sympathy for Myrtle Wilson. Her world was ashen gray before she met Tom who splashed it with a gleam of color she'd never achieve without him. Marshall couldn't condone infidelity – betrayal was betrayal. No gray area. But he accepted the desire, the insatiable pull that whispered to him as it had to Myrtle – "You can't live forever."

He should ask her to join him at his table. Afterall, they were both alone. She clearly couldn't find whoever she was looking for. Maybe she would sit with him. His thoughts fell to *The Love Song of J. Alfred Prufrock.*

And indeed there will be time
To wonder, "Do I dare?" and, "Do I dare?"
Do I dare
Disturb the universe?

This was a first for Marshall. Did he dare disturb his universe and act with such spontaneity?

And should I then presume?
And how should I begin?

Marshall's mother flashed through his thoughts. She was a beautiful woman – at least to him. She was safety and comfort and familiarity. He had trusted her once, in a life that was so very long ago. Since history had a way of repeating itself, this woman would also betray him – lie to him – ruin him.

The waiter thanked Marshall for the generous tip and offered coffee or dessert.

"I would never sleep if I had coffee now but thank you. Just vanilla ice cream, please. Toby? You don't mind do you?"

Toby's ears perked.

Marshall glanced over at the beautiful woman and their eyes locked for just a moment, but it felt like eternity. He could stare into her eyes forever. But the most beautiful woman in the world would never sit with him. Her reasons for partaking in his company would probably be all the wrong ones. People made fun of Marshall and his odd mannerisms. Surely, if this woman sat with him, it would only be as a joke.

I have heard the mermaids singing, each to each.
I do not think that they will sing to me.

This woman had what Marshall called *energy*. An energy for life that he could never possess. People laughed at Marshall, never with him. What a stupid thought. He should just leave her alone and eat his dessert. Toby nudged his foot. Marshall petted his ear and sighed. Better to simply mind his own business, watch the world pass by, and go home.

I am not Prince Hamlet, nor was meant to be;
Am an attendant lord, one that will do
To swell a progress, start a scene or two.

Marshall glanced up and his gaze, as if with a mind of its own, locked onto her mesmerizing eyes. He couldn't move. He couldn't blink. Those glassy grays had a power all their own. It was she who broke the spell when her attention turned to the menu, and she pointed before speaking to the bartender.

Marshall nodded as the waiter placed the scoop in front of him. He licked the spoon, and his eyes kept trying to sneak another peek at the woman at the bar, but he refused the desire.

She doesn't want you looking at her. You've embarrassed her and yourself. She won't talk to you. No one ever does. Just eat your ice cream. Just eat your ice cream …

Marshall shoved a spoonful into his mouth. The urge to look was overwhelming, and he gave in. Again, their eyes locked. She smiled just a little before looking away.

Smiling's a good thing.

Smiling was a good thing unless someone was about to laugh at you. Marshall didn't have the feeling that she was laughing at him. At least, he didn't think so. He wasn't sure.

In a minute there is time
For decisions and revisions
which a minute will reverse.

What if he went over to her and introduced himself? Would she talk to him or laugh? He dropped his spoon and took a deep breath. He would. He would talk to her.

As Marshall stood, a man with dark hair entered the café. Something about him made Marshall pause. The man's features wore the same expression as the woman's – searching. The man scanned the restaurant, and his brown eyes brightened. Obviously, he recognized the beautiful woman with the bandage over her eye. He kissed her cheek, the one without the scrapes. The woman caressed his face. She smiled and the whole room glowed. The woman leaned over, and the couple's lips met.

Marshall exhaled. *He's here for her.* Marshall paid and left.

It was raining. Well – not raining really, just a sort of mist that fell somewhere between a fog and a drizzle. The kind of mist that soaked a person if they weren't careful, always tricking them into believing they didn't need an umbrella. It didn't matter, anyway. Not now. Marshall had not brought an umbrella. The rain arrived as unexpectedly as the mysterious woman had.

She was beautiful.

Marshall stared up at the darkening clouds. For the first time, he felt the rain and could smell it, empowering and clean. The whole familiar city looked different now – alive, exciting, and full of possibilities. It was as if, without knowing, he had been living in a world of black and white, and now with the appearance of that apparition of beauty, his world was awash in color.

Chapter 7

Penelope, 18 October 2044, Age 25, T-minus Unknown

Penelope Hope and Everett Flach perched side-by-side on stools. The tiny bar in the Hill Café glowed with low candlelight.

"I asked Bea to be my maid of honor." Penelope leaned over and smiled, her hands clasped together on the shiny, wooden surface.

Everett placed his warm hands over hers and gently squeezed. Leaning in a little closer, he raised his brows and grinned. "Did you?"

"I mean, officially." Penelope nodded, pursing her lips. "She said yes."

"No surprise there." Everett removed his hands. "We've got a lot of details to work out."

"I know." She sat back with wide eyes. "Where do we start … the date? That seems important."

"Actually, I was thinking our first step might be to enroll."

Penelope's smile melted into a frown. She glanced around the dimly lit dining room. Everyone looked happy enough and more than likely, they were all enrolled. But the idea of enrollment seemed to cast a pall over her heart. To spend life contemplating death just didn't feel right. In fact, it felt slightly perverse. The way

Bea and Everett prodded her about enrollment, she felt as if mortality followed her around with a scythe over its shoulder. "You must have talked to Bea."

"What? No. I've been thinking about this for a while –"

"I haven't been thinking about it … at all."

Penelope's statement wasn't true. Not exactly. She had thought about it. About how awful it was. About how she wished humanity hadn't harnessed this power, if it could be called power, and if that power could actually be harnessed. Had society mastered the knowledge or had the knowledge mastered society?

"It's not something I want to know," Penelope said. "It's not *normal.* And I wish you and Bea would just give it a rest."

"It's becoming normal."

"Not for me."

"It could. Everyone we know is enrolled. We're the weird ones, Nel."

"It's just not something I want to know about. I don't need to know. It's not something *any* of us should know –"

"Being judgmental, are we?"

Penelope glared at her fiancé. "Judgmental? Knowing your deathday is a big deal. People might not think so … but –"

"Hear me out." Everett again placed his hands over hers.

"I'm listening." Penelope huffed and snatched her hands out from under his. She crossed her arms.

"It seems like the responsible thing to do. We want kids, a family. If we know our deathdays, we can make arrangements. Plan our funerals, even pay for them. We can arrange to have things sold or stored before we're even old."

"Oh, wonderful. We can start dying before we start dying." Penelope shook her head. "What an amazing idea."

"You said you'd hear me out." Everett frowned and sat back.

Penelope raised her hands. She'd listen, but she wouldn't change her mind. Was she going to spend her whole life defending herself against knowing her deathday? Would they not stop until she gave in? She wouldn't do it. She wouldn't. Knowing her deathday would only reduce the grandeur of life into a limited experience. The whole concept was counterproductive. She knew most participants believed it improved their quality of life, but they were wrong. They didn't understand how limiting the knowledge was. Bea couldn't enjoy life because she was constantly racing against the calendar, chasing the life she desired before her time ran out.

It seemed that lately, Penelope and Everett couldn't enjoy an evening of candlelight and wine without arguing over death. But if she enrolled, she knew she would fall victim to the same unforgiving notifications and counterproductive behavior she watched day in and day out from those who had enrolled. It wasn't planning so much as deprivation. They were depriving themselves of parenthood because they knew they'd die before their children reached adulthood. They deprived themselves of owning pets because they couldn't bear the thought of rehoming them to another family. They were so focused on dying, they had forgotten how to live.

People just weren't equipped for that type of knowledge. There was no way to balance living with dying. The knowledge of one's deathday tipped the scales in favor of the macabre. Time ruled, death ruled, and Penelope refused to fall in line. It was not empowerment. It was a handicap that diminished the sanctity of life – her life. It distilled everything down to ash and diluted the purpose into nothing more than the ultimate end. When a person enrolled, mortality consumed every moment.

"It would save our family so much trouble and give us more control," Everett said.

Penelope sighed. "Once I'm gone, I won't care about control."

"We have the opportunity, we should take advantage of it … together."

"Everett, what would it change? It wouldn't change the fact that we'll both die someday."

"See? That's what I mean. That right there. It changes *someday* into a date we can actually plan around."

Penelope swirled her straw in the ice and shrugged. "You sound like Bea."

"Bea's a smart girl." Everett nodded.

Penelope looked up, and her eyes softened. "I worry about what *knowing* might change."

"Such as?"

"What if *knowing* changes us? Bea may be a smart girl, but all she thinks about is thirty years from now when she's going to be dead. She's missing out on living because she's worrying so much about dying. All the wonderful things she could concentrate on are passing her by … gone because her brain is so preoccupied with her deathday."

"I'm just asking you to think about it. That's all. You never have before. You said so yourself. Just think about it. Promise me."

Penelope's straw fell from her fingers, and she rested her hands on the bar. The earnest look from her fiancé melted her heart. "Fine. I'll think about it." She sealed her promise with a slight kiss.

"Thank you," he replied.

Chapter 8

Marshall, 19 October 2044, Age 27, T-minus Age 49

The day after his eyes landed on the beautiful woman at the Hill Café, Marshall woke to find that her effect had not faded. He wondered if his world had forever changed. He walked to work with Toby at his side, and the colors of the trees and buildings looked so vibrant they were almost overwhelming. Entering the office, he aimed straight for the coffee, hoping to avoid small talk with coworkers. Head and eyes down, he reached the coffeemaker without a single social exchange. Feeling relieved, he made a cup, took a sip, and headed for his desk.

"Marshall!" Ken's voice echoed through the small breakroom.

Marshall cringed at the man's overly friendly, morning voice. It was always so irritating.

Toby glanced up and whined.

Marshall took another sip. "Ken!" He tried to match his boss's enthusiasm, though it felt somewhat contrived. He continued walking to his office. He had work to do. Surely, Ken did too.

Ken, however, followed. "It's your turn, my friend."

"My turn?" Marshall set his mug on his desk. "For what?"

"To pick up a deathday cake."

"We take turns now?"

Ken leaned against the edge of the desk. He glanced out the large, plate glass window and smiled. He spoke without making eye contact, something Marshall wished more people would do more often. "Yeah. Just makes sense if the person who last celebrated their deathday is responsible for the next deathday cake. I did yours and now you do Jeff's. Then Jeff'll do Cynthia's and Cynthia'll do Katie's. You get the idea."

Marshall *got* the idea. He didn't like it, but he got it. No reason to object. Not really. "When do we need the cake?"

"Tomorrow," Ken replied.

"Tomorrow?" Marshall glanced at his calendar and sighed. "I'll call in an order."

"Attaboy," Ken said. He patted Marshall on the shoulder before aiming for the door. "Lunch today?" Ken pointed, took an imaginary shot, and left.

Marshall sighed again. He glanced down at Toby.

Toby whined as if to say he was sorry, he didn't want to have lunch with Ken either.

Marshall picked up his coffee and took a sip. The brown swirls seemed darker, and somewhat more exciting since he had seen such a beautiful woman.

He sat at his desk and opened a drawer. It was empty except for a single framed photograph, turned facedown so he wouldn't have to look at the face. Marshall picked it up and set it on his desk. His mother's soft gaze stared back. Her blue eyes seemed to lack intensity and earnestness, although they were full of warmth and love. This was the woman of his childhood. His first and until Toby only friend. She was older now, and the photograph preserved only what he remembered. Back when Marshall trusted her. Back when she was the anchor of his existence. He wished that woman still existed. The disillusionment was disorienting.

"I miss you, Mom. I really do," he whispered.

He waited for her to reply, but of course, she remained silent. He tried to imagine what she'd say, but nothing came to mind.

"If you were here, or if I could holograph you, I'd tell you all about her … the woman from the accident. I saw her again yesterday. It was the strangest thing. When I look at her, everything feels different. Better somehow."

He sighed and picked up the photograph. Placing his thumb on his mother's cheek, he felt the gentle pressure of Toby's head on his thigh. He reached down and stroked his dog's silky head.

"Sometimes I wish I could talk to you." He smiled at the photo. "You were the only one who understood me. I trusted you."

His voice broke a little and Toby whined.

"Why did you trick me, Mom? Why did you lie to me? If anyone should've known I wanted the truth, it should've been you. And if I can't trust you …"

He placed the portrait back in the drawer, facedown. Taking in a deep breath, he sighed again. Talking to the photo rarely helped. In fact, he hardly ever looked at it. He wasn't even sure why he kept it. That was the drawer that remained closed. Closed the same way his memories were sealed. Thinking of her was just too painful.

That gaping hole behind his sternum was an emptiness he could never fill. Sometimes, he thought about reaching out to her. But how could he reach for someone he couldn't trust?

Could the most beautiful woman in the world be trusted? Could anyone? People were much easier to deal with at arm's length. The beautiful woman was nothing more than eyes and arms and hair and a white bandage across an alabaster brow. He didn't know her. Although – she seemed perfect. She was beautiful.

But so was my mother.

Perhaps it was better not to really know others. He glanced at the city spreading out in a vast grid of activity. The sun glinted off the glass buildings, casting empty shadows across the streets.

"'High over the city,'" Marshall quoted, thinking of F. Scott Fitzgerald, "'our line of yellow windows must have contributed their share of human secrecy to the casual watcher in the darkening streets, and I was him too, looking up and wondering. I was within and without, simultaneously enchanted and repelled by the inexhaustible variety of life.'"

They were out there somewhere – his mother and the beautiful woman. He tried to divert his thoughts but couldn't. He couldn't help but wonder where they were, and what they were doing.

Chapter 9

Penelope, 20 October 2044, Age 25, T-minus Unknown

Penelope stared at the black cake with the large, white letters - **RIP** - painted across the top. The *thing* looked flat and morbid. The man who had ordered it didn't sound very excited about it either.

Maybe he wouldn't show.

If he didn't, the cake would still sell before the others. Before the three-tiered wedding cake with the colorful, piped flowers, before the festive and vibrant birthday cakes. Deathday cakes sold like crazy these days. It was always *somebody's* deathday. There seemed to be more deathdays than birthdays. As if everyone had to celebrate death in order to forget that they'd someday die. The way Penelope saw it, deathday parties were just a way to cloak the macabre deadline in festivity so people could be happy and forget their fear of the future – their deaths.

Penelope puzzled over the darkness of the cake and what the emptiness actually symbolized. She shivered as a chill ran through her. The doctor's black shirt filled her vision, and it was as if the pits of hell had opened and were beckoning for her to step inside. She stepped back and stared at the white plate and black icing. Again, the doctor, with his uncaring emotions and black-white contrast, filled her vision. She grabbed a pastry bag and took a slow, deep breath before squeezing out a delicate, yellow petal to brighten the deepening shadows. People would probably balk at the flower, but the damn thing needed something. Her excuse? The flower was meant to resemble a single flower placed on a recently dug grave. A single touch to give the illusion that someone cared – that the dearly departed had been loved and would continue to be loved long after their Date of Departure. Everyone wanted their headstones adorned with flowers. Flowers meant someone still remembered.

Stroking another single petal, she whispered, "He loves me." With another stroke of the icing and another petal – "He loves me not …" – a stroke of the icing again – "… he loves me …" – a stroke of the icing – "… he loves me not."

The thought of Everett and the possibility of enrollment nudged at her from somewhere within the darkness that loomed only inches in front of her. She froze and listened to the thumping of her heart. Was her soul knocking from somewhere deep inside? A sudden pang of sadness crept across her chest. She took a deep breath and let it out slowly. Yellow icing oozed from the tip of the pastry bag and with one finger, she gently wiped it off.

"To enroll or not to enroll?" she whispered. "That is the question."

Everett loved her. After all, hadn't he asked her to marry him? Hadn't he asked her to spend the rest of her life with him? And then – asked her to find out how long that would be? She shivered. She didn't want to know when she was going to die any more than she wanted to know when he was going to die. In fact, if he decided to enroll on his own, she would forbid him from telling her his deathday.

That would be impossible, though, wouldn't it? Because he'd want to celebrate his deathday just like everyone else. And she'd probably have to make the cake. What a terrible thought.

Why is he so eager to know when my deathday is? Penelope shook her head and sighed. The whole situation was becoming just too dark to contemplate.

She leaned over and carefully added the last petal to the single, yellow flower. She had just placed the cake back inside the display when the bell on the front door rang. Cool air rushed in, stirring the sugary sweetness that saturated the place. A tall, lean man with dark hair and light blue eyes entered. Following close behind was a large, black dog.

Penelope smiled, more at the dog than at the stranger. "What a beautiful animal." She paused before raising her eyes to the man. "I'm sorry, welcome to The Cakery. How may I help you?"

The man looked vaguely familiar. He glanced at the bakery case and seemed to be contemplating something. *How odd.* Most buyers raved over her deathday cakes. But this man seemed somewhat taken aback. His eyes scanned the various sweets and lingered on the black deathday cake now sporting a bright, yellow flower. Perhaps it wasn't such a great idea after all.

"The Cakery?" he whispered, without looking up. "Clever. I'm here to pick up a deathday cake."

"You're looking at it," Penelope replied. "Just finished it. The only one I'll make today."

"I've never seen a deathday cake that looked so ... cheerful."

"Oh, the flower ..."

"It's yellow."

"Mimics a flower on a grave."

He chuckled. "The symbol for decay. Yellow, that is. At least in books."

He wasn't wrong. After all, it was Gatsby's yellow car that killed Myrtle – it was the yellow bird Abigail purported to see in the courtroom that motivated Mary Warren to turn on John Proctor – it was the yellow wallpaper that drove the woman mad. Perhaps yellow wasn't such an incongruous choice after all.

Penelope's eyes rested on the beautiful, well-behaved dog standing beside the man. "What's your dog's name?"

For the first time since entering, the man took the time to look at her. "Toby." His eyes fell back to the cakes.

"Hi, Toby." Penelope smiled at the dog and watched as a slight twinkle creased the man's eyes.

The dog looked up at her and tilted his head.

"Such a handsome boy," she said.

Toby wagged his tail before sitting on the floor.

"We've seen you before," the man said, seemingly to the cakes. "Toby and I, that is."

A puzzle-piece logo was imprinted on the dog's harness. The symbol for autism. Well, that explained the stranger's stilted speech.

"Oh? I thought you looked a little familiar."

"The accident … with the antique car? Toby and I were there. We helped you. It's what Toby does best … help people."

"I'm sorry." Penelope glanced away. "I don't remember much about that day. Thank you, though, for helping. Both of you."

She felt relieved that someone in the world, besides her, still wanted to help. The doctor at the hospital had practically ridiculed her for taking a risk to help the old woman. She didn't know what kind of risk this man and his dog might have taken – maybe none at all – but she felt happy to know they had tried to help, instead of just assuming it might be her deathday and going about their way.

Marshall opened his mouth as if to say something, but blushed instead.

"I guess I owe you one," Penelope whispered.

Marshall remained quiet.

"A favor, I mean … for helping me." She waited for him to answer, but he didn't. He simply reached down and fondled his dog's ears. Penelope sighed. "Okay then. I'll box this up for you." She set a cardboard box on the display case before sliding the black cake between the thin, white walls.

"Morbid tradition," he said more to himself than to her.

"Excuse me?" Penelope replied.

"Oh. Uh. Nothing."

"Did you say it's a morbid tradition?"

The man's face reddened. "Yes, I did."

"I've always thought that too." She smiled. "Between you and me, these cakes … these deathday things, they're my least favorite to make. Even worse to decorate. I'm sorry, but I had to add a little something. Do you mind the yellow flower?"

"It's beautiful." He shook his head. "The most beautiful deathday cake I've ever seen. I like the yellow flower." He paused. "I didn't want to buy it, but the flower helps."

"Why are you buying it, if you don't want to?"

"I *have* to. For work. For a colleague."

"Ahh. The office deathday party. Awkward." She giggled. "What about the good ol' days when people just had birthday parties, huh?"

"Yeah," the man replied with something akin to a smile replacing his frown. "We still have those at the office, but –"

"I prefer making wedding cakes or anniversary cakes or cupcakes. Actually, any cakes for that matter. But these deathday ones are the ones that sell. Supply and demand, yah know? I refuse to bake more than one a day. My friend, Bea, says I'd be rich if I'd make just three or four, but I can't do it. I just can't." Penelope loosened her stance as if surrendering to the forces around her.

The blackness of the cake seemed to be growing. As if the darkness from the pits were somehow expanding, enlarging, trying to consume her. He didn't want to buy the cake, and she hadn't wanted to make it. But it was the expectation, if not the rule. Just like enrollment. People were supposed to do it. She couldn't be a baker without baking deathday cakes. She was supposed to bake, and he was supposed to buy.

"Your friend is probably right about the deathday cakes. Business'd be better if you made more of 'em."

"She usually is … right, I mean."

"I like the flower," the man said.

"Thank you." Penelope nodded. "I like your dog."

He chuckled and looked down at Toby. "I do too."

Chapter 10

Penelope, 26 November 2044, Age 25, T-minus Unknown

Penelope froze at the door of Bea's small apartment in Shockoe Bottom. She stared at the blackness, which seemed to challenge her to enter. Her eyes scanned the panels. They seemed to darken, as if shadowing her thoughts. Each panel reminded her of a little casket. Mortality was once again standing there nonchalantly with a scythe over the shoulder.

She shivered.

Glancing over her own shoulder, she half-expected the reaper to be standing there, smiling in the dark, telling her she should know, she *could* know when he would come. It didn't need to be this way, he didn't have to sneak up on her. She could see him coming, could prepare for the swipe of his blade. All she had to do was enroll.

She sighed. She was alone. It was only her and the blackness that surrounded her. She stared at the door and shrugged off the sense of foreboding that tormented her.

"Black door, black deathday cake …" She reached for the old-fashioned doorknob and turned it. It felt cold and uninviting. The door opened, bathing her in light from inside.

Bea sat on the couch, doused in the golden glow of the late-day sun. A bridal holograph waltzed to and fro in front of her, and she looked deep in thought.

"We have a date," Penelope said, sitting on the couch beside her friend.

Bea sat straight up, eyes wide. "A Date of Departure?!"

"No," Penelope said, rolling her eyes. "And *what* is it with you and death? A *wedding* date."

"Oh, well, that's good, but –"

"But you'd rather know when I'm going to *die* than when I'm going to *marry*? Jesus, Bea."

"You know that's not what it's about. I just –"

"Yeah, you just. Aren't you going to ask when the date is?"

"When is the date?"

"June 16, year after next. So now that we have a date, we can plan."

"Speaking of a date that you can plan around –"

"Don't. Just don't. I want to be excited about my *wedding*. I'd rather not think about my *funeral*." Penelope walked into the kitchen and grabbed a bottle of water from the fridge. After sitting down beside Bea, she enjoyed a long, cool sip. The water was almost painful, and she swallowed hard.

The jolt of the unexpected coldness made her think of the stranger at her bakery a few weeks ago. The cold air that had blown in when he entered. And the black cake – that stupid blackness that seemed to be following her everywhere. Why was it that everyone she knew seemed to be stuck on knowing when the reaper would knock on her door? What if the reaper *had* been standing beside her at Bea's door? Would he have taken her then? What if the reaper were actually standing there beside her, waiting at this very moment? What if her deathday were only a few days away? She took another sip and frowned.

"Penelope ..." Bea said. "You're so sensible about most things. Why won't you listen to reason?"

Penelope glanced down and sighed. Her shoes were black. She shook her head and resisted the urge to scream. Instead, she said, "Between you and Everett ... I'd swear you're plotting together." Penelope shook a foot and allowed her shoe to fall. After chucking the second one, she laughed. *Plotting* – even her subconscious was haunting her about a future gravesite.

"We're not." Bea laughed. "If we were, it's just 'cause we love you so much."

Penelope placed the water bottle on the coffee table. She held up her hands as if in surrender. "All right. All right. Let's make a deal. Tonight, you can tell me all the reasons why Everett and I should enroll. Not that I probably haven't heard at least half of them already. After that, we talk only wedding for the rest of ... until the wedding."

"That's a long time."

"It'll be here before you know it." Penelope smiled.

Bea opened her mouth, but Penelope placed her hand over her friend's lips. "And *don't* say something morbid like my deathday could be here before I know it."

"Fine, I won't, but just know that it could be."

"Agreed," Penelope replied. "Let's move on. I want to talk about *fun* things."

"Fun things? Deathdays are fun things." Bea nodded.

"Are you kidding me?" This was absurd. "What makes *dying* so much fun?" Penelope crossed her arms.

Bea smiled. "It's not dying that's fun ... it's knowing." She cleared her throat. "First, a bucket list."

"Let me stop you right there. I don't have a bucket list, and I don't want one. Next?"

"Fine … number two – *paid incentive* …" She practically sang the words.

"Okay, I'll give you that one. Enrolling does add a few dollars to your income, but not enough to make a person rich." Penelope shook her head. "Next one? I know you want to continue."

Bea settled deeper into the couch, her enthusiasm evident. "But do you know how much it is?"

"Not really."

"It's a *good* incentive. I couldn't afford this view on just *my* salary." Bea gestured at the window that overlooked the vast expanse of the city.

Beneath the darkening sky, lights were burning on the streets and in the many windows scattered along the parkway. The world below would soon mirror the stars above, only down there, the black ribbon of the river would separate the northside from the southside.

"Never really thought about it," Penelope said, distracted by the shadows creeping over the streets.

"You should. If it weren't for *my* enrollment, I'd probably still be living with my parents."

"*Or* … you would've had the motivation to find a better job. No offense but –"

"None taken." Bea shrugged. "That *better* job, as you call it, might be more stressful, might require more hours, might eat into my free time to travel and explore and hang out with you. Lots of little things that are more important than work."

"Maybe you would've found a job you really loved." Penelope wagged her finger at Bea and added, "Find a job you love and you'll never work a day in your life."

"I could find a job I love, *maybe*. But instead, I found a *life* I love."

"A life you love *so* much you're constantly counting down to its end?"

"I'm not counting down to its end," Bea said. "I'm making the most of *my* time."

"I don't want to argue. Really good incentive. Got it."

"Reason number three … tax break. It's probably the only reason I get a refund anymore."

"Paid incentive. Tax break. Made it this far without 'em."

"And wouldn't it be nice to know how much farther you've got to go?"

Penelope rolled her eyes.

"Point taken. Not convinced yet? How 'bout this? Planning. You're a planner. Super organized and prepared all the time."

"You've already used this one on me and so has Everett. He wants us to *plan* our funerals. Buy our plots together. Sell the house we don't own yet so the children we don't even have yet won't have to."

"Right … end-of-life becomes so much easier for everyone. And … you retire young enough to actually enjoy your retirement."

"What if I learn I won't live long enough to retire?"

Bea smiled as if she knew she'd win Penelope over with this one. "If you enroll that can't happen. If you're enrolled, retirement is based on your T-minus age, how many years you have left, not how many years you've worked."

Everything her friend was saying seemed so unnatural – so morbid and backwards. It was hard to believe anyone could be so focused on death and still live happily. She sighed. "I just …"

"You just, what?" Bea scooted closer and placed her hand on Penelope's shoulder. She gazed earnestly into her eyes. "It's a good thing. Knowing your DoD is good." Bea's eyes possessed a dark yearning. "Remember when everyone first learned about the

Experiment? How many suicides there used to be? The number dropped as soon as people started enrolling. More participants, fewer suicides."

"The legal repercussions might've had something to do with that." Penelope raised her voice. "Rule number five of the *Experiment* forbids participants from attempting to engineer or alter a DoD."

"Murder was illegal before enrollment and suicide too." Bea rolled her eyes. "Rule number five wasn't what caused suicide rates to tank. As soon as people knew their deathday, they mostly stopped trying to rush it. People seem to value their lives more when they have a concrete end date. Scarcity makes things precious and life is *no* exception."

Penelope remembered. It was difficult to forget. Her high school term essay had been on the correlation between enrollment and suicide, and it still gave her the creeps. "Remember my paper –"

"Oh yeah!" Bea's eyes brightened. "Your term paper. Of course. Remember mine?"

Penelope did remember. Bea had written about the correlation of enrollment with perceived quality of life. She nodded.

"So you know that people don't live *longer* because they know their deathdays, but they do live *better*." Bea placed her hands in her lap and sat up straighter. She gave a definitive little nod, as if her last argument had done the trick, and she had just won.

What constitutes better? What metrics determine that? Penelope turned from Bea to stare out the window again.

The sun was busy tucking itself beneath the blanket of the cityscape. It shimmered dimly within the folds of the early autumn evening. Shadows were just beginning to stretch across the concrete forest. A bright light from a window in the next building over caught her eye. The white light in the otherwise darkening expanse reminded Penelope of the shiny, solitaire diamond that clung to her ring finger. Suddenly, the light darkened. Someone must've turned it off. The uniform darkness of the building against the light made Penelope shiver. Was her ring like the bright light from that distant balcony? And could her life be snuffed suddenly into darkness as unexpectedly as that light? *Well, Bea would tell me it doesn't have to be unexpected …*

"I don't understand why you don't want that for yourself … a better life." Bea's earlier enthusiasm seemed to have faded with the daylight.

"It's not that I don't want a good life." Penelope stood and stared down through the buildings. The darkened streets were barely visible now. "I'm just not convinced that knowing my deathday is the key to a life of happiness."

"Look at everyone who knows their deathdays. They're happy."

"They're always talking about dying." Penelope held back a laugh. The absurdity of the whole idea was more than she cared to contemplate.

"But they're not *sad* about it. Nobody's moping around because they're gonna die someday. We all know that much, even you. Knowing *when* is empowering." Bea's pocket emitted a gentle, metallic jingle, as if she were carrying a small wind chime. "Oh." She pulled out her phone. "It's my *Life Planner* app." She swiped across the screen, tapped a couple times, and placed the phone back in her pocket.

"What did the app want?"

"It's the timeline I set up to remind me I need to hurry up and get married if I want to celebrate my twenty-fifth wedding anniversary before I die." Bea stood and looked out the window.

Penelope wanted to ask her friend what she was feeling. Did knowing make *her* happy? Was she fulfilled knowing there was a chance she'd never celebrate her twenty-fifth wedding anniversary? Would all the deathday cakes and celebrations make up for the fact that she might never marry? Instead, she remained quiet. After all, Bea was her friend. Her *best* friend, and there was no point in hurting her just to win an argument.

"On that note," Bea said, seeming a little brighter, "let's talk wedding."

Penelope smiled, grateful for her friend's quick return to lightheartedness. "Yes," she said. "Let's talk wedding."

Chapter 11

Penelope, 27 November 2044, Age 25, T-minus Unknown

Penelope and Everett meandered arm-in-arm through the pulsating crowd of future brides and grooms enjoying the *Fall Wedding Expo* at the Koger Center. The atmosphere reminded Penelope of Christmas – a shared anticipation seemed to permeate the place. She squeezed Everett's bicep and smiled. A warm grin of affection spread across his face. It wasn't possible for her to ever be happier than she was in this moment. Anticipation and excitement raced through her heart at the thought of spending the rest of her life with that smile – and the man who wore it.

"Look here," she said, pointing to a bouquet of yellow flowers. "Forsythias! I always thought yellow would be nice and cheery in a bridal bouquet."

Everett nodded. "But our wedding is in the summer. Shouldn't we shoot for something more … seasonal?"

"Mid-June is still spring." Penelope sighed. "Technically. Besides, I'm the one who holds the bouquet."

Everett squinted and gave a playful frown. "I wear the matching boutonniere."

"Fine. Then yellow lilies. They bloom later in the year." After a moment, she added, "I'm a little surprised you even care about the flowers. I figured Bea and I would handle details like that."

Everett shrugged. "You brought me along, so I might as well put in my two cents."

"Fair enough. It's kinda cute, you caring." She gave him a peck on the cheek.

They walked along the aisles, looking through the various vendor displays – florists, bakers, salons, spas and resorts where they could honeymoon. Penelope asked questions and collected holograph brochures and QR codes. One florist handed her a yellow rose, and she carried it with joy. She would go through the materials later with Bea.

Nearing the end of the exposition, she spotted a booth for the enrollment committee. Several couples huddled around the small table. A few held hands. Others stood with their arms wrapped around each other.

Penelope held the yellow rose to her face and took a deep breath. The flower smelled clean and fresh, redolent with promise.

Everett stopped walking and watched as couples mingled around the display.

Penelope admired her rose. A single yellow flower similar to the one she had created in icing on that deathday cake about a month ago. That black-frosted deathday cake flooded Penelope's mind, drowning her cheer with its chill. She lowered the rose and frowned. Her eyes scanned the growing crowd. She didn't want to join them. She turned away, grabbed Everett's arm, and pulled him back toward the last florist.

"If you don't want forsythias," she said, "I'm sure they can make a bouquet with lilies, and their prices were reasonable. I need to ask about a few things."

"There could be more florists down this way. We haven't seen everything yet."

Penelope tugged again on Everett's arm. "Maybe …" Her eyes widened as his eyes scanned the vendor she wanted so desperately to avoid. "I liked that florist and –"

"Look!" Everett stated, resisting her tug. "The enrollment booth. Let's check it out."

The black cake again darkened Penelope's mind as she allowed her future to pull her toward her fears. She shuddered. The slogans on the display table doused her in dread.

HEAVEN IS WAITING

A sign of promise written with white script outlined in gold, a blue sky and white clouds filling the background.

ONE THING CERTAIN IN AN UNCERTAIN WORLD

The sign to the right of the table sat behind several stacks of brochures fanned out to catch the curious. They stepped up to the table, and a third sign assailed her.

ENROLLMENT: GIVING YOU AN EXPECTED END

Expected End – Penelope dropped her yellow rose and watched as a future bride – a future corpse – took a step and crushed the petals. *Expected End* – the words pulled the darkness in around her. She glanced down at the torn, yellow flower and resisted the urge to run. She glanced up, unable to bear the sight of her ruined rose, no longer a youthful promise. So carelessly crushed.

HOW LONG IS YOUR FOREVER?

Penelope shivered.

MEASURE OUT YOUR LIFE IN COFFEE SPOONS

Messages of mortality closed in around her from every angle, as if the Grim Reaper were personally tapping on her shoulder, his icy breath tickling her ear.

She wanted to savor this time with Everett and plan for their wedding. But instead, she found herself mortally afraid. It was unfair. Her deathday, although unknown, still haunted her from every shadow and every corner. She was being forced to face mortality and dread her death long before it was time, and she wasn't even enrolled.

The vendor was finishing a pitch for the eager crowd. "… 'til death do us part. So much uncertainty. But there doesn't have to be. We offer an *expected end*. You can learn how much time you have left together …" He hugged his chest and tilted his head. His smile displayed a sense of acceptance, as if it were better to simply give up, to surrender to what was on the other side. "Just live and plan accordingly. If you enroll today …" A quiet murmuring from several couples rose in excitement. A few left their names and numbers. Others asked questions.

"C'mon, Everett."

The blackness of the cake pounded through Penelope's head. Again, she glanced down at the dying, yellow rose. Had it been dying from the moment its first petal emerged, its fate sealed before it ever unfurled? Was the purpose of this flower to be snipped for a wedding expo, carried around, dropped, and then crushed only to be swept up with the rest of the dirt and dust? It would never live long enough to see a real wedding. It was just a sample. Just a display. Just a model of what could be. And that was all. It would never be anything more.

"This booth is too crowded," she said. "We can come back later if you want."

"The expo ends in half an hour," Everett replied. "Let's just wait it out … look at some brochures."

The urge to protest felt strong, but she resisted. Everett was too enthusiastic about enrollment, and besides, she was the one who had dragged him here. Not that he had been unwilling. He actually seemed pleased to be involved. His words echoed through her mind. *'If I'm here, I'm entitled to my two cents.'* Penelope stood back and allowed her eyes to wander through the excited crowd. With wide eyes and smiles of anticipation, their enthusiasm was almost catching. She took a deep breath and watched Everett as he looked over the brochures touting the benefits of enrollment.

"What can I help you with today?" the vendor asked, stepping a little closer. His name tag labeled him *Michael: Death Doula.*

"Hi." Everett glanced at the name tag and smiled. "Michael, my fiancée and I are considering enrollment."

"Not really …" Penelope mumbled, glancing away. Again, her eyes fell to the rose. It had been dying since the second the florist snipped its delicate stem, dying from the moment it was cut, its beauty stopped short, and for what? *To end up crushed on the floor? Forgotten and trampled?*

"Wonderful! Wonderful!" Michael clapped and his smile grew wider and more sinister. "Neither of you are enrolled, I presume?"

"We're not," Everett said.

"And when is the big day?"

"June 16," Penelope whispered, "2046."

"Ahh … a June wedding. Traditional. Well, you've come to the right place. Enrolling as a couple can *really* mark the start of your life together. You already know when it will begin … June 16 …" – he jotted the date on his pad – "… in your case." He nodded and winked at Penelope. "And you can know *exactly* when it will end. As we at the enrollment committee like to say, 'Enrollment … we give you an expected end.'"

There was a contrived smoothness to his voice, and his laugh seemed eerie. In many ways, he reminded her of a gameshow host or a used car salesman. Better yet, a snake –

"Did you know," he continued, "that divorce rates have steadily dropped over the last few decades? This drop directly correlates to couples' enrollment. When both partners are enrolled, couples are fifteen times less likely to divorce than when one or neither is enrolled. Divorce among enrolled couples is nearly unheard of. Isn't that something?"

Everett nodded and glanced over at Penelope.

She raised her brows and smirked. "Isn't *that* something? That really *is* something." Her sarcasm was lost on both men. "I thought the whole idea behind getting married was not getting divorced, but –"

"But if knowing our deathdays can improve our chances, why not?" Everett asked.

"I didn't know we were taking chances," Penelope replied. "I thought we were, yah know, pretty sure we wanted to spend the rest of our lives together."

"But …" – Michael raised his hand – "… wouldn't it be nice to know how long the rest of your lives together will be? That's why the divorce rates have declined, you see. Knowing the limit of their time together seems to help people cherish each day *and* each other."

"Or maybe it's just that they've already bought headstones and engraved them. Bound together by shared burial plots … how romantic," Penelope shot back.

Michael's sly smile made her cringe as he hissed every *s*.

"An *expected end* put*ssss* thing*ssss* in per*ssss*pective. What good i*ssss* fighting over financ*ssss*e*ssss* if you know you only have another fifteen year*ssss*? What differen*ssss*ce will chore*ssss* make if you know exactly how quickly your time will fly? Never wasssste time arguing."

"We already argue," Everett whispered.

"Only about this," Penelope said. "Only this." She swept her hand over the booth.

"Exactly." Everett sighed. "If we enroll, there won't be anything left to argue about."

Penelope was irritated, and she wanted to argue – but not in front of Michael. Enrollment wouldn't end arguing – it would only provide new fodder for fighting. She was tempted to start listing all the new arguments they could have as an enrolled couple – which headstones to purchase, where to buy their plots, how to execute their will, if remarrying was acceptable upon the premature death of one or the other, whose preferences weighed more based on who had less time. The list was endless.

"Well." Michael chuckled. "I'll leave you two alone to make your decision. I'll be here for about another twenty minutes or so. Here, scan our QR code. Take your time. Do more research."

"Thank you," Everett said. He turned Penelope around and they walked back toward the last booth. "Let's talk to that florist you like."

Penelope looked at Everett, surprised he had given in. "Okay," she whispered, taking his hand into hers.

They made their way back to the florist that had handed her the yellow rose. The crowd was thinning now, and many of the vendors were already breaking down their booths, packing veils and shoes and brochures into plastic crates or cardboard boxes. When they reached the florist, the woman was dismantling her display. The forsythia bouquet was still on the table. A few of the yellow petals now rested on the black tablecloth, which reminded Penelope of the black cake.

"Hello," the florist said. "You're back."

"We wanted to ask about your forsythias," Everett said. "Could you prepare forsythias for a June wedding? Is that too late in the season?"

"Of course we can provide what you need." She gestured to the golden plume of flowers delicately clinging to their tall, willowy stems. "If you'd like, why don't you take that bunch home with you? I'll be tossing them out otherwise."

"Oh, we couldn't," Penelope said. "But that's awfully nice of you."

"No, please." The florist insisted. "It will save me the trouble. I won't be able to use them again, but they'll brighten your home for a few days." The florist pushed the vase toward her. "Take them, please."

"Thank you," Penelope said as Everett cradled the vase in his arms. "You're right, they will look pretty in our apartment."

"Just think of me when you make your flower decision," the florist said with a wink.

"We will. I think we've already made up our minds," Penelope replied.

It was late and time to leave. Everett held the flowers in one hand and the door with the other. Penelope stepped into the crisp November night and breathed in the cool air. When they reached his car, Everett opened her door, and after she was settled, handed Penelope the flowers.

"Start," he said, climbing into the driver's seat.

The car's lights blinked on and the doors locked. A sensor beeped to announce it was ready for the next command.

"Home," Everett said, adding, "scenic route."

"Destination: Home. Confirmed," a female voice stated. **"Scenic route. Confirmed."** The car maneuvered out of the parking lot and onto the street.

Everett placed his arm around Penelope, who nestled into his warm embrace. The water in the vase felt cool between her legs.

"Taking the long road home?" she whispered, feeling sleepy and content.

"Forsythias?" Everett asked, kissing the top of her head before bending down and gently kissing her lips.

A warm sensation filtered through her. She loved this man and was thrilled to know she had him by her side for the rest of her life – however long that would be.

As they left the brightly lit parking lot and the dark night surrounded her, the black cake again monopolized her mind. She pushed the thought away and gently touched the flowers.

"Yeah." She smiled at Everett. "Thank you."

Chapter 12

Penelope, 14 December 2044, Age 25, T-minus Unknown

Penelope and Bea sat side-by-side with their backs against the yellow couch. Everett sat across from them in front of the large TV. Cartons of Chinese takeout littered the coffee table. Penelope sat with her feet tucked under her, pushing a piece of broccoli around her plate, coating it in savory sauce.

"We should order Chinese more often," Penelope stated. "I always forget how much I like it."

"Yeah," Bea mumbled as she chewed.

Everett was busy shoveling fried rice onto his plate.

Penelope shrugged. "Guess he agrees." She smiled, loving the time she spent with her best friend and fiancé. She was grateful they got along so well. A joyful warmth radiated through her core. In this moment, surrounded by Chinese takeout and sitting on the floor of Bea's apartment, she felt genuinely happy. There was nothing more she needed. This was the simple, beautiful life she would live. This was everything.

Bea shook the brown paper bag. "Fortune cookie time." She pushed aside the cartons, clearing the center of the table, and turned the bag upside down. Three cookies tumbled out. "Okay … everyone grab one."

Penelope chose the cookie angled in her direction. They cracked them open and pulled out their fortunes. As they ate the cookies, they read. Bea laughed and a few crumbs fell from her mouth. She wiped her face.

"Is it a good one?" Penelope asked.

"'There's only one happiness in life … to love and be loved.'" Bea rolled her eyes. "Thanks a lot, fortune cookie. I was hoping for 'Mr. Right is right around the corner' or 'True love will find you soon.' A little encouragement, not a reminder that I'm missing one of the most important things in life."

"You are *not* missing anything. I love you. And you love me." Penelope rubbed her shoulder. "You have love in your life. And happiness."

"I'm …" – Bea shook the fortune in the air – "… talking about romantic love."

"Maybe." Penelope shrugged. "But the fortune didn't specify what kind of love." She turned her attention to Everett. "What's yours say?"

Everett cleared his throat. "'The love of your life sits before you.'" He raised his brows.

Penelope winked and blew him a kiss.

"Good thing mine didn't say that," Bea said, imitating Penelope's wink and kiss at Everett. "We'd be in for some drama, wouldn't we? What about yours?" Bea asked Penelope.

Penelope held up her fortune and read. "'Enjoy yourself while you can.'" She paused, lowering the little scrap of paper to the table. She looked at Everett and Bea. "That's the worst fortune I've ever had." The warm joy she'd been savoring cooled, stifled by a sense of dread.

"A little foreboding." Everett shrugged.

"I don't think so," Bea replied.

"You don't?" Penelope asked. "It's morbid. Like saying something bad's gonna happen."

"I think it just means you should enroll."

"Of course that's what you'd think." Penelope rolled her eyes. "You would've thought that about any fortune I got, no matter what it said."

"Now hold on," Everett added. "I think Bea's onto something."

"Of course you do." Penelope huffed.

Were they ganging up on her now? It was as if the reaper was standing at her shoulder, mocking her. The creature's reflection seemed to be staring at her from inside the blank TV screen just behind Everett. It was laughing at her, gawking with a menacing chuckle – a cold, black dread smothering her joy, snuffing it out.

"Listen," Everett continued, "it's not saying something bad is gonna happen. It's saying you're young and alive and healthy, and you shouldn't waste time doing things you don't enjoy. You should make the most of the here and now. If you enroll, you can use your time wisely. You won't waste it on meaningless things if you know how much you have."

"Or how little …" Penelope whispered.

The reaper's reflection held up a stopwatch before swinging it back and forth from his bony fingers. He was taunting her now.

"Everett's right," Bea said. "When you know how much … or how little … time you have left, you can budget better. There're a couple apps for that, actually. *Every Minute Matters* and *Manage Every Minute*. I use both." Bea shrugged.

"Why does that not surprise me?" Penelope stood. She had to escape from the conversation. Not to mention the Grim Reaper's reflection. "I think I'm done."

Enrollment had ruined what would otherwise have been a lovely evening with her two favorite people – an evening she was enjoying and savoring just fine without knowing when she was going to die or having to argue about finding out.

"Suit yourself," Bea replied. "But don't think that your fortune's not true just because you don't like it. I don't like mine, but you don't hear me complaining."

Standing inside the darkened kitchen, Penelope chose to ignore Bea's comment. She rinsed her plate and placed it in the dishwasher before tossing the worst fortune in the world into the recycle bin.

Chapter 13

Marshall, 21 December 2044, Age 28, T-minus 49

Marshall had never bought himself a birthday cake before. When he was young, his mother baked one every year, but the tradition died as he grew older, and Marshall hadn't had a birthday cake of his own for nearly a decade. Unless you counted office birthday parties, which he didn't. Sometimes, he bought Toby a special treat for *his* birthday. Although he liked cooking, he had no interest in baking and felt that perhaps baking one's own birthday cake was a sorry thing to do. He was sure that Ken would laugh at the thought.

This year wasn't so much about the cake as it was about the bakery. Or more precisely, the *baker* – the beautiful woman he saw struck by the car, watched at the café, and met at the bakery while picking up the deathday cake. Besides, this was almost a big birthday, or what used to be a big birthday, when how old you were used to be paramount. Now, deathdays seemed to determine one's sense of age more than birthdays. If a person was T-minus 2, turning twenty-two might as well be turning eighty-two.

Twenty-eight – today, Marshall was twenty-eight – two years to thirty. And if you wanted to be technical, he was also T-minus 48 years, 9 months, and 19 days. And while he was celebrating dates, he might as well acknowledge that today was also his ten-year enrollment anniversary. He thought maybe all that merited a cake – even if he had to buy it for himself.

It was noon when Marshall pushed open the glass door to the bakery. Scanning the space behind the counter for the beautiful woman. It was empty. The vibration of the bells announced his arrival, fading into a single jingle as they tapped against the glass. All remained quiet except for the hum of the large refrigerator, where several wedding cakes and the day's only deathday cake waited patiently behind the foggy barrier.

As he paced, his gaze kept landing on the cakes. A small, white one trimmed with red frosting caught his attention. He stepped up to the glass and studied the intricacy of the pattern. The red icing reminded him of his bedroom draperies. Something he used to close out the bustle of the world when things felt overwhelming, when the world was too much.

A waterless vase sitting on top of the case looked incongruous next to the freshly iced delicacies. Marshall allowed his gaze to follow a trail of brownish-yellow petals that clung to the sweaty glass. Willowy, dried-up flowers that were once yellow now languished, as if defeated, in the vase. The decay seemed strangely out of place next to the lively, colorful cakes. All but the deathday cake. They fit quite nicely with that one. Marshall gently ran his fingers up one of the dead stems. He cringed when a few papery blossoms fell.

"Welcome to The Cakery," a sweet voice said. "Can I help you?" She paused before adding, "Oh, Toby. You're back."

Marshall started, then looked down at Toby, whose eyes were much braver than his.

Toby stood tall, eagerly wagging his tail.

Marshall cleared his throat. "Pretty flowers. Too bad they're dead." The pressure of Toby's weight against his leg felt reassuring.

"Thanks," she replied. "Don't have the heart to throw 'em out."

Marshall forced his eyes to find hers. Instead, his fears kept his gaze low and on her name tag – *Penelope*. "Resembles the one you added to the deathday cake that I bought a while back."

She chuckled. "Forsythias … that's what they're called."

Marshall didn't know what to say. It was his turn to talk, but his mind remained blank. Without thinking, he stated a little too loudly, "Today's my birthday. I'm twenty-eight."

"Well, in that case … happy birthday. I guess you've come for a cake?"

Marshall smiled. "You guessed right." For a second, his statement felt witty and clever, but then perhaps a little cliché. Maybe even corny. Well, he had said it, and it was too late to take it back.

"Right then. How many will it need to feed?"

"Just me." After a moment he added, "And Toby. Do you have any treats for dogs? Biscuits?"

"No. I don't sell animal treats." She paused and looked down at the dog, still wagging his tail. "Sorry, Toby."

Marshall sighed with relief when she continued talking.

"What kind of dog?"

"Toby? He's a German shepherd."

"A big dog for the city."

"We take a lot of walks." Marshall shrugged. "Sometimes we jog. Toby likes to jog."

"But you don't?"

Marshall thought. He didn't actually like jogging, but it made Toby happy. "I like it because Toby likes it. Probably wouldn't jog if Toby didn't want to."

Penelope smiled. "A boy-and-his-dog birthday party. How about this white-and-red one? It's small. You'll get about four or five pieces. Eat birthday cake for a week."

"Where'd you get the flowers?" Marshall asked, hoping they weren't from the dark-haired man at the café, or any man for that matter, unless he was her dad or brother.

Penelope hesitated. "Oh … a wedding expo last month. The vendor gave them to me at the end of the night. I thought they'd brighten the place up. They take up too much space in our apartment. Nowhere to put 'em."

Marshall winced. *Our* apartment? A wedding expo? Maybe the wedding was for a friend. Maybe she was a maid of honor. Maybe she was marrying the man from the café. Maybe … maybe … maybe … Marshall looked for her left hand, but it was deep inside her apron pocket.

"My fiancé wasn't thrilled with the idea of forsythias at first," she said. "They're a spring flower and won't be in season on our wedding day, but he gave in."

It was his turn to talk, and again he didn't know what to say. She had a fiancé? Marshall felt an unfamiliar emotion building behind his chest. Disappointment, yes, but something more, a new flavor of disappointment. It was jealousy.

She stood silently behind her counter and smiled before adding, "That's why I like 'em. I like it when spring arrives and the forsythias bloom. People used to say the robins were the first sign of spring. I say it's the forsythias. Of course, they both start appearing in February these days …" She waited again.

Marshall felt his face warm, and knew it was probably turning red.

"Twenty-eight?" she asked.

Marshall nodded. "And T-minus 49. T-minus 48 years, 9 months, and 19 days, if you want to be exact."

"You're enrolled? You're a participant?"

Marshall tilted his head and frowned. "You're not?" He had never met anyone who wasn't enrolled. He knew that non-participants were around, but not many. They occupied the status of unicorns in the collective consciousness. He felt almost privileged to have met one.

She shook her head. "No." She paused before resting her elbows on the glass case. "Tell me … what's it like?"

"Being enrolled?"

"Yeah. What's it like to know? I kind of like *not knowing*. My best friend and fiancé think I should enroll. Believe it or not, Everett … that's my fiancé … isn't enrolled yet either. He wants us to enroll together."

"It would give you another anniversary to celebrate. Your enrollment date. Mine is today. Ten years."

"Uh … happy anniversary?"

"Thank you." Marshall said it not because he was grateful but because he knew that's what people were supposed to say when someone wished them a happy *something*.

"Bea and Everett keep saying that enrollment is a *thing* and it's romantic. Not many couples get the opportunity to enroll together, and we should take advantage."

"Maybe," Marshall replied. "It's rare to find a non-participant, much less two. And even more rare … two that want to marry each other. It would be special to enroll at the same time … at least unique. But what if you discover that your life will end before it officially starts? Now that's morbid."

"You don't recommend it?"

"Most seem to find it helpful," Marshall replied.

"But do you?"

Marshall had never considered it before. It just was. He had made the choice. He was living with the consequences. Whether it was good or bad didn't matter. He couldn't go back.

"I don't know." Marshall paused. "Could I buy that white-and-red cake please?"

"Of course." She slid the cake into a box and set it on top of the display case. Another petal fell from the forsythias. "On the house. Happy birthday." Penelope smiled.

"Really?" Marshall watched as she lowered the white box into a paper bag with the bakery's logo.

"Sorry it's not prettier wrapping. No gift bags." She shrugged. "But I have this." She pulled a thin, yellow ribbon from under the counter. Snipping off a few inches, she tied the handles of the bag with a bow. "There. Looks a little more festive." She pushed the bag toward Marshall.

He wasn't sure what to do. He knew people were supposed to protest when someone offered to pay for something. But he also knew that not accepting a gift was rude. He looked at the paper bag with its yellow bow.

"Happy birthday …?" She paused as if waiting for something.

After a moment, Marshall realized she was waiting for his name. "Marshall … my name is Marshall."

"Penelope." She smiled.

"I know. Your name tag."

"Oh." She chuckled, glancing down. "Happy birthday, Marshall."

"Thank you," he said, wishing she didn't have a fiancé. He carefully picked up his birthday present and nodded. As he walked into the December afternoon with Toby at his side, Marshall realized he was smiling. A long time had passed since someone had given him a birthday present.

Chapter 14

Penelope, 21 December 2044, Age 25, T-minus Unknown

Penelope watched as Marshall walked down the sidewalk with the brown paper bag dangling from his fingers. It reminded her of a young child's lunchbox. When he turned a corner and disappeared, she smiled.

He's an odd duck.

But there was something about him she liked. What it was exactly she had no idea.

Authenticity?

Yes, that was it! There was something genuine and sincere about the man with the dog. Marshall acted with an honesty unnatural to most. So many picked and chose what to say or display about themselves, preparing 'a face to meet the faces that they meet.' But not this guy. And his dog! What a gentle, calm presence. His caramel-colored eyes seemed to love you right away. She understood now what Nick meant – how he felt – when he saw Gatsby smile. Toby's gaze had the same 'quality of eternal reassurance.' It seemed he 'understood you just as far as you wanted to be understood, believed in you as you would like to believe in yourself.' He was comfort in a coat – a soft, furry, black coat. She hoped they'd be back.

She glanced at the clock – 3:56 – and pulled a snack from the fridge, yogurt and an apple. Bea insisted she ate her fruit.

Penelope wished she knew what to do about enrollment. It was a normal thing to do nowadays, by everyone else's standards. People found out their deathdays the way they used to find out the gender of their babies. Now, of course, most parents chose the gender through the Department of Population Control. The DPC. It was a great way to monitor the number of boys and girls. It wasn't a perfect science. Despite the name, they didn't use it to control the population. For now, it was still acceptable to allow nature to take its course, but parents who didn't choose were considered backward and old-fashioned, an inconvenience to the efforts of the DPC.

Penelope wondered how much longer the option of surprise would be permitted. By the time she and Everett were ready to be parents, she imagined the DPC would simply assign a gender for their baby and that would be that. Choice and surprise, forgotten luxuries of the past.

Heck – that might be true with DoDs. We might be mandated to find out when our bodies are going to call it quits. Well, we're dying from the moment we're born, aren't we?

T.S. Eliot's poem surfaced in Penelope's mind.

There will be time, there will be time
Time for you and time for me,
And time for yet a hundred indecisions,
And for a hundred visions and revisions.

But how much time?

She studied the dead petals on the bakery case. They had faded and withered to practically nothing. They were as good as dead the moment they were trimmed from the bush. Their petals, once so bold and robust, were now etiolated and papery. The flowers had died. One day, she would die too. And Everett would die. She took a bite of the apple. Maybe Everett and Bea were right after all. Perhaps she should find out when the reaper will come for her.

What would it change?

A loud crash echoed through the bakery. Penelope started and glanced out the window. A man wearing a green jumper waved as he tossed a trashcan to the curb. Penelope waved back.

"I've gotta stop doing this."

As the truck drove to the next stop, the squealing brakes made her wince. Today was the shortest day of the year. Shadows already stalked the city, stealing away the sunlight from the streets. A lone streetlamp blinked across the street.

Penelope shivered. Outside in the fading daylight, she imagined something tall and dark emerging from the shadows. Again, the reaper entered her mind, and a chill ran up her back. Taking another bite of her apple, she held her breath. The sound of the bakery door opening and the dinging of the bell crashed through her thoughts.

"Hello? I need a dozen cookies, please."

Penelope coughed and caught the apple in her hand. She glanced out the window again, but the street was vacant. Snow had begun to fall.

"Excuse me?" the woman stated.

Penelope looked at the woman and smiled. "Sorry. Was just thinking."

"About what?" the woman asked.

"How long it's been since I've seen snow … and our deathdays. What changes when we know the number of remaining days? I mean, the number wouldn't change."

"One thing certain in an uncertain world!" the woman parroted. Her eyes twinkled like the eyes of a child. "I still have lots of years to go, and I'm already in my seventies!" The woman's eyes widened. "What about you?"

Penelope took another bite of the apple and chewed slowly, staring at the old woman. If this woman wasn't going to let the reaper sneak up on her, why should she? Maybe there'd be a certain freedom in knowing. Before she could change her mind, Penelope grabbed her phone.

"Excuse me for just a moment while I call my fiancé."

Chapter 15

Marshall, 29 December 2044, Age 28, T-minus 49

Marshall stared at the last slice where it waited for him in the open cakebox. The forsythias he had bought from the corner florist drooped in a cup beside it. They were past their ability to drink. The withered petals were as dry as the edges of the stale cake. He couldn't stop thinking about Penelope. Nor could he forget her nagging question. *What's it like to know?* He never answered her because he had no answer. He still didn't know what it was *like*, because there was nothing to compare it to. He sat and ran his finger across the cake. The frosting no longer stuck to his skin. He took a bite, and the staleness made him shiver. After a few more bites, he still could not think of an adequate response.

What was it like not to know?

Now that was a more complex question. Since he had known for so long, he could not remember. No one could *un*know once the date was revealed. Not even in the deepest recesses of the imagination could a person erase the information. At least, he couldn't.

What he could remember was a passage from *Tess of the d'Urbervilles*. Thomas Hardy, ahead of his time, had managed to put words to some participants' desires to enroll.

'There was a date of greater importance to her than all those … that of her own death … a day which lay sly and unseen among all the other days of the year, giving no sign or sound when she annually passed over it.' Tess wonders – *'When was it? Why did she not feel the chill of each yearly encounter with such a cold relation?'*

How lucky was Tess not to know, not to have been born or imagined or written into the pages of a book before someone could answer that question, *'When is the day?'*

For Marshall, it was October 10. And with the help of his Annual Deathday Diary Entry and those obnoxious office deathday parties, he often felt the *chill* of each yearly encounter. He wouldn't miss it if *he* didn't know the date – if October 10 could just *'lay sly and unseen among all the other days,'* could be just another day with no particular significance to his life.

Or his death.

Enrolling was different now than when he'd enrolled. Back then, a decade ago, it was an experiment. He would one day die. Everyone would. The difference now was that most people knew when. Death was no longer a someday. Death had a date. It was reality.

The *Experiment* wasn't an experiment anymore. The hotline number no longer rang. Participants' DoDs were now handed out at the enrollment office. The focus groups had long since disbanded, though participants were still required to maintain the practice of composing and submitting ADDEs. Participants in what had been the initial control group were given the option of learning their deathdays. After seeing the perceived benefits, most were all too eager for the information.

There was a freedom in knowing.

Marshall swallowed another mealy bite and held back a cough. He closed the lid and placed the box on the counter. He would save that last bite for tomorrow. It was rather sad to know that after tomorrow, there'd be no cake left.

There was a certain freedom in *not* knowing.

Chapter 16

Penelope, 3 January 2045, Age 26, T-minus Unknown

"I'm glad we decided to do this together, Nel," Everett said, holding open the door of the enrollment office on West Cary Street so Penelope could enter.

She smiled at him, ignoring the nagging sense of doubt that gnawed at her. "So am I," she lied. Yesterday she'd turned twenty-six. Today, she would turn T-minus who-knew-what. T-minus she-would-know-soon-enough.

"This is going to make our life together much easier to navigate."

"Mm-hm."

"I promise," Everett said. "You're going to be glad we did this."

"Everett," Penelope said, touching his arm and stopping him in the narrow hallway that led to the waiting room. "One thing has been on my mind …"

"Ask me anything."

"If you're so excited to enroll, why didn't you do it years ago? What were you waiting for?"

Everett's eyes crinkled at the edges in the way Penelope loved. "You," he said, kissing her. "I was waiting for you. The one and only."

"What if I had already enrolled? Most people enroll long before they're engaged."

"That would have been a shame because I … *we* … would have missed out on this rare experience. This is a one-in-a-million opportunity. It's how I knew we were meant to be together, the fact that you weren't enrolled." He rested his hands on her shoulders and looked into her eyes. "I knew … but then when I discovered that you didn't know your deathday, then I *really* knew. That was my sign. I mean, for two people not enrolled to meet … and then fall in love? Talk about the perfect match. What were the chances?"

Penelope resisted the urge to argue they could still be a perfect match without enrolling. Though she didn't share his enthusiasm, she did love it. And she had to admit that there was something *pretty special* about it. He was right about that. They were unicorns. Probably one of the last remaining couples to take advantage of the *allegedly* romantic experience of enrolling together. Who knew? Maybe she'd end up finding it romantic after all. *Only one way to find out …*

At the end of the sterile hallway, so typical of government agencies and hospitals, Everett and Penelope found themselves standing at a counter with a sheet of glass separating them from the workers on the other side. They waited for someone to acknowledge their presence, but no one did. After a moment, Everett tapped on the glass.

A Felix 1, a rectangular box balancing on a single wheel, stopped what it was doing and turned its silvery, square head. "Hello! Thank you for visiting the enrollment office." It pressed a button on the wall, and the glass shield lifted. The Felix 1 opened the door on its chest, revealing a touch screen. "Please listen carefully to the following options. If you are currently enrolled, please press one. If you would like to enroll, please press two. If you –"

Everett pressed two.

"You have pressed two. If you are enrolling alone, please press one. If you are enrolling with another, please press two."

Everett pressed two.

"Thank you for your interest in enrollment," the Felix 1 said. "Heaven is waiting." The cheery, metallic voice continued, verifying Everett and Penelope's full names, weights, eye and hair colorings, skin tones, shoe sizes, waist and chest measurements, occupations, home addresses, and annual incomes. "Please wait while I store your information." There was a pause. "Please enter the door to your left."

A soft click sounded, and the door opened, revealing another Felix 1. Penelope and Everett stepped forward, and the door closed softly behind them. The lock clicked back into position.

"Please wait here," the second Felix 1 said.

Penelope looked around. The walls were painted an inoffensive, if dull, beige. Five uninviting folding chairs sat against one wall. Opposite them, a wall-sized screen soundlessly re-played the benefits of enrollment. A larger-than-life couple shopped for headstones. A man dove headfirst out of an airplane as the clouds streamed past. The image was so dizzying that Penelope lowered herself into one of the unforgiving chairs. A woman gleefully used her *Life Planner* app to map out her bucket list while a man exuberantly viewed his participant stipend on the *Participant* app.

"Wow!" Everett gasped with a gleam of fascination in his eyes as he watched the images on the screen. His look of complete awe gave Penelope the chills.

A Felix 2, a newer and more evolved model – shinier with a larger viewing screen, entered. "Good afternoon."

Penelope stood.

"Please give me your hand." The Felix 2 held out its hand, and from its metal finger extended a thin needle. It pricked Penelope's middle finger, and a small red drop formed. The Felix 2 soaked it up through a tiny tube that fed into the silver, rectangular box.

Penelope frowned and sucked on her finger.

The Felix 2 handed her a cotton swab that smelled like alcohol before asking Everett for his hand to do the same with his finger. After a few moments, the Felix 2 dinged and said, "We are in the process of retrieving your Date of Departures. We hope you will find the waiting room comfortable." The Felix 2 spun on its axis and wheeled away.

"This isn't very romantic," Penelope stated.

"Nel … we're about to find out how many decades of wedded bliss we get to share. What's not romantic about that?"

The Felix 2 returned. "I have your Date of Departures. Ladies first. Penelope Rae Hope, your Date of Departure is … January 30, 2046."

At first, Penelope wanted to hear the date again. *This has to be a mistake.* One year away? Then she decided she didn't want to hear anything, especially numbers. Her gaze dropped and she fixated on the Felix 2's single, black wheel, which seemed to vibrate as the Felix tried to balance itself. A smarter design would have included two wheels or maybe even four. Much more stable. The constant movement made her feel a little dizzy. January 30, 2046 was a little over a year away. Twelve months. She glanced up at Everett, and her stomach clenched. He didn't meet her gaze. His face was pale and his eyes wide. He remained speechless, mouth agape.

The date again flashed across her vision – January 30, 2046, twelve months from now! The number twelve was a symbol of space and time. She had read that somewhere. Was it Newton or Einstein? No, that wasn't right. Maybe Kant? The Vedas ran through her mind, and an image of a Hindu monk appeared before her.

"Follow your desire as long as you live," the monk whispered, before vanishing from her mind's eye.

Penelope blinked several times. "Twelve months?" she whispered.

Da Vinci's *Last Supper* now consumed her view. A copy of the painting had hung in her grandparents' dining room, depicting Jesus' last meal. She'd grown up looking at it and wondering who the people were. She thought about the colors and the shadows and had often wondered if anyone was hiding somewhere in the darkness. The darkness always frightened her. Where would she have her last supper? Who would be at her table?

"Congratulations, Penelope Rae Hope! You are T-minus 2 years," the Felix 2 said. "You will be T-minus 1 on January 30, 2045, in three weeks and six days! And now for the gentleman. Everett Sebastian Flach ..."

The Felix 2's metallic voice faded. Penelope felt defeated and weak. The folding chair creaked from her weight as she sat, and her eyes darted across the room, as if the other chairs were somehow mocking her. A pregnant woman on the screen joyously planned out each day of her family's lives right down to the last. No one on that screen looked as if they felt the pressure of passing time. Her time had just been reduced to the number twelve. What could that possibly mean? The people on that screen still held to their dreams, their hopes, their plans, their remaining time.

There will be time, there will be time
Time for you and time for me,
And time for yet a hundred indecisions,
And for a hundred visions and revisions.

Something heavy pressed against Penelope's chest. It was difficult to breathe. All the time she did not have was suffocating her.

"There's *one* thing certain in an uncertain world," the Felix 2 said.

Penelope leaned over and promptly vomited onto the robot's single, black, wobbly wheel.

The cold, fresh air against her face somewhat soothed Penelope's reeling stomach. She leaned on the car and took several deep breaths. Both doors opened, and Penelope dropped onto her seat.

"Start." Everett glanced at Penelope with a blank stare. "Bea's," he ordered.

The car whirred gently out of its spot and headed for Shockoe Bottom.

"I'm going to die," Penelope whispered. She pressed down on her window button as another wave of nausea rolled across her soul.

"It's too cold outside." Everett pushed his button, and her window raised.

Penelope turned her head away from the outside world and concentrated on her fiancé's eyes. "'It's too cold outside?' That's all you can say? 'It's too cold outside?' I'm dying. I can have my fucking window open if I want it open." She pressed the button but nothing happened. "Fuck!" she screamed. "Unlock my damn button!"

Everett stared straight ahead and didn't blink.

She pounded on the button with her fist. As her hair fell across her face, she yelled, "I can have my damn window open if I want it opened. Damn it, Everett. Unlock my fucking window. Open it! Open it!" Her fist continued to pound against the button until her eyes filled with tears. As her vision blurred, she placed her head against the window and cried.

"We're all going to die," Everett said, his voice cold and flat. "All of us. I'm going to die."

"When Everett? When? Not in twelve fucking months. Not in a single, short, shitty little year!" She drew a slow, shaky breath. "I *knew* I didn't want to know. I fucking knew it."

"Your life is just shorter than mine, that's all."

"Do you hear yourself? Don't you care? I'm going to die. *Soon.* Your fiancé. Your almost-wife. You'll be a widower before you're even married, unless we move the date up."

Everett didn't respond. The car's gentle droning filled the silence. Everett cracked Penelope's window just an inch or so. She took a deep breath and savored the feel of the cool, fresh air.

"I won't leave you," Everett whispered. "If that's what you're worried about. This changes nothing between us. You were always going to die someday."

"We didn't know *someday* was in twelve months!"

"We can talk about it in the morning," Everett whispered. "Stay with Bea tonight. I need to think."

Chapter 17

Penelope, 4 January 2045, Age 26, T-minus 2

Penelope awoke in Bea's bed. She watched as her friend's chest gently rose and fell with the slow, nighttime breaths of a sleeper. Penelope thought about their childhood sleepovers, and all the happy times they had spent heedless of their mortality. Too young to worry about death or dying – or anything for that matter. Assuming they'd be young, carefree, and fearless forever, because what else was there to be? Well, Penelope reasoned, she would be young forever, in her own awful way. She'd never grow old.

Quietly, she pulled the blankets aside, stood, and walked to the window. The moon hovered above the city, keeping a late-night vigil over the inhabitants. Its candlelight glow burned warmly through a gossamer curtain of clouds. The moon was here long before she was and would be here long after she was gone. The city lights twinkled cheerily below, and for a moment within the stillness, she almost forgot how limited her time was. She was part of the night. Part of the darkness. Nothing and everything, all at once. No beginning. No end. No limits or measurements of time. Penelope sighed and wiped her eyes.

"There will be time … but not for me. Time for you, Bea, but no time for me." A tear rolled down her cheek, and this time, she didn't wipe it away. "'And time for yet a hundred indecisions' … maybe a few … and for 'a hundred visions and revisions.' No, Mr. Moon, I don't think so. For me, there won't be any time."

She shivered and hugged herself. Glancing down at the city far below, she sighed. The black ribbon of the river still coursed through the city. In the middle of the night like this, it looked like nothing more than a rift between the north and south sides of town – a gaping tear in the city's infrastructure. A black chasm. If one were to step too close, one would fall in and disappear forever. A deep loneliness, black as the inky river below, spread through Penelope's chest. At daybreak, she would have one less night left in her life.

"Penelope?" Bea's voice sounded groggy and muffled.

"Hi." Penelope sat on the edge of the bed and breathed in deeply.

"I'm sorry. I never thought –"

"I know and it's fine. Thanks for letting me stay here."

Bea sat up. "We should spend as much time together as we can now that we know …" Bea frowned and stared at her hands.

"That I don't have much time?" Penelope wiped away another tear.

"I thought you'd have more. T-minus 30 seemed kinda hard to beat. I just assumed … me before you."

Penelope shook her head. "T-minus 2. Almost T-minus 1."

Bea pushed away the blankets and grabbed onto Penelope. Their tears felt warm against their skin. Together, they cried.

"Oh, Penelope!" Bea whispered. "What will I do without you?"

Penelope felt along Bea's spine, and she counted. When she reached twelve, she paused and concentrated on the warmth of her friend's life, and the softness of her friend's shirt, and the way her engagement ring kept snagging on the fabric.

"Keep living," Penelope whispered. "For the both of us."

Chapter 18

Penelope, 4 January 2045, Age 26, T-minus 2

A little before lunch, the doorbell buzzed.

Bea glanced at her phone and sighed. "It's Everett," she said, as she tapped on the screen. "The door's open."

Everett entered, barely glancing at the two friends sitting across from each other at the small dinette, their coffee mugs steaming in front of them. Penelope wiped her eyes and tried to smile. She knew he'd be able to tell she'd been crying. Bea pushed her mug around as if considering the perfect placement.

"Good morning, ladies," Everett said.

Penelope frowned at his obvious and failed effort to sound cheerful – normal. She stood and left her mug on the table, following Everett to the small entryway that faced the kitchen. She placed her hand on his arm. She needed a touch of solace, some reassurance.

"We need to talk." He looked away. "Maybe we could go for a walk."

Penelope studied his handsome face. Perhaps it was his strong jawline that made her want him so much. Or his brown eyes that twinkled in the afternoon sun and seemed to light the path that she was to travel into forever. Maybe it was his smile. Now, his frown reminded her that yesterday's tomorrow was actually today, and *that* yesterday seemed a lifetime ago.

He refused to look at her. Refused to acknowledge her touch. She felt as if that black chasm from last night had opened up between them. He was light-years away from her.

"I'll dress."

She released his arm and headed for the bedroom to pull on a pair of jeans and a hoodie. Something didn't feel right. Something didn't feel right at all, and it wasn't her heart she was thinking about. It was Everett's.

Stepping into the foyer, she glanced over at Bea still pushing her mug back and forth across the table. "Can I borrow a jacket?"

Bea nodded.

Penelope selected a tweed peacoat too formal for her outfit, but she didn't care. Everett held the door, and they stepped into the hallway. Without words, they aimed for the street.

"Where are we going?" Penelope asked as they stepped onto the sidewalk. She kept her hands inside the peacoat's pockets and her eyes glued to the ground.

"Shiplock Park."

"Okay."

The day was cold and gray with thick clouds obscuring the blue sky hiding just behind them. Every now and then, a gust of wind drove a parade of errant leaves tumbling into their ankles. The water in the canal looked brown. No turtles sunned on the dead logs along the shore.

"I've been up all night," Everett said. "I'm not sure I can do this."

Penelope kept her gaze on the gray pavement.

"Nel?" He held her arm and tightened his grip ever so slightly.

"I heard you," she whispered.

"Can *you*?"

She looked up at him and frowned. "I don't exactly have a choice now, do I?" She paused and stared at her shoes. "But I guess you do."

"Everything is more complicated."

"Complicated? I thought enrolling was going to make our lives so much easier to navigate. Isn't that what you said?"

Everett winced and looked out over the water.

"We never should have enrolled," Penelope whispered. "I never wanted to know. What if we didn't know?"

Everett took in a deep breath and shifted his stance. "I can't stop thinking about burial plots. I'll outlive you by … I might meet someone after you're … then what do I do? She'd probably want to be buried with me. But then there's –"

"You've found a replacement already?"

She had felt it. She knew he would leave. The moment he told the car to aim for Bea's, she knew it was over. He was walking a path by himself, and she would have to find her own. Her path was short. His ran for many more miles – decades.

"What?" he asked.

"You've found a replacement. A newer model that should last longer?"

"No. I haven't met anyone. I'm speaking hypothetically. Even if we moved the date to this summer, Nel, we wouldn't be married a whole year before …"

Oh, there will be time. Lots of time. Just not for me. Indecisions and a hundred revisions. So that was it. She would be revised right out of Everett's life. "I guess everyone is right."

"Right about what?"

"Knowing allows you to plan ahead. And that is what you're doing." Penelope shook her head and turned away. "Did you download the *Life Planner* app? Bea loves it. Says it really helps."

"Penelope, I –"

"What? You what?"

"People will talk," Everett said.

"People will *talk*? Talk about what?"

"Our T-minus ages. We could be judged for our poor decision."

Penelope bit her lip, her eyes concentrating on a swirling eddy in the water. "The stigma!" She threw up her arms. "Of course." Rolling her eyes and shaking her head, she sighed. "The age remainder gap. No one cares about age difference when people get married. Not anymore. You could be in your fifties and I could be twenty, and no one would care. As long as we're both comparably close to *death!* Is that it, Everett? We're not comparably close?"

Everett didn't reply. Instead, he looked away.

He had made up his mind. Probably the moment that metal contraption spewed out the date. Then again, she probably never had him in the first place. She was always going to die on January 30, 2046. She just hadn't known it.

Penelope watched as a paper bag tumbled across the dirty sidewalk, wrapping around the trunk of a cherry tree. "Alright," she whispered. "Alright, Everett."

"Nel …" Everett reached out. "It was never meant to be."

"I suppose not."

Penelope took a step and sat on a cold metal bench. A chill ran up her legs and into her back.

Everett touched her shoulder. He bent over and gently kissed the top of her head. As he walked away, Penelope thought about the door that had just closed. A door that her future husband had just locked behind him. A lock to which she didn't have a key.

"T-minus 2." She shook her head. *Who will buy in for just one year?*

Chapter 19

Marshall, 14 January 2045, Age 28, T-minus 49

Marshall didn't have an occasion to buy a cake today. He just had a desire to see Penelope. Besides, Toby was out of biscuits and maybe, since he'd mentioned it, The Cakery would have some to sell. He scratched Toby's velvety ears and studied his trusting, golden eyes.

"Let's find some biscuits."

Marshall had been thinking about her question – about what it was like to be enrolled – and maybe he had an answer. He had tried all morning to think of a reason for a cake, but nothing came to mind. At least he could say he came to answer her question.

As he walked beneath a gray winter sky, Marshall somehow felt warmed, as if a small flame was glowing from somewhere inside him. Stale Christmas lights still burned inside a few shops. With New Year's Eve long passed, the bulbs no longer lit the windows with a festive cheer, or signified joy, or anticipation of the coming season. Instead, they revealed the laziness of the overwhelmed shop owners. Marshall felt annoyed at people who didn't take their lights down within a respectable window of time.

The cold, however, seemed to lift his spirits, and he felt a giddiness that thickened as he stepped closer to the bakery. But the unfamiliar joy was replaced with disappointment as he reached for the door.

Brown paper covered the glass. The Cakery storefront was dismal and gray. The sign looked somehow out of place above the empty windows. A handwritten note taped to the door stated that The Cakery was *Closed*. That was all. Not *Closed for Repairs*. Not *Closed for Renovations*. Not *Closed: On Holiday*. Just *Closed*. It felt so – definite.

Marshall took a step back and held his breath. As he released the pent-up excitement, an emotion close to betrayal rose up inside him.

"Tricked!"

Marshall didn't like tricks. Why had she not told him she was planning to close? He promised Toby some biscuits, and Penelope was the sweetest thing – the only sweet thing – in his life besides Toby. Her presence colored his otherwise-dull world. Colored it in cheerful yellows and now everything was gray again. That was the only word he could think of to explain how he felt – gray. He stared at his reflection and frowned.

A small tear in the paper grabbed his attention. He leaned in, cupping his hands around his eyes to block out the glare. The darkened room was ashen, and the display cases were empty. No longer did they boast colorful, celebratory cakes. The refrigerator that once glowed with a garish, white fluorescence slept somberly in the twilight, and dust particles drifted through the light that crept through the cracks. On the glass counter beside the now-silent register, a bouquet of dead forsythias was the only thing decorating the room. Paper-thin petals littered the counter, the stems nothing more than brittle sticks, standing naked in the glass vase like meatless bones.

Marshall lowered his head, and Toby lowered his tail. They walked home together along the graying streets under the heavy, gray clouds.

Chapter 20

Penelope, 26 January 2045, Age 26, T-minus 2

"Alright, Penelope," Bea said, throwing the living room curtains wide open, exposing the cityscape. "It's morning."

Penelope blinked, groaned, and rolled over. "Another one? Again?"

"Another one," Bea repeated. "Again."

"One less sunrise for me." Penelope pulled the blanket over her head. "Hooray."

Bea sat on the edge of the couch near Penelope, who pretended to have fallen back to sleep. "It's not gonna work. I've been thinking about it for days, and you can't keep this up."

Penelope didn't respond, just kept breathing. *In and out. In and out. How many breaths do I have left to my name, anyway?*

"Penelope!" Bea tossed a pillow at her friend's head. "I said, it's not gonna work. I know you're awake. Get up!"

Penelope opened one eye and focused on Bea. "What's your problem? I don't have anywhere to go. Let me sleep."

"No."

"Yes."

"No, Penelope. I mean it. Get up."

"No."

"Yes!" Bea yanked the blanket off Penelope.

"Bea! Seriously? What are you doing?"

"Get dressed. Go outside for crying out loud. *Do something.*"

Penelope sat up and rubbed her eyes. "I do … things," she said, knowing she didn't sound convincing.

"What things?"

"I get up. I mean, at some point. And I look out the window. Sometimes I drink coffee. When you're not here, I nap."

Asleep, she could forget she was dying. Asleep, she wasn't afraid of dying. Maybe sleeping was like death – except sleeping could become waking – death couldn't become life.

Bea stared at Penelope and raised one brow. "What kind of life is that?"

"A short one."

"Penelope! What's happened to you?"

"I think we all know what *happened* to me, but if you want me to rehash it for you –"

"Penelope, stop!" Bea paused. "Don't you ever get bored?"

"When I get bored, I sleep."

"Don't you ever miss baking? Or … reading?"

"Not when I'm asleep." *I don't miss anything when I'm asleep. Not baking. Not reading. Not Everett. Not my whole ruined life …*

"This has got to stop."

"It will," Penelope said. "In twelve months and four days."

Bea sighed.

Penelope waited.

"Is this really what you want to do for the next twelve months?"

"And four days," Penelope added. "Twelve months and *four* days." Right now, every day counted.

"And they're all you have left." Bea paused. "You know what? You're *not* dead yet."

Penelope squinted and frowned.

"Well, you're not!"

"Yet."

"Do something with the *yet* for God's sake! Get off my freakin' couch!" Bea walked across the room and stared at a few pictures on the wall. She sighed, turned toward Penelope, and smiled sadly. "I mean … at least for a while. You can come back tonight and sleep on my couch if you want to. But for now go do *something*."

"Alright, fine. Today I'll celebrate."

"Good. Celebrate what?"

"A milestone."

"Okay … what milestone?"

"Everett-Dumped-Me-Day. And the day I started living with you. I think I'll commemorate the occasion. It's been almost a month, hasn't it … with a visit to the scene where it all took place. Can I borrow a hoodie? I'm going to Shiplock." Penelope stood and held out her hand. "Hoodie?"

Bea pulled hers off and hesitated before handing it over. "Penelope, this isn't exactly what I meant. I was thinking maybe do something fun."

"Fun? You don't think going to the *park* sounds like *fun*?"

"Penelope –"

"No, Bea. No. You are absolutely right, just like you were about *enrolling*. I should definitely go do something." The statement about enrolling was mean. She knew it before she'd said it, but she couldn't help herself. It felt good to *be* mean.

Bea didn't protest or speak a single word in her own defense. Instead, she sat on the couch and stared at the floor.

Penelope thought about apologizing, but the idea was only a wisp. She walked past Bea into the foyer, closing the door behind her without saying another word.

Chapter 21

Marshall, 26 January 2045, Age 28, T-minus 49

Marshall and Toby always walked the Capital Trail to the office. It wasn't the fastest route, but it was the prettiest and the quietest. Although it felt a little lonely with the bare trees and the barren ground, the red berry bushes and the sweet aroma of the canal water made Marshall feel better about things – even on these biting, blustery mornings.

When the trail bustled with people, Marshall loved to *people-watch*. Most never talked to him, and he liked that. He could just observe how they interacted. Mothers pushing strollers and ogling at a baby he couldn't see. Children wanting to pet or talk to Toby and Toby obliging. The slight breeze from a runner passing by, a faint scent of laundry soap or perfume or shampoo left in their wake. Cyclists, heads down, gliding past, bicycle chains sounding a familiar rhythm.

Today, however, the trail looked deserted.

Toby stopped walking and lifted his front paw, informing Marshall that they were no longer alone.

"What is it, Toby?" Marshall glanced around and spotted someone sitting on a bench under the sleeping cherry trees. She seemed to be the only person in the park aside from him and Toby.

He took a deep breath. Would he have to give a greeting since they were the only two there and he had to pass by? Would she acknowledge him? Marshall hoped not. Maybe he could get by without an interaction if he just put his head down and walked as quickly as he could, keeping his eyes glued to the path. Avoiding eye contact usually meant he could avoid conversations.

Taking a deep breath, he let it out slowly. "Okay, Toby. Let's go."

They approached the bench, and his eyes defied him, falling on that beautiful face. It was Penelope, the baker. The one with the dying flowers. The one from the Hill Café. The one from that unfortunate incident with the antique car. The most beautiful woman in the world. He surprised himself when he stopped in front of her, smiled, and said, "Hello."

Penelope looked up. Her eyes were red and swollen. She held a tissue to her nose. "Hi." She reached to scratch Toby, but he ducked and stood behind Marshall. Her hand fell to her lap.

"Sorry," Marshall said. "He's working."

The beautiful woman remained silent.

"Funny I should run into you," Marshall said, wishing he hadn't said it. It wasn't actually funny. There was nothing funny about running into her. He wasn't laughing. She wasn't laughing. *Funny* wasn't the right word. "Fitting, actually. Do you remember me? I'm Marshall. I bought that cake at your bakery for my birthday." Marshall waited for her to speak, but she didn't respond. "I've been thinking about your question, and I have an answer."

"My question?"

"Yes. Your question. The one about what it's like to be enrolled. You asked me that question at your bakery. I've been thinking about it, and I have an answer. I think I know what it's like." Marshall wasn't sure what she was thinking as he finished his sentence. It was difficult to read people, but she almost looked surprised.

Penelope patted the empty space on the bench.

Marshall tilted his head and thought for a moment. Shrugging, he sat and remained quiet.

"Okay then," Penelope said with a slight smile. "What's it like? To be enrolled."

Marshall stared at Toby. His mind whirled in all directions at once. *Is she being sarcastic? Or does she honestly want to know?* He allowed his mind to search through his references and determined several possible outcomes. She no longer owned the bakery, so the chances of running into her again would probably be slim.

"Cold today," he said.

Penelope laughed. "Yes, it is. Now, do you have that answer for me or not?"

"You really want to know?"

"I really want to know," she said with a slight sniffle.

"Okay, knowing is like when I savored each bite of my birthday cake, knowing that each bite took me closer to the last. I knew exactly how many bites I had left before the whole cake was gone."

Penelope didn't say anything.

Marshall paused and kept his eyes on Toby. It was her turn to say something. That was how conversations were supposed to work, but she wasn't saying anything.

"Knowing that," Marshall whispered, "almost ruined each bite."

Penelope remained quiet.

Marshall thought about his mother. Sometimes people are laughing at you, but sometimes they are laughing with you. Sometimes people cry when they are sad, but sometimes they cry when they are happy. It is polite to show interest in people by asking them questions about their life.

His mother's voice lingered as he remembered that this beautiful woman was planning her wedding. Feeling a nudge, as if his mother were standing behind him, he took in another deep breath and said, "How's the wedding planning coming along?"

"Wedding planning." Penelope scoffed and rolled her eyes. "Ha!" She shrugged and a tear fell. Wiping her eyes, she laughed. "Wedding planning," she said again and laughed harder. "Now that *is* funny."

Funny? How could planning a wedding be funny? If planning a wedding was so funny, then why was she crying? Her smile had disappeared, and the corners of her mouth seemed weighed down by a large frown.

"My coworkers loved the deathday cake I bought at your bakery. Do you remember? You added the yellow flower. I've tried to go back a few times, but –"

"I closed it."

"Yes, it was closed." Marshall paused. "They didn't understand the flower. My coworkers are like that. They never understand. I got it."

Penelope looked up and wiped her eyes. "No … no. Of course they wouldn't understand." She huffed, glanced at the canal, and shook her head. "There is no wedding to plan for anymore. Bea was excited to be my maid of honor. It's always been our plan, yah know?" She hesitated before laughing again. "What a fool I am."

"I don't think you're a fool," Marshall said.

Penelope shrugged. "You don't even know me."

"I know you like forsythias and hate deathday cakes."

Penelope chuckled. "Yes, I do."

"I know you bake cakes … really good cakes. And you can make delicate, little flowers out of frosting."

"Also true." Penelope smiled.

"And I know you're not enrolled."

Penelope stared at the canal again and frowned.

Marshall scratched Toby's ear and waited.

She shrugged.

Marshall smiled. "You see, I know you a little."

"How old is Toby?" she asked.

"Seven. But no T-minus age. They don't enroll dogs."

"That's a good thing."

"I have to go to work now," Marshall stated.

"Oh, right. Of course."

"Maybe we could talk again? On purpose next time?"

Penelope laughed and nodded. "I'd really like that, Marshall. That place in Church Hill? The Hill Café? You want to meet me there?"

Marshall felt his stomach churn, but it was a good churn. He smiled. "Tuesday evening at seven?"

"Done." She used her hoodie sleeve to wipe her nose.

For all the puffiness around her eyes and rawness around her nose, she was still beautiful in Marshall's eyes.

Chapter 22

Penelope's Annual Deathday Diary Entry

Date: January 30, 2045

Entry No. 01

Everett left me. I guess I'll start there. It was the day after we enrolled. How is that for romantic? We were supposed to be married next year. June 16th, 2046 would've been our day.

God, there are so many dates to remember now. My birthday. My deathday. My enrollment anniversary. The day Everett left me. The day I would've married him, my *would-be* anniversary. I'll live most of those dates one more time. One more birthday. One more enrollment anniversary. One more day-that-Everett-left-me.

I never used to walk around and look at people and think, "I wonder how old that person is." You could pretty much guess someone's age, within a few years, by their appearance. It was easy. But the T-minus age, now that's a whole different thing. I look at people and have no idea what their T-minus ages are. And I wonder. I really want to know. Most of them have so much more time than I do, even the really old ones. And that's so strange. So counterintuitive.

Everett dropped me off at Bea's the night we enrolled, and I just haven't left. I mean, I've been out to pick things up from our apartment and close the bakery, but that's about it. I've become the proverbial *guy on the couch*. And I'm okay with that. Bea is too, I guess. I mean, she hasn't said anything about it one way or the other, at least not now that

I've started to leave the apartment sometimes. So, here I am. I can survive off my paid incentive for the rest of my life. It's not like I have much time left.

Where would I be right now if I weren't sitting here in this chair, in this room, writing this ADDE all alone? If I didn't know that in exactly one year, I'll be dead? Bea found me a death therapist, one who comes to you. I asked him that question. He didn't know the answer any better than I do. But he told me it didn't matter, and I should stop thinking in what-ifs. Said before my next session I needed to come up with an answer. So I did. I said I'd be happily planning my wedding day with Everett, maybe looking ahead to starting a family, ignorant in my bliss and blissful in my ignorance, baking cakes and brownies and going about my short, lovely, little life. And do you know what he said? He said, "Now I want you to visualize how your current situation is actually better than where you would've ended up." Actually *better*? He said I needed to reframe my thinking and not to worry, he'd give me the tools I needed. I don't need to reframe my thinking. I don't even need to know where I'd be if I weren't right here. What I want to know is this: *What does it mean to be dead?* What *is* it to be dead? Where am I going in exactly one year? They say enrolling gives you an expected end. Bullshit! I have no idea what to expect, only when to expect it.

What else? I've been thinking about my parents. It's been a while, honestly, since I thought about them. When my parents divorced, Mom was awarded custody. Dad had visitation rights. But that arrangement lasted only a few days. Mom died in a car crash just two weeks after she won the custody battle. Everyone thought Dad would enroll me without Mom to tell him not to. But he didn't. I don't think anyone knows why. I never asked. But once, just after the divorce, I asked my mom why I couldn't enroll. Most of my friends were enrolling and encouragement to enroll was everywhere -- the TV, the Internet, posters in the hallways at school, etc.

"All this technology," she said, "it's taking us farther away from what's real." I didn't understand her then. But she was right. When was the last time anyone went to a beach or set foot in a forest? But we all sure know a hell of a lot about a Felix and virtual or augmented reality chairs. I've gone to the woods in one of those. It's realistic, but it's not *real*. Life has sort of become like that for people now—not real. Look at Bea. She has fabricated this grandiose idea of what life is supposed to be. But her fantasy is so far from reality that she can't enjoy what she's experiencing right now. She's too busy chasing a life she wishes she had. I'm not gonna do that. I refuse to let my life become a series of disappointed dreams and missed milestones that are marked in red X's on a *Life Planner* app. I wonder what Mom and Dad would think of me now. Of the fact that I'm enrolled.

What a waste of time this is. I have so little of it left, and I'm mandated to spend it like this? Reflecting on knowledge I wish I didn't have? Writing my first, also my last, my *only* ADDE? If I'm being honest, I don't know what to make of all this. I've only been enrolled for a few weeks. And it has changed everything. Absolutely everything. The life I had planned is gone. And what am I going to do with the life I have left?

Signed: Penelope Hope, Participant No. PH01302046

Chapter 23

Penelope, 31 January 2045, Age 26, T-minus 1

Penelope sat across the table from Marshall and smiled. She liked the way Toby rested his head on Marshall's feet, and the way Marshall's blue eyes darted from face to face without ever really looking at anyone – except for her. It felt as if his soul was reaching for her through his eyes. He would set his gaze just above the hostess' brows or just below the waiter's nose. But for her, his gaze was penetrating. It was as if he could single her out in the room and erase everyone else. She felt beautiful. For the first time in a very long time, she felt wanted. The sense of actually feeling anything had evaporated almost as fully as the life she had planned with Everett. It felt good to be desired again.

"My friend Bea couldn't believe I had plans tonight," she said, taking a peek over her menu.

"Why?"

"I haven't been out much lately."

"Why?"

"It's been rough since my fiancé and I split."

"What happened?" Marshall asked. "Why the break up?"

Penelope laughed and placed her menu to the side of the table. "Loaded question." When Marshall didn't respond and instead gazed at her with honest concern, she shrugged. "Just wasn't meant to be."

"Wasn't meant to be?" he repeated, furrowing his brows and nodding.

As he buttered another dinner roll, he squinted at the menu. Penelope studied his strong jawline that chewed in time with his thoughts, the muscles under his ears bulging and relaxing.

"Do you think anything is ever meant to be?" He looked up at her as he spoke. "Getting hit by that antique car … was that meant to be? Or running into each other at the park? Meant to be or happenstance? In life, is it fate or design? Or serendipity? Perhaps coincidence? A grand plan? What's the point of getting engaged if it wasn't meant to be?"

Penelope felt breathless. She'd been thinking about these questions recently. More than ever before. In particular, the last one. "I … I don't know," she replied. *We didn't know it wasn't meant to be.*

Marshall folded his hands in front of him and gazed into her eyes. It was impossible for her to break the link as she listened to his recitation. "'Let us go …" he whispered, "'… through certain half-deserted streets … streets that follow like a tedious argument of insidious intent to lead you to an overwhelming question ... oh, do not ask, What is it?'"

"'Let us go and make our visit.'" Penelope finished the stanza.

Marshall nodded, turning his attention back to his menu. "I always order the meatloaf." He placed his menu on top of hers. "The gravy's good. Why did you close The Cakery?"

Penelope smiled and shook her head. He certainly wasn't socially graceful.

Marshall clasped his hands and again raised his brows.

"Wasn't making money," she lied and glanced at her lap. "I guess my refusal to bake more than one deathday cake a day came back to bite me."

He laughed and she looked up. She hadn't meant to be funny.

"Bite me," Marshall repeated, shaking his head and folding his hands. "Cake. Bite me." He glanced up at Penelope and smiled. "Funny."

"Yeah," Penelope replied. "I guess it is. I get it." She smiled and a warm comfort flowed over her. He wasn't judging her, he was actually curious. Unabashedly curious. And straightforward. And certainly not like anyone she'd ever met. She liked him. Marshall was refreshing. Or maybe it was just the change of scenery. Maybe Bea was right. She should have gotten off that couch a long time ago.

"Your one-deathday-cake-a-day policy was a rather clever business model. Your friend Bea was probably right that making more of those cakes would've made you more money, but who knows? Supply and demand and all that. One a day makes them more novel, more desirable."

"Knowing your deathday is so commonplace, so mundane," Penelope added. "It's anything but novel."

"Doesn't mean the cakes can't be."

"Hence the flower."

"Touché." Marshall chuckled. "The flower was a novel touch. No other bakery places a flower on their deathday cakes. Now that The Cakery's closed, no one puts a flower on a deathday cake. No one seems to have thought of it except you."

Their waiter returned. Staring at the man's nose or lips, Marshall ordered the meatloaf and gravy, and Penelope ordered the salmon with mashed potatoes and asparagus. Her dinner tonight would be a steep upgrade from the tubs of ice cream, bowls of cereal, and bags of chips that had sustained her existence on the couch. For the first time in weeks, she had her appetite back. And it felt good to want to eat. It felt good to feel pretty, and it felt good to feel hungry and maybe, just maybe, it felt good to be alive – if only for a little while.

When they finished their dinner, Marshall asked Penelope if she'd fancy a walk to Jefferson Park where they could see the entire city underneath an expanse of stars. Everything would look like the scene of a model trainset – pristine and distant.

"I'd like that," she said. It'd been almost a month since she'd seen a view of the city different from the ones out of Bea's apartment. A new perspective on things might be in order.

They climbed the concrete steps in silence. The whisper of cars on the streets below grew more distant as the sound of dry leaves rustling in the cool night grew more real, more immediate. She was out of breath when they reached the top, but Marshall seemed as if the steep climb hadn't affected him at all.

"I guess I'm a little out of shape," she said, feeling embarrassed.

He didn't respond. He sat in the brittle grass and gazed at the city. She sat beside him, secretly thrilled that Toby had elected to rest his head on *her* feet. For a few minutes, they were quiet. The grid of blocks forming light squares, and the black outline of streets streaked with white headlights and red taillights, felt more real than the blackness that haunted her. Everything glittered or twinkled, and she was happy.

Penelope took a deep breath and caught the scent of dried leaves and pine. She closed her eyes. Bea was right. She should have gotten off the couch sooner. Much sooner. But there was no point losing more time regretting the time she'd already lost. She could only move forward. The days on the couch were of the past. In some respects, today felt like the first day of the rest of her life.

"Toby and I come here sometimes," Marshall said. "Look at that black sky. At the black river where the city lights suddenly stop and the water starts."

Penelope nodded. A few forlorn lights in the blackness, probably boats floating on the water, reminded her of something that had broken free to set off on its own solitary adventure. She thought of fireflies or perhaps satellites traversing the night sky.

She shook her head. "And they say that heaven is waiting," she whispered.

"What is heaven waiting for?" Marshall asked. "I've always wondered what that slogan meant."

Penelope smiled. The phrase was just an idiom. A catchy slogan that gave the religious a reason for enrolling. They were standing in line for God's plan – the belief that *He* had to give an expected end. No harm in knowing when that expected end was. Knowing wouldn't change *His* plan. Knowing wasn't playing God. It was growing closer to God. It was accepting *His* will. It was exchanging a sense of chance and human frailty for certainty in *His* plan. To know was to have faith and place oneself entirely in *His* care. To stop trying to exercise human control over the divine. *His* plan. The faithful who enrolled weren't counting down to death, but to a rebirth in the afterlife. World without end. The justifications were endless.

Surely, an omnipotent God didn't have to wait. Time waited for no man, so why would heaven? It didn't make any sense. And if they were all waiting to enter heaven, what was heaven waiting for?

"For us to hurry up and die so we can get there, I guess," Penelope replied. "I mean, that's the idea."

"That's ridiculous. Why would heaven wait for anyone? Isn't it supposed to be perfect with or without us?"

"Heaven ..." Penelope watched the slow crawl of a green light across the dark water. "Heaven is here. Heaven is in every sunset and sunrise. In every beautiful part of human nature." She took a deep breath. The crisp night air felt cool, the wind on her skin invigorating, sending a wave of goosebumps down her arms. She relaxed into the whispers of the dried oak leaves. "What a gift it is to be here. What a gift to live in this world with rainbows and snowfalls. How could heaven be anywhere else? What could be better than this?"

"A world where we don't know," Marshall replied.

Penelope had almost forgotten that Marshall was sitting beside her. She had dissolved into her new appreciation for this world and her life. "A world where we don't know what?"

Marshall looked at her and smiled. "A world where we don't know how little time we have left. A world like yours, like Toby's. A world without a countdown."

Penelope shivered, pulling her knees to her chest, resting her chin. The green light she'd been following across the water vanished into the inky darkness. She stood and brushed off her pants. "Walk me down?" she asked.

Marshall stood and Penelope linked her arm with his. His body felt sturdy and warm and safe. Together, they made their way back to the city far below.

Chapter 24

Marshall, 3 February 2045, Age 28, T-minus 49

From the small table in his kitchen with his breakfast in front of him, Marshall looked out the floor-to-ceiling window that offered a view of the far western edge of the city – white sky, gray buildings, black river. On the other side of the water, the buildings seemed shorter and sat farther apart before giving way to the forest. Marshall had never been to the forest. In fact, he had never left the city – never considered it as a possibility. He enjoyed all the adventure he needed from reading, which he supposed was better than everyone's AR or VR. At least it exercised his imagination a little. But maybe he should visit the tall trees while he had the chance – before they were gone. Or before he was. Maybe Penelope would like to see the forest with him. Maybe she had already visited the tall trees. Maybe she could tell him about it. He squinted, trying to see all the way to the forest. Instead, everything blurred together. All he could make out was the blackness of the river mixing with the greener edges of the trees. Toby looked up, seeming to shrug.

"Have you been to the forest, Toby?"

Toby's ears perked, and he cocked his head from side to side, his brown eyes intelligent, inquiring.

"No, of course you haven't. Since I've never been, neither have you."

Marshall tore the crust from his toast and handed it to Toby, who used his front teeth to delicately accept the offering.

"What would we do in the forest? What does anyone do in the forest?"

Toby lay on the floor and chewed on his crust, holding it between his front paws.

"I've read about it." Marshall leaned back thoughtfully. "Hiking and camping and swimming and boating and orienteering. Maybe Penelope would like some of those things. Think Penelope has ever hiked or fished or climbed a tree?"

Toby swallowed the last bit of crust and looked up at Marshall.

"I know. Maybe I should ask her."

Toby wagged his graceful, black plume of a tail, and Marshall rubbed him between his ears.

"What would you call Penelope and me? We've been on one date. Does that mean we're dating?"

Toby stood and stretched. It was time for their morning walk. Coffee, toast, and a short jaunt to the office.

"Maybe I should ask her." Marshall grabbed his jacket.

Toby yawned and shook his head, the tag on his collar jingling.

"Do you think I'm her boyfriend?"

Toby barked and panted. He spun in a circle as if chasing his tail.

"I should ask her," Marshall said as he placed his plate and mug in the sink. "I like her, Toby."

Toby continued to spin.

"I see things in full color with her. I wonder about things. I notice things." He sighed. "Things I never saw before. Enrolling didn't change things as much as Penelope has."

Marshall thought about the day he enrolled. Ten years had passed, and everything had remained the same until he'd met Penelope. She meant more to him than living or dying. She gave his existence a purpose.

He remembered leaving the enrollment office where he had signed the paperwork. If he hadn't called within twenty-four hours, his enrollment would've been automatically voided.

He'd walked a few blocks and crossed West Cary Street to Shyndigz, one of his favorite Richmond desserteries. Back before he'd discovered The Cakery. He and his friends, by which he meant people who'd needed his help with schoolwork, sometimes ate cake and pretended to study there, by which he meant he'd given them the answers to the assignments.

He had ordered an oatmeal cream pie and sat at a table under the decorative, twinkly lights and plants. He'd downloaded the *Enrollment* app as instructed and waited. The dropdown menu had included screens dedicated to basic information about each experimental group.

Experimental Group A	–	those who were told their DoD
Experimental Group B	–	*his group* – those who were told their DoD and were mandated to make entries into an Annual Deathday Diary
Experimental Group C	–	those who were not told their DoD

If he'd wanted to proceed, he would have to agree to the rules of the *Experiment,* of which there were seven. Marshall had found no reason to balk at any of them. He'd tapped the screen and agreed to follow the rules for the rest of his life – of which he would soon know the exact duration. He'd checked his watch. It had been 10:05 a.m. when he'd arrived at Shyndigz. It was now 10:15, and the aroma from the oatmeal cream pie had made him hungry.

Would he rather know sooner or later? Before or after he ate the large cookie? If he confirmed his enrollment, much of his life would be like this. A countdown of sorts. Everything calculated.

He had checked his watch again – 10:30, and taken a bite of the oatmeal cream pie.

I'll wait to call the hotline.

He had taken another bite and selected another option on the app. The benefits of participating in the *Experiment* had included partial funeral expenses. Options from three local funeral homes were listed. A pseudo-life insurance policy. A pension to a beneficiary of his choice. Reduced rates on life-planning packages from three life coaching companies. The names of the companies had been listed just above the funeral homes.

Ironic.

Marshall had glanced out the window and sighed. He didn't have any beneficiary, and once he was dead, he wouldn't worry about expenses. He'd shrugged and taken another bite.

In a font one size larger and one shade darker than the rest of the benefits listed, he had read, *One thing certain in an uncertain world.* Was knowing when he was going to die the greatest benefit of all?

Marshall's fork had clanked against the porcelain plate. He had mindlessly finished the pie, which meant there was no excuse not to call the hotline.

He had contemplated about following through with the process. He could have simply decided not to call and that would have been that. He'd go on living the same way he had for the last eighteen years. But he had come this far. Had spent the entire morning on the process, visited the enrollment office, filled out the forms, swiped through the app, took a blood test. Half a day of his life was gone, swallowed up in deciding whether or not to discover when it would all be gone, like the oatmeal cream pie he had just devoured.

This had been the first significant decision of his adult life. He couldn't back out. It was 11:00. He dialed the hotline. He waited for someone to answer. His concept of a minute had changed. He had to remember the date and time for his ADDE. Each second had felt as if it were peeling away from his life like sheets on an old desk calendar. He had held his breath.

"Hello!" A cheerful, somewhat robotic voice had answered, accompanied by a musical, metallic sound. "Thank you for calling the hotline." There had been a pause. "Please listen carefully to the following options. If you are a newly enrolled participant, please press one. If –"

Marshall had pressed one.

"Welcome *new* participant!" Again, a robotic voice. "We are so very happy to hear from you. Thank you for your enrollment. In order to proceed, we must verify your identity. What is your full name?"

Marshall had watched as several people walked past the window. "Marshall John Milton."

"You answered … *Marshall* … *John* … *Milton* … is this correct?"

Marshall had replied *yes*.

"Birthdate … year … month … day with zeros."

Marshall had answered.

"Happy eighteenth birthday, Marshall … John … Milton."

Marshall had looked at his phone and squinted.

"Date of enrollment?" the voice had asked.

Marshall had replied.

"Thank you, Marshall … John … Milton. Please hold."

Again, Marshall had waited. Two people had crossed the street as a gray drizzle moistened the asphalt.

His phone had chimed a cheerful tune. "Marshall … John … Milton, your Date … of … Departure is … October 10 … 2093. Thank you and remember, *heaven is waiting*. Press zero to return to the main menu, otherwise, you may hang up."

Marshall hung up.

Marshall had lived eighteen October 10s in ignorance. He almost felt as if the date had somehow betrayed him, as if it should have revealed itself to him instead of lying by omission, keeping itself secret, crouching inconspicuously among the other dates on the calendar.

Eighteen October 10s – he would live another fifty-nine. At age seventy-six – almost seventy-seven – he would somehow die. Twenty-one thousand four hundred seventy-eight sunrises. Twenty-one thousand four hundred seventy-eight sunsets. Twenty-one thousand four hundred seventy-eight breakfasts, lunches, and dinners. Maybe, depending on the time of day that he died.

Marshall had enrolled during the early days of the *Experiment*, and things were not that precise. They could pinpoint the date, but not the time or cause. Those two mysteries remained. *Only one thing certain in an uncertain world.*

There was a certain freedom in not knowing, replaced by a certain fear. What deadly *thing* would happen to him on October 10, 2093?

Toby faced the door and barked.

"I should just ask her." Marshall clipped the leash to the collar for their morning walk.

Chapter 25

Penelope, 6 February 2045, Age 26, T-minus 1

Bea and Penelope reclined on the couch with their heads at opposite ends, their knees bent, and a plate of cookies on their laps. Bea's feet were cold against Penelope's.

"You should put on some socks," Penelope said.

"Why?"

"Cuz, your feet're freezing."

"They'll warm up." Bea wiggled her toes under the fleece blanket.

"At least stop touching me. You're making *me* cold."

"Suit yourself." Bea pulled back her feet and sighed.

"Thank you."

"You know what? You used to bake these for me. Now I have to buy them at the store," Bea said, holding up a cookie. She swallowed and sighed. "*You* used to *bake* them for *me*, remember?" She bit into the second cookie.

"Yes, I remember."

"You should do that again."

"Do what again?"

"Bake."

"Why?"

"Cuz you're good at it." Bea shrugged. "And ... because I want homemade cookies." She started on her third.

"I just haven't felt like it."

Bea set her plate on the coffee table and leaned forward. "Can I ask you something?"

"Anything."

"Do you ever wonder what comes after?"

"After? You mean after we die?"

"I didn't want to say it, but yeah." Bea nodded.

"I try not to."

"Sometimes I just can't help it." Bea sat back and pulled up her knees, resting her head. She stared at Penelope.

"Don't know, don't care," Penelope replied.

Bea's eyes refused to move. It was as if her gaze had somehow locked permanently onto her face. Penelope needed to give her friend a better answer. Bea would not accept the fact that she didn't care, because Bea knew that she did. The day that Bea had ripped her from her hibernation and forced her off the couch was the day she'd come back to life. Now, she was being forced into the darkness again – a place she didn't want to visit, not even for a brief moment.

"As far as I'm concerned," Penelope said, leaning forward to match Bea's posture, their faces just inches apart, "I have only now. Only this moment. Tomorrow no longer exists for me." She sat up straighter and took in a deep breath. "I have to live for the present. I can't live in an uncertain or unknown future. I used to think I knew what the future held ... a life with Everett ... The Cakery ... kids. Turns out I was wrong. Now, I realize I don't know my future. I only know how little of it lies in front of me. But I have no idea what it holds. Darkness? Oblivion? After my deathday, I don't know what comes next. And it scares me." She leaned back against the cushions and pulled the hair from her face.

"Think of it this way." Penelope glanced around. "See the dark foyer?"

Bea nodded.

"That's my life right now. All I see ahead of me is darkness, every second creeping closer. And when I feel the pressure of that darkness as it extinguishes more and more of the light, I have to turn away and live for the moment. If I don't, that darkness will swallow me. I'll end up back on this couch, paralyzed with fear of the future and what's in the dark." She looked through their reflections at the city. "I'm afraid of the future. I'm afraid of what comes next."

Bea wiped away a tear.

"I don't want to miss anything while I'm still here, while I'm still living. I don't know what comes after, but I do know that if I allow myself to walk into that darkness, think about it too much ..." – Penelope pointed back to the foyer – "... that darkness wins, and I lose the moments I have left. Like this one ... look at that sky." She pointed at the window. "The sky won't ever look like this again. Every moment is unique. I'll never get this moment back." She inhaled, allowing the air to completely fill her lungs. "I don't want to ponder what lies beyond. It's the one thing certain in an uncertain world ... *this* moment. If I had a hundred years left, this would still be the only time I can see this sky, this way. Those clouds will blow away, and there won't ever be others like them ... not *just* like them. There'll be new clouds just as beautiful, but they won't be *these* clouds in *these* shapes. We only get one life, Bea. And mine isn't very long. I don't want to spend what's left thinking about what's next. I just want to focus on what's now."

Penelope stared into the rosy horizon surrendering to the velvety dusk. She tried to memorize the texture of the clouds, the way the sunlight hit their undersides just so – all that would be over in just a matter of minutes. That radiant, glowing sky would be dark.

Bea rested her head against the sofa. She too stared at the sunset and sighed.

Penelope inhaled deeply again. "All I have is now. *This* is the only thing I can count on. The now and the darkness that is coming for me. After that … I don't know." She touched Bea's arm. "But … I do know I have three cookies left. And after *that* will be a glass of milk."

Bea smiled.

Penelope smiled back.

They each bit into another cookie. Penelope savored the chewy chocolate. When all that remained were crumbs, she looked at her empty plate.

"I'm afraid, Bea," she whispered. "Mostly, I'm just afraid."

Chapter 26

Penelope, 7 February 2045, Age 26, T-minus 1

Penelope stood in the kitchen, hand-mixing a thick, dry dough. Bea hefted a large shopping bag onto the counter with an obnoxious grunt, tossed her device onto the table, and plopped into the closest chair. Penelope turned, cradling the bowl in one arm, her other hand still stirring. She started, nearly dropping the bowl when she saw Bea.

"God, Bea!" Penelope stopped stirring and grabbed onto the bowl with both hands. "How long you been sitting there? Scared me to death."

"Impossible. At least today, anyway."

"Shut up." Penelope flicked a little dough at Bea. It landed on the table in front of her.

Bea scraped it off with her finger and tasted it. "That's good." She smiled. "Wait a minute. Are you … *baking*?"

Penelope shrugged. She set the bowl on the counter. "Maybe."

Bea stood. "You are! You're baking again! Peanut butter?"

"Peanut butter dog biscuits."

"I just ate dog biscuit?"

"It's human-grade, you'll be fine. It won't kill you." She paused for dramatic effect. "Well, not today, anyway."

"Touché. Dog biscuits for what?"

"For fun, and … for Toby."

"But you don't bake anymore. And you don't have any fun. So, it's impossible for you to bake for fun. We just talked about this."

Penelope glared at her friend. Bea was right. Penelope hadn't thought about baking ever since Everett called off their engagement. And she certainly hadn't considered having any fun, at least not until her date with Marshall. At one point she had convinced herself that there was no more fun to be had – that the next several months were merely there to be endured until – until what came next – whatever that was.

"I have fun," she stated.

"Since when?" Bea squinted.

"Since …" She had to think. With the wooden spoon poised above the mixing bowl, she sighed deeply. "Since I started seeing Marshall."

Bea bit her lip and raised her brows. "Oh, so it's *Marshall* that has you having fun, is it? And the baking?"

"I told you … for Toby."

"And who's Toby?"

"Marshall's dog."

Bea hefted herself onto the kitchen counter. "Let me get this straight, cuz it's rather confusing."

Penelope laughed. "Nothing confusing about it."

"Oh, yes there is. I just spent the last month trying to figure out how to get your sorry ass off my couch, but Marshall has you smiling and baking after just *one* date? Without even *trying?*" Bea scooched closer to her friend and leaned forward with a serious expression. "Tell me … what's *he* got that I don't?" She hopped off the counter.

"A dog."

Bea huffed. "And …?"

"And I like him. A lot." Penelope paused. "Marshall, I mean. But I like his dog too."

"I can tell. Fun? Baking?"

"I like him more than Everett."

"But you *loved* Everett."

Penelope sighed. "I thought I did. Now I'm starting to think maybe I didn't. Maybe I just *thought* I did. Maybe calling off our engagement was the best thing that could've happened to me. Meeting Marshall allows me to see things more clearly, to reframe my thinking. Just like that death therapist said, the one you made me see."

Bea stared at Penelope.

"You don't understand?" Penelope asked.

"I guess I wouldn't know, would I?"

Penelope wiped her hands on the kitchen towel and stood beside her friend. "But you will. I know no one likes to think so anymore, but these things take time. You can plan things and you can know things. But you can't plan or know when you'll fall in love. No *Life Planner* app is *that* good. *Together Forever* can help. But what if your soulmate isn't on *Together Forever*? What if he isn't even enrolled? You can do everything in your power to bring about the result you want … the person, the wedding, the marriage … but some things just aren't within our reach to control."

"You're not helping."

"I'm trying."

"I know."

Penelope smiled. "Maybe you need to think on a smaller scale."

"How do you mean?"

"Instead of searching for Mr. Forever, just look for, I don't know … a nice date for Valentine's Day?"

"And see how it goes from there?" Bea shrugged.

"You only have so much time, and you're spending it trying to craft the perfect life. Instead of enjoying the life you have, you're busy worrying about a life that doesn't exist. There's nothing wrong with wanting to get married before your deathday, but don't act like your life isn't complete just because you're single."

Bea leaned her head on Penelope's shoulder, and the familiar weight felt comfortable.

"When did you get so fucking wise?" Bea asked.

Chapter 27

Penelope, 9 February 2045, Age 26, T-minus 1

A tall woman in her mid-fifties placed their meals on the table. She looked like she had been pretty once, and Penelope thought about her mother. Her mother had been pretty too.

"Can I get you anything else?" the woman asked.

"I think we're good," Marshall replied.

"She reminds me of my mother," Penelope said as the woman walked away. "Has a similar name, too … June. That's close to Joan."

"What about your dad?" Marshall stabbed his fork into the meatloaf.

"Victor. Joan and Victor. Or at least that's how it used to be. They divorced when I was in school. I think I was about thirteen."

Marshall didn't respond

Penelope took a sip of her drink. "My mom died shortly after their divorce. I don't see much of Dad anymore."

"I don't see my parents at all." Marshall impaled another chunk of meatloaf.

"Why not?" Penelope pushed a tomato across her plate. *Why did I order a salad?* She wanted the meatloaf. The least she could've done was add salmon to her greens. Too late now. She lifted her fork and prodded the lettuce.

"My mom and I don't talk." Marshall chewed.

Toby shifted under the table, and she smiled as his fur brushed against her leg. Penelope watched as Marshall ate. He was so methodical, so organized even when he was eating his dinner. It was almost entertaining.

"Sorry to hear that," she said. When he didn't respond, she picked through the lettuce and took a bite.

Marshall pierced another hunk of meatloaf, and a metallic clink rang when his fork struck the plate. He swallowed and gulped down some water. He wiped his mouth with a napkin, placed the napkin back on his lap, and looked up. "We haven't seen each other in years. Since before I got Toby."

The dog's ears perked at the sound of his name. Penelope wished Marshall would slip him some meatloaf. Maybe her too. *Why did I order the salad?* How terrible to be Toby at that moment, assailed by the inescapable, stale smell of decades of fried food and not a morsel for him. He nosed around on the floor, sticky with old spills. She wasn't much better off with just her salad. She eyed Marshall's meatloaf jealously, and then, not sure what to make of the matter-of-fact tone he'd used and not at all enticed by her salad, she put her fork down for a second time.

"Why?" she asked.

"She lied to me," Marshall said, sprinkling salt over his grilled vegetables. "About my dad."

Penelope leaned back. "Must've been a pretty serious lie."

"It was." Marshall nodded. "A big one." He raised his brows, but not his eyes.

Penelope waited for him to say more, to explain. But Marshall just sat there exchanging the salt for the pepper. He chewed his food, and his eyes never left his plate.

"What was it?" she asked.

"What was what?"

"The lie?"

"Oh, she said that my dad had died."

"Did he?"

"Did he what?"

"Die?"

"No. That was the lie. She told me he was dead, but he wasn't."

Marshall's mother had lied to him about his father being dead? He had said it the same way someone might talk about the weather. "It rained yesterday" or "it'll be sunny tomorrow."

She coughed and took a sip of her water. "Your mother told you that your father was dead, when he was still alive?"

Marshall nodded. "Truth was … he didn't want me." His eyes met Penelope's for the first time since their meals had arrived.

"He didn't want you?"

"Nope. And Mom told me he was dead."

An inexplicable sadness crept through heart, seeping into her ventricles and filling them with a sort of inky blackness. Seemingly unaffected, Marshall stared into her eyes. He smiled and placed another piece of meat into his mouth. Did his mother's lie, which was designed to protect him, hurt him more than the knowledge that his father didn't want him?

"Maybe it wasn't a complete lie," Penelope said.

"She said he was dead. He wasn't. That's a lie."

"Things aren't always that black and white. Maybe your mom was trying to protect you."

Marshall looked up. "Protect me? From what?"

She thought about her own lie, a lie by omission. The truth was, she would be dead soon. And Marshall didn't know. "The truth," she whispered and glanced over at the window.

It was dark outside, and the customers' reflections enlivened the black glass, obscuring the outside view. Her own face stared back at her. The empty shadows under her eyes and cheekbones made her look tired, hollow. She glanced away and told herself that she was just protecting Marshall from a truth that would only hurt him. A truth that pushed her closer to the grave with every sunrise, every sunset, every breath.

Penelope's wasn't a complete lie. Just a partial one. It wasn't the same as what his mother had done. Not really. His mother had lied directly – told a deliberate untruth. Penelope had merely neglected to say anything. Then again, they both had the same motive – protection. Marshall was the one who assumed she wasn't enrolled. She just didn't correct his assumption. So, was that a lie? In that moment in the park with the pain so fresh and raw, her heart and stomach had not allowed her to admit the truth. The hurt was still too deep. Too strong. She had barely come to terms with it herself. And it wasn't like there'd been a good time to say something. Was she really being dishonest? Was omission a lie? At what point was she obligated to tell him the truth? Was there such a point? Was her deathday any of his business?

She could argue it wasn't. But a nagging guilt scraped away at her gut. Somewhere within the deepest and blackest part of her inner soul, she *was* lying. And not just to Marshall but to herself. Who was she protecting from the truth?

Maybe it wasn't a question of protection. Maybe she was just being selfish. Everett had left her because of her DoD, Marshall would leave her too. The truth was dark. Too black and ugly. She couldn't allow herself to think about it, because the truth was that this time next year, she would be dead.

"The truth?" Marshall laughed. "You can't protect someone from the truth. The truth is just the truth … it's there … it's real. No matter what someone tells you … or doesn't tell you. I'd rather just know because the truth, you know, will come out eventually. You can't hide from the truth."

Penelope studied Marshall's eyes. He was so candid, so honest. Maybe she didn't have to be delicate. Maybe she should just tell him things. Match his matter-of-fact with a new straight-forward way of talking. That was how he was. Maybe she should try it. Maybe she'd be able to convince herself if she spoke the words.

"Marshall, what if she was trying to protect you from the fact that your father didn't want you? To spare you from the pain of losing him."

He laughed. "What's the difference? The truth hurt more when I discovered that my mom had lied. She was the only one I trusted. She was supposed to be my friend." He paused. "The longer a lie hides the truth, the more the truth hurts when it's finally told."

Penelope's gaze fell to her salad as a pang of guilt ran through her. *'I should have been a pair of ragged claws scuttling across the floor of a silent sea.' I'm not any better, am I? Not any better than a lowly sea creature. Not any better than a mother trying to protect her son with a lie.* She looked up at Marshall and smiled weakly.

Chapter 28

Marshall, 10 February 2045, Age 28, T-minus 49

The sky had exchanged its vibrant afternoon blue shirt for a pale lavender nightgown. Marshall sat in front of his large, wooden desk, situated directly in front of his office window. The last of the day's diffused, white light skulked through the glass, barely illuminating the room. The building across the street reflected the last glow of the setting sun.

Almost quitting time.

The shorter days of winter provided him with a natural reminder of the time. Clock watching could wear a person down. The workday seemed simpler in the winter months. Darkness came swiftly now, a natural notification that the workday was winding down. Things were a little more challenging during the summer months. He often found himself falling back into his obsession with watching the clock. How many more minutes until lunch? How many more minutes until he could leave for the day? How many more minutes until his DoD? Time – time – time –

Time for you and time for me,
and time yet for –

"Thought I would find you here." Penelope's voice echoed off his window.

Marshall started and Toby lifted his head, softly whining a greeting. Marshall smiled and Penelope's two-dimensional figure flickered before materializing into a stable and solid – if not translucent – Penelope. As she stood between his desk and the window, Venus shimmered in the sky from behind her right eye.

Toby's tail thumped.

Marshall cleared his throat. "Penelope? Hi." He stood.

No one had ever holographed him before.

"Sorry … am I interrupting? I thought you'd be wrapping up for the day."

"I am."

"Is now a good time to graph?" she asked.

"Graph?"

"You know … *holograph*?"

"Is that what they call it?"

"Yeah." She smiled.

"Okay."

"Is now a good time?"

Marshall wasn't sure when a good time to graph would be, but he guessed now was as good as any. "Sure."

"I wondered what you were doing for Valentine's Day," she asked.

Valentine's Day? What was he doing for Valentine's Day? He'd never made plans for Valentine's Day before but assumed he'd spend it with Penelope. After all, wasn't that what happened when you loved someone?

Loved someone?

How easily that phrase had come to mind. Did he? Love her? Was that what this was? Was this what it was like? He had nothing to compare it to, not personally, not first-hand, but –

"Because Bea is sort of seeing this guy she met on that *Together Forever* app. Not serious enough to do a just-the-two-of-them Valentine's Day ... but serious enough to *do* Valentine's Day, and she asked if we would want to double date. I told her I'd have to ask, so ... I'm asking."

Marshall struggled to keep up. The sound of her voice was a beat or two behind the movement of her lips, her hand gestures, and her facial expressions. Marshall had learned, somewhat and with great practice, how to decipher what someone might mean or how someone might feel based on gestures and volume and pace and facial expressions – but when the timing was all wrong, it made reading and understanding harder than it already was.

"You're asking what?"

"I'm asking," Penelope repeated, "if you want to go on a double date on Valentine's Day ... you and me with Bea and this guy from *Together Forever.*"

A double date? With a stranger? Socializing and strangers were not things Marshall enjoyed. Socializing *with* a stranger was even worse. Then again, he loved Penelope. And Bea had been kind to him. Would it be so bad? Before he allowed himself to fully consider the answer to the question, he replied, "Yes, of course."

Penelope's graph squealed a beat after her hands clapped. "Bea's going to be so happy," she said. "Thank you, Marshall." She blew him a kiss, and the graph blinked, leaving Venus hanging alone in the black winter sky.

Chapter 29

Penelope, 14 February 2045, Age 26, T-minus 1

"This is fun, right?" Bea said, popping her head into the bathroom.

Penelope had left the door ajar as she finished applying her makeup. She leaned over the counter and inspected her face before turning and smiling. "Yeah, Bea. Yeah, it's fun."

Accepting the affirmative as an invitation into the room, Bea pushed the door the rest of the way open and stepped in. They locked eyes in the mirror.

"Feels like college all over again," Bea said. "Getting ready to go to parties … remember? We'd play that Black Eyed Peas song and dance around the dorm, gettin' the party started before we were even dressed. We should do this more often."

"Yeah," Penelope replied. "Those were such *good* days." She remembered those days fondly. The days before she knew how numbered they were. She sometimes felt like she had led two lives. One before enrollment and the other after. There was a definite demarcation between the two. A clear *then* and *now*.

Bea wrapped an arm around Penelope's shoulders and squeezed. "*These* are such good days too. Let's have fun."

Penelope met her friend's eyes and smiled.

They arrived at Havana 59 to find their dates waiting outside. Marshall stepped forward and smiled. He held a bouquet of forsythias. Toby whined and wagged his tail.

Penelope stared at the flowers, and her heart raced – he remembered. Everett ran through her mind and she flinched. One of her last delusional moments involved a vase of forsythias. Was this a hint of what was to come?

"Happy Valentine's Day," Marshall said, his voice rich and warm.

Her face flushed, and she felt embarrassed to meet Marshall's eyes. "Happy Valentine's Day." She forced herself not to look away. Holding the flowers, she sighed. "You remembered."

"How could I not?" he replied.

Bea grabbed her date's arm. "Looks like you guys already met? Boris, Marshall? Marshall, Boris?" She gestured to each man respectively.

Marshall nodded.

"Good," Bea said. "I'm starving."

A young hostess led them to a table at the front of the colorful and crowded restaurant. The street outside looked busy with the hustle and bustle of the holiday.

"So," Boris said as he settled into his seat. "What's with the dog, Marshall?" He nodded at Toby.

"Toby?" Marshall replied. "He's a service dog."

"Yeah? What service does he provide?"

"Lots of things. Let's me know when someone is approaching my door, calms me down when I'm nervous –"

"Why do you have him?"

"Marshall's autistic," Bea said, looking over at Marshall and smiling.

Boris nodded and grinned. "That's cool, man."

Marshall seemed to be studying Boris as he spoke, looking unfazed, which made sense. To Marshall, the truth was just the truth – the simplest of things. He was autistic. And that was that.

"It is?" Marshall said. "Is it cool? Never felt cool. Not a word I would use to describe it."

Bea shrugged.

"Toby's a dog," Boris stated, "and he's allowed in here with us. Now, *that's* cool."

The hostess handed them menus and ice water. "Your waiter, Donald, will be with you shortly." She nodded before walking to the next table.

"Donald?" Boris snickered. "Really? *Donald?* What kind of a name is Donald? I've never met anyone named Donald before."

Marshall squinted at Penelope and frowned.

She leaned over and whispered, "I guess he thinks the name's funny."

Without matching Penelope's inconspicuous volume, Marshall replied, "But *his* name is Boris. *That* is a much more awkward name than Donald. At least Donald could go by Don or Donnie. What kind of a nickname can you come up with for Boris? Bore?"

Penelope laughed. It was somewhat absurd that a man named Boris was laughing at a man named Donald. Even more amusing was Marshall's unconcealed puzzlement at the irony.

Boris turned to Penelope and Marshall. "What?" he asked. "I can't help what my name is."

"I don't suppose Donald can either," Marshall stated.

And ... he had a point. Donald and Boris had only their parents to thank. Or blame.

"Marshall's … uh … Marshall has no filter," Bea said, smiling at Boris and patting his leg. "He doesn't mean anything by it. He's not … he's not making fun of your name."

"Oh, no," Marshall said. "Not at all. Boris is a dignified name. It means wolf or snow leopard."

Boris' gaze bounced between Marshall and Bea. Penelope leaned forward and winked at her friend. When their eyes met, the two burst into hysterics.

"Good evening," their waiter said. "I am Donald and will be serving you this evening. Can I interest anyone in a mojito?"

After ordering drinks and appetizers, Boris made what Penelope considered an admirable attempt at reconciliation. "So … how did the two of you meet?"

"In a bakery," Marshall replied. "Penelope's bakery. Well … it *used* to be her bakery. She called it The Cakery."

"You *met* in a *bakery*?" Boris asked. "By coincidence? Chance?"

"Yeah, I had to buy a cake."

"You met in person?" Boris asked.

"Yeah." Marshall sounded exasperated. "At The Cakery."

Boris frowned and nodded a few times before glancing around the table. He spread his napkin over his lap and chuckled. "Okay. That's kinda cool. Sorta analog and old school. I dig."

Marshall shook his head and frowned. "What do you dig?"

Boris paused for a second. "It? I dig … it." He waved his hand through the air.

"What's it?" Marshall asked.

"No, I mean … I dig it … the concept. It's a phrase … an old school phrase from back in the day. I was … I was making a joke. Sorta."

"Oh." Marshall shrugged and took a sip of his drink.

Tears welled in Penelope's eyes and she smiled. She shook her head at Bea, who appeared equally, if not painfully, amused. The entire evening was quite absurd.

"And you two met on *Together Forever*?" Penelope asked, wanting to turn the conversation back toward a semblance of normality.

"Yep. The app," Boris replied.

Marshall remained silent.

"Well," Bea said, reading over her menu. "I think I'll have the seared duck."

Penelope nodded and giggled.

Marshall laughed. "The duck! A joke!"

"A joke?" Bea repeated.

"Because of Donald? Our waiter?" Marshall replied. "Donald Duck."

Boris nodded. "I *like* you, man."

Penelope shot Bea a *what-the-hell-is-going-on-here* look, and Bea responded with a *what-have-we-gotten-ourselves-into* shrug. The absurdity of their evening was entertaining. Penelope looked forward to laughing about it later when they settled in for the night.

Bea unlocked the apartment door. They felt happy and exhausted as they peeled off their coats, draping them over the chair. Simultaneously, they dropped onto the plush cushions of the couch.

"What a night!" Penelope said, smiling. "That was fun … a lot of fun."

"Yah think? Even with Boris?"

Penelope laughed. "Even with Boris … Boris the Bore. I mean, tell me the best part of the night wasn't listening to him trying to talk to Marshall?"

"True. That was pretty damn funny. But a date alone with Boris? Let's just say … the nickname Marshall gave him fits … Boris the Bore. Marshall on the other hand …"

Penelope raised her brows and grinned. "Yeah …?"

"I can see what you see in him."

"Yeah?" Penelope settled deeper into the couch.

"Yeah. He's just … Marshall. What you see is what you get. It's appealing. It's special."

"Yeah, it's special."

"Have you kissed yet?" Bea leaned closer.

"Not yet. But … it might happen soon."

"Not if you don't make it." Bea smiled.

"What do you mean?"

"You think Marshall's gonna make the first move?" Bea shook her head. "If you believe that, then you'll be waiting forever."

"Please. I'm not *that* old-fashioned. I'm not *waiting* on him. I'm waiting for the *right moment*. It has to *feel* right."

"And what were you saying about not being old-fashioned?"

"You know *exactly* what I mean." Penelope pulled a pillow from behind her and smacked her friend with it. "I'm going to bed." Penelope stood and walked toward the bathroom.

"Hey!" Bea called, still laughing. "You need to at least download the *Bucket List* app."

Penelope stuck her head out of the bathroom. "The what?"

"The *Bucket List* app."

"What kind of a morbid suggestion is that? Is that even a thing?"

"It's a thing. Kinda like my *Life Planner* app. Anyway, you could add *Kiss Marshall before I die* to your list."

"You're lucky I'm in a good mood," Penelope replied. "There was a time when a comment like that would've driven me deeper into the depths of depression and despair."

"Don't be so melodramatic," Bea replied. "Seriously, though, get that app."

"Bea!" Penelope splashed warm water on her face and relished the freshness of her naked skin. "I'm not making a bucket list … and I'll still kiss Marshall before I die."

Chapter 30

Marshall, 15 February 2045, Age 28, T-minus 49

Marshall sat in his office, staring out the window and thinking about Penelope. Valentine's Day would have been the perfect day for a first kiss. After reading up on what he should or shouldn't say to lead up to the first one, he felt more confused than ever. Something about her eyes seemed to be right, but he hadn't said a thing about her eyes. Hadn't even come close to a kiss. He blamed Boris, but not for any legitimate reason. Just because Boris was an easy out. When would his next opportunity to –

"Marshallllll!" Ken pushed the office door open, and it banged against the wall. "How's it hangin', buddy?"

"Hi, Ken."

"You, uh, enjoy Valentine's Day?"

"I did."

"Celebrate?"

"Double date."

Ken took a step back with his eyes widening and an odd grin growing across his face. "Really now? A double … fucking … date? Good for you!" He chuckled. "You're serious? You actually went on a date? With a girl?"

"Yes. An actual date. With an actual girl. In fact two girls. And Toby."

"Fuckin' yeah, man!" Ken clapped Marshall on the back.

Marshall winced.

Ken was in his personal space – standing a little – a lot – too close. Marshall gritted his teeth. He took a deep breath as he felt Toby press against his legs.

"What's this?" Ken sauntered over to a piece of paper taped to the wall. "Kinda old school, huh? Paper and tape." Ken laughed. "Wait a minute, I know what this is …"

"… that's the part I know! The coffee spoons part. Isn't that fucking cool?"

"Isn't what cool?" Marshall asked.

"That we can *do* that?"

"Do what?"

"Measure out our life with coffee spoons."

"What?"

"Oh, Marhsall, you really have to get with the program. When we enroll, our days become measured. We know exactly how many evenings, mornings, and afternoons we have left. We can plan our lives right down to the last ... little ... detail. We can measure it one coffee spoon at a time. That's fucking power."

Marshall shook his head. *Fucking power?* He closed his eyes and sighed. "That is not what that line means."

"Sure, it is."

"No, it is not. Not at all."

"Yes, it is, Marshall. Ask anyone. Fucking anyone."

"That poem was written in 1915. People didn't enroll back then. How could a line from something written over a hundred years ago refer to knowing our deathdays now?"

"Well then what do you think it means?"

Marshall took in a deep breath and released it slowly. It didn't matter what it meant. Or what *he* thought it meant. The world had already made up its mind, and Ken had made up his.

"You know what? You're probably right."

Ken winked and pointed two fingers at him. He walked out backwards and closed the door.

Marshall looked at Toby and whispered, "In the room Ken comes and goes, talking of Michelangelo."

Chapter 31

Penelope, 17 February 2045, Age 26, T-minus 1

Marshall's apartment was spotless and spartan. The only remotely messy aspect was a disorderly stack of books sitting on an end table next to the couch where he and Penelope reclined. At least eight books teetered in a precarious Jenga-like stack. Toby was curled up in his dog bed beneath the book-bearing table.

Penelope read through the titles.

David Finch	*The Journal of Best Practices: A Memoir of Marriage, Asperger Syndrome, and One Man's Quest to be a Better Husband*
Michael Finkel	*The Stranger in the Woods: The Extraordinary Story of the Last True Hermit*
John Milton	*Paradise Lost*
Edward Abbey	*Desert Solitaire*

Old textbooks formed the base of the unwieldy stack.

"You like to read," she said. "No fiction … just real life."

"Nonfiction, mostly. I enjoy biographies and autobiographies. And textbooks if they're about an interesting subject. Although most of the ones I have are outdated. It's more like reading history. I like philosophy too … sometimes."

She smiled. "My favorite is American literature. Steinbeck and Fitzgerald and Hemingway. And Hurston. The dark romantics."

"Do you like T.S. Eliot?" he asked.

"I *love* his piece about time."

"Time?"

"You know … 'there will be time, time for you and time for me and time –'"

"'… for yet a hundred indecisions …'" Marshall stopped.

They had leaned in closer with each word of the poem. She cast a glance into his eyes and allowed her gaze to fall to his lips. When she looked back up, she froze. His eyes had never left hers. His gaze felt intense – sincere – hungry.

He lifted her chin, tilting her face slightly upward. "'For yet a hundred indecisions,'" he whispered as if trying to encourage himself. He leaned in closer, and his lips met hers. A slow, gentle, and almost questioning kiss.

She placed her hand on the back of his head and pulled him in, whispering, "'And for a hundred visions and revisions, before the taking of toast and tea.'"

He sat back and rested his hand on her thigh. "What about the coffee spoon line? What do you think that means?"

"The coffee spoon line? The one the *Experiment* hijacked?"

"You don't think it means –"

"That we should be planning our lives bit by bit, spooning up each monumental moment with a proverbial *single* coffee spoon? No. That's not what Eliot meant. C'mon, he wrote that poem somewhere between 1910 and 1911. It's all been misconstrued, taken out of context."

"That's exactly what I was trying to tell Ken today."

"Ken?"

"This guy at work who says 'fuck' a lot but doesn't actually do any fucking thing, at least as far as I can tell … except barge into my office for lame conversations. I owe him a lot, though. I try to be nice, even though I can't always tell if *he's* being nice."

"Owe him?"

"Yeah. He's the one who sent me to buy the deathday cake. The day I first came to The Cakery. The day I first talked to you."

Penelope smiled, a warmth rising in her chest. She leaned in and kissed Marshall again.

Chapter 32

Penelope, 18 February 2045, Age 26, T-minus 1

The soft glow of an overcast winter day illuminated the room through the large picture window. Penelope rested on the couch with a book on her lap. The sun was busy burning its way through the morning's cover. But with temperatures as cold as today's, the distant star didn't stand a chance. The sun struggled against the clouds, becoming nothing more than a white dime high above the city, fatigued by its effort. And to think that just a few days ago it was over seventy degrees.

Stranger and stranger, this weather. Penelope pulled her eyes away from the book and glanced out the window. The filtered light didn't seem to hurt her eyes.

"Whatcha doin'?" Bea asked, shaking her coat. "So damn *cold* outside …" – she walked into the room – "… are you looking at the sun?"

"Yeah."

"You should never look directly at the sun," Bea stated. "You'll go blind."

"It's not that bright today."

"Still, it's bad for your eyes."

"I'm pretty sure I'm going to die before I go blind from looking at the sun."

Bea shrugged. "Fair enough. Stare away." She sat next to Penelope, pulled a throw from its place on the couch, and tucked it around her legs. "What're you reading?"

"Just a poem I like. Marshall likes it too. Thought I'd revisit it."

"What poem?"

"*The Love Song of J. Alfred Prufrock*. Remember it? From high school?"

"Not really. Let me guess … Emily Dickinson?"

"No."

"Langston Hughes?"

"Not even close."

"Don't tell me. Uh … Frost?"

"Eliot. T.S. Eliot."

"I would've gotten to him eventually."

"No, you wouldn't."

"Maybe not." Bea looked out the window. "What's it about?"

"Want me to read it to you?"

"Sure." Bea settled deeper into the couch, nestling between the cushions and gazing at the city.

When was the last time two friends sat together and read poetry? Years? Maybe a decade? Unless it was for a school project, but that didn't count. People used to read poetry all the time for fun. The Fireside Poets and all that. Now what did they do? Play on apps?

Penelope didn't know the answer. But she did know that, aside from their time in school, she and Bea had never read poetry together. Not for recreation. She looked over at Bea and smiled. She was glad that, at least for the moment, they weren't swiping away on their devices. Or sending each other holographs. Both were more convenient than an actual flesh-and-blood visit, but neither as fulfilling. Right now, this moment, was real. It was flesh and blood and friendship and books. Right now, she was sitting on a couch reading poetry to her best friend in a warm room on a cold day.

If only we had a fireplace.

Penelope took in a deep breath and let it out slowly. "'Let us go then, you and I,'" she said, reading from the book, "'when the evening is spread out against the sky, like a patient etherized upon a table …'"

Bea rested her head against the pillows and stared up at the ceiling. "That's a little morbid. Reminds me of being in a dentist chair."

Penelope shook her head and continued reading. "'… and indeed there will be time to wonder, Do I dare? and, Do I dare? …'"

"What's he daring us to do?" Bea asked.

Penelope glanced up. "He's not daring us to do anything. He's having an inner struggle." She went back to reading. "'… do I dare disturb the universe? In a minute there is time for decisions and revisions …'"

"Now that's a deep thought," Bea whispered.

"What is?" Penelope rested the book on her lap.

"Disturbing the universe. Who really believes one little person could do *that*? We're not that important. Was this guy some kind of egomaniac or something?"

Penelope didn't respond, but allowed her eyes to fall back to the lines. She focused on one, *'in a minute there is time.'*

Sixty seconds worth of time in every minute. Sixty minutes in each hour. Twenty-four hours in each day. Three hundred sixty-five days in each year. She couldn't count her remaining time in years anymore. The largest unit she could use was a month. How much could she achieve and experience within each of the remaining minutes? How could she make the most of the time? How much time did someone need for a hundred visions and revisions?

Penelope allowed her eyes to move down a few lines. "'For I have known them all already, known them all … have known the evenings, mornings, afternoons, I have measured out my life with coffee spoons …'"

"I know that part!" Bea sat up.

"Everyone knows that part," Penelope said, without removing her eyes from the page.

"It's that saying for enrollment. 'Measure out your life in coffee spoons.'"

"I know. I've heard it." Penelope looked up, irritated at the constant interruptions.

Bea frowned. "Sorry."

Penelope looked back at the book and continued. "'I know the voices dying with a dying fall beneath the music from a farther room. So how should I presume?'" She slowly flipped the page as she read through the stanzas. "'Till human voices wake us, and we drown.'" Penelope closed the book and sighed.

"I never knew the rest of it," Bea said. "It's pretty morbid actually. And I didn't know the coffee spoon line came from a poem."

"I don't think many people do. But Marshall did. And so do I."

"So what's that poem supposed to be about?"

"Loneliness, isolation, identity, insecurities." Penelope sighed.

Bea leaned over. She rubbed her legs and rested her head on her knees. "I guess it makes sense that Marshall would relate to it. I imagine things can get pretty lonely when no one understands you, and you don't understand them."

Penelope hadn't thought of it that way, but Bea was probably right. The poem reached Marshall on a personal level, always feeling like he was on the outside looking in.

"Speaking of Marshall …" Bea's tone grew playful. "Have you two kissed yet?"

"Yes, we kissed." Penelope sat the book on the coffee table.

"And you didn't tell me?"

"I was going to –"

"When?"

"When did we kiss or when was I going to tell you?"

Bea laughed. "When did you *kiss*?" She shook her head.

"Yesterday, on our date. When we were in his apartment."

"Yesterday? And you never said anything? When were you going to tell me? You know I've been waiting for you two to kiss."

Penelope smiled and her stomach fluttered with a sense of anticipation. "I've been wanting to tell you, but you've been busy, and I wanted –"

"I have time now. Talk! Is he a good kisser?"

"Sooo good." Penelope sang the words.

"How did it happen?"

Penelope recounted the whole story. As she finished, a mellow tone hummed through the apartment from the kitchen.

"Oh!" Penelope said, jumping up. "I almost forgot my cakes."

"Cakes …?"

"Yeah, cakes. The sweet, frosted desserts you eat with a fork. The ones we have for birthdays and weddings, and morbidly enough, deathdays?"

"I know what a cake is. You're baking? Again?"

Penelope smiled. "Is that a bad thing?"

"No … no no no no. It's a *good* thing. I'm just surprised, that's all. But in a good way."

"Come try the brownies I made this morning."

Bea stood. "You baked brownies this morning too?" She followed Penelope into the kitchen.

"Uh-huh. Here, try this." Penelope handed Bea a little brown confection.

"It's not for Toby is it?"

"No and it's really good. I mean, I think it's good."

Bea took a bite and nodded enthusiastically. "You think right!" she said, licking her fingers.

"Yeah?" Penelope couldn't remember the last time she'd felt so happy. In fact, she was pretty sure she'd never been this happy. Even when she'd thought she was happy back in her pre-enrollment days with Everett. The only thing that tainted everything now was knowing she had an expiration date. A date that left her very few remaining days.

"Thank you, Marshall!" Bea sang. "That was delicious."

"Did you just say, 'thank you, *Marshall?*'"

"Yep. I'm pretty sure I owe him for these brownies. I can't *wait* to see what you'll make after you two … yah know." Bea raised her brows.

"Oh my God. Get your mind out of the gutter."

"I'm just saying … if you make brownies this good after kissing, I can't imagine what a little sex will do. It's gonna be *goooood.*"

Penelope relented to Bea's playful banter. "The sex or the baking?"

"Both, I hope."

Penelope swung a dishrag at Bea's legs, and they laughed the kind of laugh they hadn't shared since high school. Penelope was conscious of a lightness of heart she hadn't felt since then. One she hoped she would feel for as much time as she had left. "It's fun, isn't it?" she asked.

"What's fun?" Bea wiped away a tear.

"Just … being alive."

Bea placed her hand on Penelope's arm. "Yeah." She nodded. "Yeah. It's pretty fun."

Chapter 33

Penelope, 24 March 2045, Age 26, T-minus 1

After arriving home from an evening with Marshall, Penelope closed the door behind her. She leaned against it and smiled.

"Do tell." Bea's voice echoed from the shadows of the living room. The glow of a screen reflected blue against her face. "More dessert baking?"

Penelope started and sighed. "I wasn't expecting to find you home." Her eyes followed the dark line that separated her from her friend. Did she dare cross that dark line? Was it there to remind her that her finish line edged ever closer? Was it edging closer to her or was she edging closer to it? Did it matter?

Shrugging off the morbid thoughts, she laughed and flipped on a light. "I had a good time. I really did."

"Did you guys finally … *do* it?" Bea raised her brows several times. "Please tell me you did." Her hand made a dismissive gesture at the screen and it fell dark. She faced Penelope and smiled. "Well?"

"No. We didn't."

Bea tossed up her hands and slapped them on her knees. "Why not?" She looked at the ceiling as if petitioning for divine support.

"You're so dramatic, jeez. These things just … take time."

"You don't exactly have a lot of time."

"Bea!"

"Well, you don't. And you know it. All I'm saying is, you can't really afford to take your time."

"Bea!"

"Come *on*. Don't you want to know if he's good in bed?"

"Belinda!"

"Well? Don't you? 'Cause I kinda do. Just sayin'." Bea shrugged. "Besides … I'm looking out for you. Remember the day you came home from Jefferson Park? Your first date with Marshall? You told me you wanted to do everything you had time to do. You said you didn't want to waste a minute. Not even a second. How many weeks have you already wasted *not* banging him? That's a lot of missed fucks, yah know."

"Bea! I know exactly how little time I have. But Marshall doesn't –"

"Wait … what? You haven't told him?"

"Well, no … he doesn't think I know my deathday. I didn't tell him I'm enrolled."

"Penelope –"

"He might not understand why I'd be moving so fast. I don't want him to get the wrong idea. He might think I'm using him."

"Well, aren't you? I mean … if you haven't told him –"

"I'm not using him. I like Marshall, and I think he likes me. I don't want to hurt him."

"Right. Right. So you're protecting *him*. You're just gonna take things nice and slow and never mention that, 'oh, by the way, I have less than a year to live.' What if he wants to make plans like me? You're just gonna lead him on?"

Penelope stared at the floor. "He might stop seeing me like Everett did," she whispered.

"He might stop seeing you?"

"He might not want to see me anymore if he knows how little time I have and that I didn't tell him. Everett didn't want me after he found out. Marshall might feel the same way."

"He might. But Marshall isn't Everett."

Penelope stared out the window overlooking the city. She watched as the headlights dodged about like little fireflies on a summer's night. She thought about what Bea had said and cringed. Bea was right. Marshall wasn't Everett.

Over the last few months, Penelope had realized a few things about Everett. He was selfish and shallow. And he probably never really loved her. Not the way a husband was supposed to love a wife. Not *'til death do us part* type. A *'til enrollment do us part* type. Marrying him would have been a disaster. She would have married a man who wouldn't love her the way she *wanted* to be loved. The way she, the way everyone, *deserved* to be loved.

Now, in a way, she was playing Everett's role in Marshall's life. She wouldn't be able to stay with him, not for the long run. Only 'til death do us part, which was much sooner than Penelope would like to think about. She was letting Marshall fall for her not knowing that her time was limited, so she could experience love, so she could in some way pretend she wasn't so close to her end. If their love was just beginning, surely the rest of her life was too.

She was like a patient etherized on a table, nearing the day's end, willfully oblivious of the approaching darkness. Was she living a fake life, lying to Marshall? A life she was never entitled to? Trying to exist in a world that wasn't real and never could be? The only thing that made her better than Everett was that she was falling in love with Marshall. Falling harder than she'd ever thought possible.

It was hours before she drifted off to sleep, those familiar verses echoing through her mind.

There will be time, there will be time
Time for you and time for me,
And time yet for a hundred indecisions,
And for a hundred visions and revisions.

Chapter 34

Penelope, 25 March 2045, Age 26, T-minus 1

"Good morning." Bea stood in the threshold between the bedroom and the living room. She stretched and yawned.

Penelope closed her eyes tighter, fighting against the pale sunlight that splashed across her face. She'd never pulled the curtains closed last night.

"Morning." Penelope sat up and rubbed her eyes.

"You look tired." Bea strode across the room to the kitchen and started the coffee. "Want some?"

Penelope glanced over. "No thanks."

"You sure? Always wakes me up."

"Mornings wake you up."

"I like the way it smells." Bea sat on the couch and took in a deep breath over her mug.

"You could just get a candle."

"I could … but it's the whole *ritual* I love."

"The ritual of pressing a button and waiting thirty seconds while the coffee sputters into a cup? That's not much of a ritual."

"I like the warm mug in my hands and the steam in my face and the sound of the spoon when I tap it on the edge … like this …" Bea gently tapped her spoon against the mug. "Not just the smell."

"I've measured out my life with coffee spoons," Penelope whispered. She thought of the way she savored the texture of a dense cake or the way the soft petals of a rose felt against her cheek. "You're right. A candle isn't real coffee, just like AR and VR aren't reality."

Bea took a sip and winced. "Hot."

"I've been thinking about what you said last night. About how Marshall isn't Everett."

Bea nodded.

"And I'm falling for him. Like, really, really falling. I don't know who I'm more grateful to for bringing me back to life … you or him."

"I'll take the credit, thank you."

"I'm sure you will." Penelope smiled but her eyes filled with tears. "I'm going to have to stop seeing him."

"Why?"

"Because he's sweet and sincere and innocent and fun and –"

"Horseshit! Nothing you just said is a good reason to dump him."

"He deserves better."

"You're going to break it off instead of just telling him the truth? You're not even going to give him a chance to prove himself, to make the choice on his own?"

Penelope shook her head. "I couldn't stand it if he left me like Everett did. I don't want my vision of him sullied. If he's anything like Everett, I don't want to know. Besides, he deserves someone who has more time. Breaking it off will spare us both. If he's going to leave me, I don't need to know … and he doesn't need to know that I lied. I need to quit before we're in too deep. I can't damage him."

"Damage him?"

"He's kind of … fragile."

"Fragile? Marshall's anything but fragile." Bea laughed.

"If he finds out I lied … all trust would be broken. Not just in me, but in everyone."

"Don't take this the wrong way, but I don't think he'd look for someone else. He's a little –"

"Strange? I know. He comes off that way sometimes."

"Sometimes?"

"Well … most of the time."

"How about *all* the time. Not that I don't like him. You know I do."

"I know you do … the thing is … he'd feel just as betrayed if I dumped him as he would if I told him the truth."

"Okay, let me get this straight. You don't want to lie anymore, but you don't want to tell the truth either. You don't want to dump him, but you can't keep seeing him. That pretty much covers everything. So … what *are* you gonna do?"

"Make *him* want to dump *me*."

Bea snorted and rolled her eyes. "You just totally contradicted yourself. Do you understand what you're saying? Are you losing it?"

"If he dumps *me* cuz I'm being a bitch, it's different than if he dumps me because I'm enrolled and going to die soon."

"So, what … that won't hurt as much?" Bea asked.

Penelope wiped her eyes and nodded.

"Good luck with *that*. It'll hurt no matter what happens. Besides, who in their right mind would dump you?"

"Everett did."

Bea shrugged. "Exactly my point."

"I need to find a way to make him not want me anymore." Penelope stared at her hands, waiting for her friend to provide some ideas or at least advice. When Bea didn't respond, Penelope looked up and frowned.

Bea stood. She walked up to the kitchen counter with coffee mug in one hand and her phone in the other. She set down the mug and swiped across the glossy phone screen, looking preoccupied.

Penelope cleared her throat.

"Sorry … I was checking an app."

"Which one?"

"My favorite … *Together Forever.* The one that pairs you with people who share a deathday close to yours."

Penelope sighed and rolled her eyes.

"It's genius. It really is. My *Life Planner* keeps reminding me that I'm running out of time to meet my marriage goal." Bea swiped a finger across the screen a few times and handed it to Penelope.

"'Never live without the one you love,'" Penelope read the words. She looked up and frowned. "Really?"

"I think it's a pretty good idea." Bea shrugged. "Well, it's not for everyone. When are you gonna get Marshall to dump you?"

"We're supposed to see each other tomorrow. So tomorrow, I guess."

Tomorrow – another date to add to the list of somber anniversaries that seemed to sum up her abbreviated life.

Chapter 35

Marshall, 26 March 2045, Age 28, T-minus 49

Marshall wasn't sure how to tell Penelope he wanted their relationship to be exclusive. He didn't know what to call it. He'd asked Toby, but Toby just wagged his tail and offered a toy for a game of tug-of-war.

"Who can I ask?" Marshall whispered.

Toby gave the toy a ferocious shake.

"Ken? Toby, don't be smart," he said, as if Toby had made the suggestion.

Asking her to be his girlfriend felt somewhat juvenile. Back in high school, his classmates said they were *talking* to someone when they were actually probably already sleeping together. He'd never understood that. He talked to a lot of people, and he never slept with any of them. How could just talking to someone turn into such intimacy?

With Penelope, he was beginning to understand, but it was still all a bit perplexing. He'd heard about people *talking* to each other all the time. He'd ask a classmate to study once, and they'd reply with *I can't. I have plans with the girl I'm talking to.* When he'd finally gathered enough nerve to ask a girl to a dance, which happened only once, she'd responded with *I'm sorry, I'm already talking to Andrew.* He'd been so confused he'd made the mistake of voicing his confusion.

"Actually, right now, you're talking to me," he'd said.

At first, she'd just stared at him with what he'd thought might be bewilderment and then laughed as if he had said something funny. Marshall had laughed too, vaguely sensing that it was the right thing to do. But he'd left the encounter no less befuddled than he'd been before.

His mother would probably know the right thing to tell him to say, but he couldn't ask her. Marshall would just have to tackle this on his own. Things had been going splendidly so far. There was no reason for that to change.

When Marshall's car slowed to an automatic stop in front of Bea's building, Penelope was already standing on the curb, wearing a red peacoat. Toby stood on the back seat and whined, his feathery tail waving.

"I know, boy," Marshall said. "I feel that way too."

He didn't have to – he could have just pressed the button to open her door – but Marshall wanted to step out and walk around to the passenger side. But before he could, she yanked the door open and sat without a word.

Marshall looked at her. She refused to face him. She didn't even acknowledge Toby when he rested his chin on her shoulder. She just stared straight ahead. Definitely not the behavior he was used to from Penelope. But he remembered his mother telling him things about bad days, bad moods, times of the month. Maybe it was just his nerves. Maybe she and Bea had argued. She would tell him all about it on the way to Lewis Ginter Botanical Gardens, and by the time they were on their way home, they'd be laughing about it. Marshall reached over Penelope's shoulder and scratched Toby's head as a sort of consolation. He pushed the door button, and the door silently lowered with a gentle click as it sealed.

A visit to Lewis Ginter was Penelope's idea. She'd said she was tired of the unseasonably cold weather and wanted to feel the close, dank warmth the greenhouse offered. Their ride was devoid of the usual conversation. Marshall tried to gauge Penelope's mood, but he didn't know what to say or do. He could rarely gauge anyone's mood.

"You won't need that coat where we're going," he said.

"Hmm," Penelope replied, offering a weak smile. She gazed out the window.

"It'll feel like summer."

"That's why I want to go. I already told you that. I can't believe this cold snap. It's almost April. It's absurd. Just last week, the highs were in the mid-seventies. Makes the fifties feel like freezing."

"We could grab some dinner after? Dot's Back Inn is close."

"I won't be hungry."

"Okay." Marshall stared out the window unable to comprehend why for the first time talking to Penelope felt like such an effort. It was normal for him to struggle when talking to people. He just wasn't used to struggling with Penelope.

The car pulled into the spot nearest the entrance and its hum dulled to a whir before cutting off. He opened the back door for Toby, and started for the passenger door but before he could reach it, Penelope had pressed the button and let herself out. Marshall pushed the button to close it. He tried to take her arm, but she didn't seem to notice. She forged toward the entrance.

That must've been some argument with Bea. Toby trotted beside Marshall as he hurried to catch up with Penelope. It was as if she were in a hurry. The door closed behind her just as Marshall reached it.

But that was okay, because it wasn't her job to hold it open for him. He opened the door, letting the warmth of the visitors' entrance envelop him. He caught up with Penelope at the front desk and managed to take her arm. He was relieved when she didn't pull away, but disappointed when she scanned her own thumbprint to pay for her admission. He had wanted to pay for them both. They walked arm-in-arm in silence for several minutes. Each step was torture for Marshall. He was looking for the perfect time, the perfect place, or the perfect plant. But it was beginning to feel as if nothing about this day was going to be perfect enough for his question.

Maybe he was reading her all wrong. He wasn't good at reading people. Books he could read and understand, yes. He was very good at books and numbers but not people. They were much trickier. They had too many gray areas. Crying when they were happy *and* when they were sad. Laughing when they were kind *and* when they were cruel. It was difficult to tell the lies from the truth. He wished someone had trained Toby to do that.

The area was adorned with showy, red flowers that were fragrant and florid. The heavy perfume was sweet, made sweeter by the hot, humid air. The aroma was almost overpowering.

Penelope stopped walking and gazed up at Marshall. Her eyes searched his in a way that concealed a heavy emotion. But what was it?

Toby sat at Marshall's feet and leaned slightly against his leg. The pressure gave Marshall a little boost of confidence, and he sensed that this was his moment.

"Penelope, am I … can I be … your boyfriend?" he asked.

A wave of relief swept over him, and he could've laughed for the weight that had lifted from his chest, but something in Penelope's reaction kept him quiet, stifling his joy.

Penelope remained quiet.

Toby whined.

"You thought today was a good day to ask me that?" she asked, her voice low and flat and ominous.

Marshall hadn't planned for such a reaction. He wasn't even sure he understood what it meant. "I don't understand."

"Let's sit," she said. "It's so damn hot in here."

Marshall had never heard Penelope Hope say a curse word, and it was a little like watching someone spill red wine on a white tablecloth yet managing not to stain it. The words were incongruous with the delicate lips that had just spoken them. Something was wrong.

Penelope struggled to pull her arms free from her coat. "Shit," she whispered. She freed herself from the fabric and tossed it at Marshall.

They sat on a bench tucked away amongst lush, tropical plants. Marshall rested his hand on Penelope's knee. She placed hers, cold even in the heat of the greenhouse, atop his and lifted his hand from her leg, setting it firmly on the bench.

"I'm not in the mood," she whispered.

If that was all then that wasn't such a problem. He could just ask again on a different day, when Penelope was in a better mood. That was easy enough. Tomorrow, even.

"Okay," he said. "Are you free tomorrow?"

"I'm not free tomorrow."

"Maybe the next day?"

"Marshall. Just take me home. Why did we even come here? It's so hot. Toby's panting. I'm sweating." Penelope stood, snatched her red coat from Marshall, and draped it over her arm. She took a few determined steps down the pathway.

"You wanted to come here," Marshall said, standing to follow. It was strange that she had forgotten that Lewis Ginter was her idea, and precisely because it would be so hot.

"What?" Penelope stopped and stood combatively in the middle of the stone path.

"You asked why we came here. We came here because you wanted to. You said you wanted a break from the cold."

Penelope stared at him. Had she really forgotten?

"Well, break's over," she said. "It still feels like winter outside. Take me home, please." She walked toward the exit.

Toby stood and waited to see what Marshall would do.

Marshall followed, feeling perplexed, with Toby in step. Maybe Penelope had been a trick all along. Maybe she'd been good at pretending to be sweet, but all along she was mean. Or maybe he'd been blinded by love. It had taken him a long time to understand that concept – *blinded by love.* What did love have to do with going blind, exactly? And if the two conditions were connected, why weren't more people blind? Was love really that rare? Or maybe she just had a huge fight with Bea or a bad night's sleep. Or any number of other things. Maybe she just wasn't in the mood like she had said. He knew exactly what that felt like. It happened to him every time Ken walked into his office. *Oh God,* Marshall thought. He hoped Penelope would never feel about him the way he felt about Ken.

"Are you *coming?*" Penelope demanded, standing at the exit, her hand on the door.

Marshall felt relieved. No, she must not feel about him the way he felt about Ken. If she did, she certainly wouldn't wait for him. Marshall would sooner walk home in the cold than sit in a car with Ken and count the number of times he heard the word fuckin'.

Chapter 36

Penelope, 26 March 2045, Age 26, T-minus 1

Marshall held the door, and Penelope stepped into the cold. Beyond the confines of the warm cocoon, the bitter winds of winter had returned. Penelope stopped and looked back at the fogged windows of the greenhouse, opaque with just frosted hints of green, red, and brown. Several petulant leaves, tired of their confinement, pressed flat against the sweating glass. Penelope shoved her gloveless hands deep into her pockets and looked up at the sky. It was smooth and white, without texture, as if someone had cast a bedsheet over the world and taken the time to iron out the wrinkles. The only variation in the endless white was a weak, bright spot where the sun glowed trying unsuccessfully to penetrate the cloud cover. A dying flashlight pressed up against the taut sheet that covered the city. March was a difficult month to live through, straddling winter and spring. Her life felt somewhat like March – in transition.

"I'll walk." Penelope stepped off the curb and into the parking lot.

"It's cold," Marshall replied. "And it's not walkable. How would you cross the highway?"

"I have a coat, and I'll be fine."

"I would rather drive you home." Marshall's eyes widened. His brows furrowed, and he shook his head.

Penelope stared into the traffic and shrugged. He was right about the highway. She nodded. "Okay."

Despite her less-than-pleasant treatment of him, Marshall opened the door and waited until she was settled. He opened the back door for Toby, then took his own place on the driver's side.

Penelope felt the gentle pressure of Toby's head against her shoulder and his breath in her ear. She wanted so much to kiss his soft, black face, and press it close to hers. When she ignored him, he whined and pulled away. Settling on the backseat, he stared at her with his droopy eyes. She felt a little piece of herself die.

Breaking Marshall's heart was bad enough, but to break the dog's too? A tear rolled down her cheek. She wiped it away and wondered what she had done to deserve such torture.

Marshall pressed the power button, and after a few beeps and buzzes, the car hummed to life.

"Penelope's," Marshall stated.

The car maneuvered its way into the traffic on 95 South, finding its place with ease amongst the other metallic capsules.

Penelope stared out the window, allowing the world to blur. Imagining her life without Marshall masked the city in a dull gray. Familiar sights no longer felt welcoming, but instead seemed like cruel reminders of what could have been. Once their relationship ended, Marshall's office, his apartment, his hardcover books, and Toby would be off limits, no longer a part of her life. She'd never be able to go to Shiplock Park – or the Hill Cafè – or even Lewis Ginter. Too many precious, painful memories would stalk her. They were no longer her places. They had become a part of their relationship, and when that ended – so would everything else – casualties of love. It was a cruel trick of the universe, happiness ending in sorrow, happily ever after just a myth, a wish, a trick.

The stuff of fairytales, no less make-believe than unicorns and monsters. *I wanted to believe. I have only myself to blame. I deceived myself again.*

A scream hunched down inside her chest, humming to itself, thrumming at her ribs like guitar strings. If she took a deep breath now, it would escape. She tightened her lips against it, grinding her teeth.

As they came to a stop in front of Bea's apartment, the car idled and announced ... **"Arrived at Penelope's."**

Marshall jumped out and opened her door.

She found his old-fashioned chivalry endearing, though a little less enthusiasm on his part would have been less painful. Surely, he would show some cruelty, some unkindness – at least a light sense of frustration with her negative attitude. After all, she had been mean to Toby. There was no excuse to behave coldly to a helpless animal. And she'd just spent the entire date being, for lack of a better word, a bitch. Everything he did for her only heightened her awareness of the quality of the man she was pushing away, the kind of love she might have nurtured if she had more time.

Marshall closed the car door and followed her to the sidewalk. When he reached for her hand, she jabbed it into her pocket. She turned and gave him the iciest stare she could muster. At least, she hoped it looked icy. With Marshall standing in the street and her on the sidewalk, they were now eye-to-eye. She searched his stunning, blue eyes but could only focus on the blackness of his pupils. She wanted a hint of what he might need to hear to get on with his life and leave her behind – to make it his choice. But, as usual, Marshall was unreadable. She looked past him and at the car.

Toby's gentle, dark eyes stared at her from the backseat. Her heart was melting, and if she didn't run inside right now, the courage to make a clean break would fade.

"Thanks for the ride," she said, turning around to walk into the apartment complex.

The gentle thud of the lobby door sounded from behind her. She didn't have to turn around to know that Marshall was still standing there in the cold wind. He would simply wait and watch her disappear into the recesses of the building. His loving gaze felt warm against her back as if his protection and love would follow her everywhere. It took all her resolve to keep walking.

Inside the apartment, Bea sat on the couch with her feet tucked under her. She was licking a blue sucker and watching something idiotic on TV. Penelope took off her coat without announcing her presence, draping it over the back of the chair.

"How'd it go?" Bea smiled. "Did he dump you?"

Penelope rested her hands on the chair, looked up at the ceiling, and took in a deep breath before answering. "Not yet." A heavy, drawn-out sigh filled her with a sudden desire to disappear into the blackness that was slowly consuming her reality. "He asked to be my boyfriend."

Bea pulled the sucker from her mouth and laughed. Her tongue and teeth were stained a deep blue.

Penelope stared at her and frowned.

Bea's laughter subsided to a soft giggle before she pushed the sucker back between her lips. As the candy clicked against her teeth, Bea whispered, "Backfire." She turned off the TV. "You need a new plan. I could've saved you a lot of trouble and told you no one would dump you over one bitchy day."

"You think maybe I need a few bitchy weeks?"

"Can you *be* bitchy to Marshall for a few weeks? I don't think so. You love him too much."

Penelope sat, feeling deflated. She rested her elbows on her knees and her head in her hands, staring at the silent TV. Her reflection stared back. From somewhere behind the figure inside the reflection, something dark and evil lurked behind her, skulking in the shadows. Something that would one day pull Penelope into the pits of hell. Especially, if she continued to act the way she was acting.

"No," she whispered. "And I can't be mean to Toby anymore either. I need a different plan."

"You *need* to just tell him," Bea said, pulling the sucker from her mouth and pointing it at her friend. "Didn't you say the only reason you *weren't* telling him was because you were afraid he'd break up with you?" Bea waved the sucker through the air. "Voila!" She chuckled. "It's what you want. Boom … done deal."

Penelope sighed. "I guess that would be the kindest option … for *him* anyway," she whispered. "Just not what I wanted."

"What *do* you want, Penelope?"

Penelope *wanted* to be with Marshall. Maybe even marry him. She wanted to reopen The Cakery and bake cakes – even deathday cakes, if that was what sold. She wanted to buy a house and travel and bake Bea's wedding cake and camp in the forest and maybe raise a child. She hadn't known it before, but she even wanted to grow old – to notice the first gray hair or lament the first wrinkles. Would they have been crow's feet? Laugh lines? Or maybe those long, ugly, deep creases that would eventually stretch across smooth brows. Even those she could've been grateful for if they signified more time. She wanted all the things she had thought were givens. Aging seemed like such a privilege now that she knew she'd never grow old. She turned her face away from her translucent reflection in the TV and looked at Bea.

"I want more time."

Chapter 37

Penelope, 30 March 2045, Age 26, T-minus 1

As usual, Bea was right. There was absolutely no way Penelope would be able to maintain a nasty façade around Marshall – not when he made her so happy, so giddy, and feel so warm. Being with Marshall was like coming home. He and Toby were impossible *not* to love. She tried convincing herself to just stop seeing them – ignore Marshall's calls and notifications. Refuse to answer his graphs. Pretend to not be around if he showed up.

Bea offered to cover for her. Tell Marshall that Penelope had moved away or was seeing someone else or whatever she wanted. But she just couldn't do it. Was it too much to ask to be happy, even if just for the next several months? And wasn't *she* also making *him* happy? Wasn't that worth something? Couldn't his happiness justify hers?

Or was it her destiny to be miserable until she walked into that dark abyss? Maybe she had no right to be happy, no right to exist in the world of the living. What right did she have to plan for a future? Maybe her soul already belonged with the dead. Maybe she should start living like she was dying, making those morbid plans everyone had to make sooner or later. For her, it just happened to be sooner.

Despite her misgivings, when Marshall called a few days later to walk the Capital Trail with him and Toby, Penelope agreed. She loved that trail, especially in the spring – the way the cherry trees at Shiplock Park ballooned into bloom, their full, round branches resembling pink cotton candy atop spindly trunks. Besides, over the last few days, the weather had finally turned and it was starting to feel like spring.

With her arm tucked tightly under Marshall's, Penelope inhaled deeply and stared rapturously at the pale blue sky. Cherry blossoms drifted through the air like little, blushing springtime snowflakes.

"What a beautiful day," she mused.

Marshall chuckled and shook his head.

"What?" Penelope asked. "What's so funny?"

"You."

"Me?" She smiled and a little laugh bubbled in her chest. "I'm being serious. It's beautiful today."

"I know you're serious. That's not what's funny."

"Then what's so funny?"

"What a difference a day makes."

"What do you mean?"

"You were so grouchy the other day, and now here you are smiling and happy and acting normal again."

"It was cold the other day, and now here we are warm and lovely and it's spring again."

"What were you so upset about?"

Penelope wasn't sure what to say. She hadn't really been angry about anything. It had all been an act, and she wasn't accustomed to lying – not outright, anyway. She replied with the first thing that came to her mind. "Bea and I had an argument. I'm sorry I took it out on you."

"I knew it."

"Knew what?"

"I knew you must've had an argument with Bea. What was it about?"

Annoyed at both his prying and the prospect of having to concoct and remember another lie, Penelope changed the subject. "Why are you always so direct with your questions? Some things are just none of your business, you know."

His gaze lowered and he frowned.

She was already inflicting pain with her deceit, and now she was hurting his feelings in their conversation. "Even if you *are* my boyfriend." She added the last few words hoping to give his ego a little boost and soften the bite of her words. She felt guilty encouraging their relationship, digging the grave of Marshall's happiness a little deeper, one selfish deception at a time. Still, her heart warmed at the sheepish smile she saw on his face.

"Your boyfriend?"

"Yeah," she said, squeezing his arm. "My boyfriend." She bit her lip and smiled up at him.

"I like that."

Penelope did too.

Marshall was quiet for a few moments as they continued to walk, and Penelope wondered what he was thinking. After a while, she received her answer.

"One reason I'm so direct," he said, "is because I don't know how not to be. I'm not very good at what my mother would've called *niceties*. I don't see how they fit into actual conversations … *productive* conversations. I don't see the sense in saying a whole lot of unnecessary things. Small talk is silly. But sometimes, even when I can tell I should use a nicety, I just don't. It feels like a lie."

"Why do you feel that way?"

"Because I don't really mean what I'm saying, and that's a type of lie. I don't like being lied to, so I don't want to lie to anyone else. I know how it feels." He looked at Penelope. "It doesn't feel good."

Penelope squeezed Marshall's arm, managing a weak smile. She felt sick to her stomach.

Chapter 38

Penelope, 3 April 2045, Age 26, T-minus 1

Penelope and Marshall sat on opposite sides of Bea's couch. They faced each other with their legs intertwined and their heads supported by pillows. Marshall was lost in the pages of a book, and Penelope liked watching the tiny, almost undetectable reactions to what he was reading as they flickered across his face – a subtle twitch of an eye, a quick furrow of the brow, the faintest glimmer of a smile – dancing like ephemeral flashes of light on a ceiling when the sun shines on a puddle of water.

"What are you reading?" he asked, looking up without warning.

Penelope laughed. She'd been so absorbed in watching him, she'd almost forgotten that he knew she was there. His directness startled her.

"Your face," she replied. "I was reading your expressions. Well, not reading exactly … just watching."

Marshall closed his book, leaving his thumb between the pages to mark his spot. He tilted his head as if scrutinizing her remark. "And … what did you see?"

Penelope wasn't sure how to answer, so she asked her own question. "What are *you* reading?"

"Nonfiction."

"Mm-hmm. Usually is. What about?"

Marshall's even-toned skin blushed a slight pink, and he averted his gaze when he whispered, "Marriage." His eyes darted back to her, then down at the book's cover, and then back up at her. "And how to raise kids. It's about being married with kids."

He seemed nervous. And he wasn't hiding it very well. In an attempt to explain himself, he started to ramble.

"It's just … well … I never thought I'd have a family of my own. It didn't seem like that would be an option. I mean … I'm different. I don't understand people, and they don't understand me. Then I met you, and it seemed like, maybe … maybe I could be a husband and dad someday. I want to learn about it. Do it right … cuz I never really thought much about it before … before I met you."

Penelope couldn't imagine a situation in which she would feel like a more detestable human. Here was a man – the one she loved – who believed he would marry her someday, raise children with her, and – and she *didn't have time.*

Before she could respond, Marshall took in a deep breath and continued. "I could do it, I think. I could be a good husband and dad. I can learn to do anything if I study. But I can't do it alone. I'll need help." Marshall paused as if trying to find the right words. "I'd want to make sure my children could make friends and understand things. Things I never could. To relate to others and have them relate back. You could teach them that."

Penelope tried to meet Marshall's gaze. Instead, she looked out the window. All the bad things, the dirty things, were seeping up from the pit and melding into her soul.

I am 'the pools that stand in drains'
and 'the soot that falls from chimneys.

There was no time for a hundred indecisions or revisions. There was no time for any of the things he wanted. She had taken their relationship too far. She had led this wonderful man to the edge of the dark abyss that she was trying so desperately to avoid and simply shoved him in. Now, she was staring down, wondering if he would ever find his way out.

With her eyes watching the clouds, she whispered, "Marshall … I like you. I really do. A lot. And I want you to be my boyfriend, but …" – the untruth behind her words made it hard to say – "… but I think we're moving too fast."

"Too fast for what?" he replied.

"Too fast for me."

"Why?"

"I don't know *why*. It's just a feeling," she lied.

"I don't have that feeling."

"But I do. And it takes two … we both have to be on the same page for it to work. And you're ahead of me. Family and kids … I'm not even planning our next date yet, and you're ahead by ten chapters, planning our whole life."

Our whole life. Our life.

It sounded perfect. She swallowed back her tears. She didn't mean anything she was saying. In fact, everything was the exact opposite of what she meant. She was lying to him – again. *It's for his own good,* she told herself. *It'll spare him even more pain later. Sometimes, you have to be cruel to be kind.*

Marshall was staring at her. She could tell by his reflection in the window.

"It's like … it's like you've read ahead and you're on page ninety-two and I'm still on page five. I don't know what you've already read, and you can't forget what you've already read. There's a big gap, and I can't close it."

"Yes you can," he said, in his characteristic, matter-of-fact manner. "If I put the book down for a while, you can catch up. Then we can read it together."

Penelope wiped away a tear.

"I can wait," he replied. "I don't want to rush you. There will be time, remember?"

No! There wouldn't be time! There wasn't any time.

Penelope knew what she should do. Tell him no, there *was* no time. She should walk away. Break his heart now before their lives, hers so short and his so long, became even more entangled. Instead, she heard herself whisper, "Time for you and time for me," and felt Marshall's warm embrace, dissolving any resolve she might have felt.

When Bea arrived home just after dark, Marshall pecked Penelope on the cheek, bade Bea good evening, and sauntered out of the apartment with his book about marriage and children tucked snugly under his arm. Penelope closed the door and leaned against it. She sighed. Bea set her purse on the kitchen counter and frowned.

"Why all the heaviness?" Bea asked. "Did you have a fight or something?"

"Hardly," Penelope replied. "He mentioned that he might want to marry me and have children."

Bea laughed.

"It's *not* funny."

"So …?" Bea asked. "What happened?"

"I tried to break it off. Sorta."

"And?"

"Didn't work."

"You can't dump him, and he definitely won't dump you. You're just gonna have to tell him. He'll understand. Everyone's enrolled."

"It's not the fact that I'm enrolled that's the problem. It's the fact that I didn't *tell* him I'm enrolled."

Bea shrugged. "So tell him now."

"He'll think I lied to him."

"You did."

"It'll hurt him."

"Too late. Tell him the truth," Bea replied. "Give him time to plan, to prepare."

Penelope thought about Marshall's words, spoken in the glow of the late afternoon, and how he would need help. He wanted his children to have two parents, someone to teach them how to be sociable. Their child, if there were even time for a child, would grow up in a single-parent home. If she didn't tell him, she'd be double-tricking him. But if she did tell him, it could ruin everything.

"Bea … what if he never knows?" Penelope asked weakly, trying to convince not only Bea, but also herself, that what Marshall didn't know – might *never* know – couldn't hurt him.

"He'll know when you die, you idiot! Can't hide that now, can you?"

"He'll know I died. But he doesn't have to know I knew when it was gonna happen."

"Listen to yourself. Are you for real? Do you know how deceitful you sound right now? You'd be turning *me* into a liar too. I'd have to play along with this stupid, little stunt until my own deathday. It is still lying to Marshall, and you'd keep lying to him from your grave."

Bea was right. She'd be knowingly breaking Marshall's heart, leading him directly into grief.

"*Ignorance is bliss*, right?" Penelope was working hard to convince herself. "He would be happy. What he wouldn't know, wouldn't hurt him. I could live the life I want for as long as I have, and he could be happy."

"He could be happy? Right. Until January 30, 2046. What about after that? He'll have … what … forty-seven years of misery? Or is that forty-eight?" Bea counted on her fingers. "Something like that. Anyway, you think Marshall's gonna find someone else? Never … he'll miss you forever. For the rest of his life. Half a century. Now that's cruel."

Penelope was losing the battle with Bea and with herself. "Better to have loved and lost than never to have loved at all," she tried.

"Honesty is the best policy."

"Ignorance is bliss," Penelope countered, wishing that she had never enrolled.

"Used that one already."

Penelope stared out the window at the black river, an artery of pulsating water. It would keep flowing long after her own blood dried up. The heartbeat of the city would go on even after her heart fell silent and stilled. "I'm gonna have to tell him, aren't I?"

"Yeah. You're gonna have to tell him."

Chapter 39

Penelope, 6 April 2045, Age 26, T-minus 1

Penelope understood that she would have to tell Marshall and soon. That she probably already should have told him. If she didn't say something soon, her resolve would again melt. She promised herself that she'd tell him the next time they were together, and today was that next time. They sat across from each other at the Hill Cafè. Penelope absentmindedly stirred her ice water with a fork, trying to decide if she should say something before their meal arrived. It wouldn't do to tell him while they were eating. She could wait until they paid. Or –

"What's it like," Marshall asked, "not to be enrolled?"

Penelope stopped swirling her water, and her eyes widened. Was the man a mind reader? What was it like not to be enrolled? It was enjoying life as if immortal. It was freedom from the constraints of time, from an inescapable sense of mortality that darkened every day. It was savoring each bite of the cake assuming another would follow – enjoying it right up until the end. Maybe knowledge was power. But ignorance was bliss. And if Penelope had to choose, she'd pick bliss.

"You should know," she said. "You enrolled when you were eighteen. Don't you remember what it was like before?" Was this her opening, her time to spit out the truth? While they were on the subject of enrollment, maybe her admission wouldn't seem so out of the blue. "There's something you need to know."

"Okay."

"You might get mad." She waited for him to say something reassuring, like how he could never be angry with her, but he simply looked at her, expectant, so she continued. "You think I'm smart and pretty and *good* –"

"You are. You're all of those things."

"No, Marshall. I'm not. I'm anything but perfect. And you need to know that –"

"I know you're not perfect." Marshall chuckled and rolled his eyes.

Had it been anyone else, Penelope would've thought they were teasing, but this was Marshall, and he was being candid. She smiled.

"You're definitely not perfect," he repeated. "Remember that day at Lewis Ginter? That was definitely *not* perfect." He chuckled again. "Doesn't matter. Besides ... some things are none of my business, even if I am your boyfriend. You said so yourself."

"But this concerns you. You need to know." She took in a deep breath. One large enough to hold the weight of what she was about to say.

"Whatever it is," Marshall added, "doesn't matter. You're not perfect. I'm not perfect. Toby's the closest to perfect. But I love you anyway."

The big breath escaped Penelope's mouth in one long exhale, emptied of its message. "You what?" she said weakly.

"I love you."

"I love you too." But she hated herself.

Chapter 40

Penelope, 16 April 2045, Age 26, T-minus 1

Marshall sat on the ground propped up on his elbows, Toby at his feet. Penelope reclined in the soft grass, her head resting on Marshall's lap. She stared up at the leaves above Marshall's head. She watched the bright, white sun alternately appear and disappear as the breeze disturbed the leaves, rearranging them on a whim – revealing the light – then hiding it. She wasn't thinking about anything in particular. She hadn't been thinking about anything at all. She was simply existing. Maybe that was what death was like – not oblivion – not heaven – not hell – just a sort of disembodied mindlessness, an existence without pain or pleasure or thought or obligation or foresight or hindsight. Maybe to be dead was just to be – the simplest form of being. An existence devoid of self-awareness.

Might not be so bad.

"Have you thought about reopening The Cakery?" Marshall asked.

Toby lifted his head and looked at them before gently resting back in the grass.

"Not really. Why do you ask?" The truth was she had thought about it. In fact, she thought about it all the time, but there just wasn't any time.

Marshall pointed to the small shop down below. "It's right *there.*"

Penelope followed his finger to her old storefront. From her perspective, high up on the hill, it looked like Marshall could brush it away with the gentlest of movement – just flick it off the block like a crumb off a kitchen table.

"Yep." Penelope squinted through the sunlight. "It's right there."

"Where we first spoke."

"You needed a deathday cake for someone at work."

"Yeah." Marshall sat without talking for a few moments before adding, "I wish you'd reopen it."

"Why?"

"Why not?"

Penelope hesitated. She could tell him the truth right now or –

"Penelope!" a voice yelled.

It was a familiar voice, one she'd heard say her name many times before but in another life.

Toby sat up, alert, ears perked in the direction of the sound, nose slightly lifted to pick up a scent.

Penelope and Marshall both turned, and there, walking back into her life like she'd invited him, was Everett. "I thought that was you." Everett sat in the grass a few feet away. "How have you been?"

For a moment, Penelope couldn't speak. Here she was, Marshall sturdy and supportive on her left, his solid body warm and firm beside hers, and Everett a few feet away on her right, a seeming lifetime between them. Seeing him, a ghost from her past, again – in the flesh – was a little like realizing what she'd thought was merely a bad dream was actually a reality. Like she had told herself in her presumed sleep, *'it's only a dream; it's only a dream, you're okay'* only to realize it wasn't, and she was awake, and the nightmare was the truth. "Fine," she choked. "I've been fine. I'm doing well."

"Stopped by The Cakery a couple times."

He would. Everett would possess the gall not only to try to see her again, but to fish for information about the choices she'd made after enrollment.

"Not there anymore."

"I see. You closed it."

"Yeah."

"Too bad. You can make some mean cakes."

"She made very nice cakes," Marshall stated.

Penelope patted Marshall's leg.

Everett leaned over, holding out his hand to Marshall. "Everett," he said.

A low growl rumbled deep in Toby's throat.

"Marshall," Marshall replied, not reaching to meet Everett's offer.

"Right," Everett said, lowering his hand.

The fur on Toby's back bristled.

Penelope glanced around, rubbing her arms. She hoped Everett didn't plan to stay long. If he didn't leave soon, she and Marshall and Toby would have to. She'd say Bea was waiting for them at the apartment. Hopefully, Marshall wouldn't blow her cover with his inability to be anything but literal and honest.

"So, Penelope. What have you decided to do with your remaining time?" Everett looked at the city and smiled.

Penelope winced. She looked over at Marshall to see if he'd picked up on it. But he simply rested his head against hers, staring into nothing.

"Same as anyone, I guess," Penelope replied. "Live."

Everett chuckled. "That's good. Have you made any plans?"

"Have you?"

Everett shrugged. "I have time," he said. "I'm in no rush." He looked at Marshall.

Was he jealous? What right did he have to be jealous? He'd left her. She had almost begged him to stay for the little time she had left, and instead he walked away. "Have *you* met anyone?" she asked.

"I meet lots of people," Everett replied.

Penelope wished he would get up and leave.

"I called, you know, but Bea wouldn't let me talk to you."

"Bea's a good friend," Penelope replied.

"She encouraged you too, yah know. It wasn't just me."

Penelope's heart pounded, and her grip on Marshall's thigh tightened. *Marshall can't find out, not this way.* She glanced at Marshall. He was still looking at the city. But he was clenching his jaw. The muscles below his ears were bulging and relaxing, bulging and relaxing.

"True," she said. "But she's still my friend and a big part of my life. And you're not." She challenged his stare.

"Whatever," Everett said after a few seconds, hefting himself up. "I would've thought you might be happier to see me. I can see I was wrong. Good seeing you. Nice meeting you … Marshall."

Without looking in Everett's direction, Marshall offered a brief nod of acknowledgment. Everett scoffed and walked away.

"Who was that?" Marshall asked.

"Everett."

"He told me his name," Marshall said. "I meant who is he to *you*?"

"My ex-fiancé."

"Not difficult to understand why you called that one off. He didn't even ask what Toby's name was."

Penelope laughed. She braced herself for more questions but none came. She wriggled back down into the grass, resting her head on Marshall's lap.

"Penelope," Marshall said after a few seconds. "Have you ever been to the forest?"

She craned her neck to look at him. "A long time ago. My mom used to take me. We'd camp … spend the night in a tent. She called our trips Back-to-Nature weekends. 'Let's get back to nature,' she'd say. And I knew we were in for a weekend in the woods."

"What was it like … the forest?"

Penelope closed her eyes and took a deep breath. She smiled at the memory of her mother and of the forest. It had been a long time since she'd thought about either. She let out a long, nostalgic sigh. "Well … when you first get there, you can still hear the city and the cars. But once you're in deeper, the noise just fades away. All you can hear are birds and bugs. You know, buzzing and chirping and clicking. Little animals rustle in the leaves. Maybe a squirrel or something small. It's shady even on hot days. The sun shines through the branches, and the rays are like the ones in photographs or paintings. Your footsteps are quiet because the pine needles steal away the sounds. The air smells different … fresher. Like dirt and rain and pine."

"I've never been to the forest," Marshall said. He sounded wistful, his gaze drifting from the city to the distant trees.

She sighed and whispered, "We should go sometime. We can camp just like I used to with my mom."

Marshall's eyes darted from the faraway forest to Penelope. He squinted and nodded. "Okay."

"Yeah? When?"

Marshall smiled. "Next month?"

"Done!" Penelope could hardly contain herself.

She hadn't realized how much she'd missed the forest until Marshall asked her about it. Now, she couldn't wait to exchange the concrete maze for the endless tangle of trees. She'd have to find a tent – did they even make them anymore? And a few other things – a backpack, some food, a solar phone charger.

They would build a campfire and cook over the open flames. They would lay awake and listen to the sounds of the night creatures. If they were far enough away from the city lights, they might even see the stars. It had been a long time since Penelope had seen a star. She didn't want to die without seeing a star at least one more time.

Chapter 41

Penelope, 13 May 2045, Age 26, T-minus 1

Penelope bent over an oversized backpack, doing her best to convince it to stay closed. It had been a long time since she'd walked the forest and even longer since she'd camped. There must've been an art to packing, a skill she had once known and long since lost. She didn't know whether she was bringing too much or just packing unwisely. Maybe a little of both.

She groaned as she fought with the clips and buckles, and after a few more tries, she won. Not without wondering how she'd reclose it after she had to open it for something. But by that time, Marshall would be with her, and he could help. Surely the two would win against the one.

"Makin' an awful lot of noise over there," Bea said, rounding the corner into the kitchen and switching on the coffee maker.

"Packing," Penelope whispered between huffs.

"For what?"

"Back-to-Nature Day," Penelope replied. "Marshall and I are going camping. I've been talking about it all week." She laughed.

How could Bea forget? She had to be tired of her ceaseless talks about stars and pine trees and campfires.

"This whole time I thought –"

"What? That I was kidding?"

"No … that you meant the AR forest … *augmented reality*? You know … like what everyone else does. Not the real thing with all the crawly, nasty, little critters."

Penelope rolled her eyes and stared up at the ceiling. "Oh come on. AR? You know me better than that."

"Why do you have to be so weird?" Bea wrinkled her nose as she pulled a mug from the shelf. She breathed in the morning aroma of coffee and sighed. "Smells good."

"It's not weird to want to experience a real forest, Bea. People used to do it all the time. There used to be a lot of parks and campgrounds. You should remember. You sometimes came with Mom and me on our hikes."

"Even back then people thought it was weird."

"No, they didn't. I bet when your parents were little, your grandparents took them to a state or national park or something similar."

Bea shrugged. "Maybe." She took a sip of her coffee. "But *my* parents never took *me*."

"Then it's a good thing I did."

"Maybe." Bea shrugged and took a longer drink. She swallowed and exhaled. "Still, the AR forest is more convenient."

"I want the *real* deal. Marshall's never been."

Bea lifted her mug as if to toast. "Ahh … normal."

Penelope shook her head and laughed. "He's definitely not normal. But that's one thing I love about him."

Chapter 42

Marshall, 14 May 2045, Age 28, T-minus 49

Marshall leaned against the closet door, surveying the items on his bed. An extra shirt. Extra undershirt. Extra pair of socks. A few condoms – he'd pack those discreetly. Extra underwear. Water bottle. Solar charger. Sleeping bag. Three books – he was almost through with one and didn't want to be without the next. Trail mix. A compass – that was hard to find, since everywhere he looked, people kept telling him to use a navigation app. No one could fathom that their phones might die, the charger might fail, cell service might not reach. He'd scoured the city's antique and oddity shops all week, and finally found one at the history museum's gift shop, which in and of itself, was something of a relic. They still had human cashiers instead of *Felixes*.

"You know," the cashier had said, "this is the first one we've sold since I've worked here."

"How long have you worked here?" Marshall had asked.

"Two years. Seems that kids don't know what they're for even after visiting the museum. What're you buying it for? Don't really need these things now." The cashier then turned it around in his hand as if inspecting it.

"Camping."

The cashier had looked at him and smiled. "You know, we sell a few great AR programs for that. We just received one that features Glacier National Park … while it still had a glacier. Imagine that."

"I'm going into the, uh, *real* forest," Marshall had replied. "With my girlfriend."

He'd never imagined being able to add that phrase to anything he might do. And it felt good. He would have to say it more often.

The cashier had raised his brows and frowned. "Good luck." He'd handed Marshall the compass.

Toby whined behind him, startling Marshall from his reverie.

"What, Toby? Am I ready? I think so. I'm not sure. I've never done this before. Any of it. Never been to a forest. Never hiked. Never camped." Marshall sighed. "Never spent the night with a woman, much less the most beautiful woman in the world."

Toby rested on the floor like a sphinx, looking up at Marshall expectantly, ears high.

"Yeah. First time for everything right, Toby?"

Toby tilted his head.

Marshall loaded his pack with his things. On the nightstand was the stack of his most recent reads. They were older books. It was hard to find anything new – in print – about camping or hiking or most anything really. But he managed to find a few as recent as the 2010s.

Ian Kerner	*She Comes First: The Thinking Man's Guide to Pleasuring a Woman*
Harris O'Malley	*New Game +: The Geek's Guide to Love, Sex, & Dating*

Though Marshall wasn't sure if that last one applied to him. He knew he wasn't like everyone else, but he wasn't really a geek either.

Nicholas Sparks *The Notebook*
James Salter *A Sport and a Pastime*

On the top he'd left, very deliberately, *Camping for Beginners: The Ultimate Guide to the Best Experience in Your First Outdoor Adventure.* He hadn't read that one yet. Plus, it was just a decoy to hide the others. Penelope and the compass would guide him through the woods, but he didn't want her to have to guide him through anything else.

Chapter 43

Penelope, 20 May 2045, Age 26, T-minus 1

It was the first predicted weekend without the chance of rain. So, after an hour or so of what could only be described as urban hiking, Penelope and Marshall finally paused at the edge of a newly mowed field, about a quarter mile wide, which served as a buffer between the city and the forest. Toby whined at their feet, his tail swaying in excited uncertainty. It was a strange border, this stretch of lawn. At least, Penelope thought so. It wasn't really designed to keep anything in or to keep anything out. No fences. No signs. Just a line where the mowing stopped, and the shorn, tame grass gave way to the wild.

If a person had been responsible for maintaining this vernal border, Penelope would've wondered if he'd ever been tempted to just step off his mower and walk into the woods. But that was silly – people didn't mow anymore. Self-propelled mowers did that now. Programmable according to the acreage, the fencing, and how high and thick the grass was.

She looked over at Marshall and smiled. He stood, eyes wide, mouth slightly open, staring into the shady, green realm they were about to enter. Behind them, the whir of traffic buzzed. In front of them, only the birds and crickets sang.

"Should we go?" she asked.

Marshall nodded.

She linked her arm with his, and together, they took their first step, Toby at their heels.

A few miles into the forest, Penelope glanced over at Marshall. He was shifting his backpack uncomfortably from one shoulder to the other. Strange, since he was so fit – more fit than she was – and she wasn't struggling. She stopped walking.

"You okay?"

Marshall wiped a thin layer of sweat from his forehead. "Yeah. Good." His breathing sounded labored.

"You sure? What do you have in there, anyway?"

"Just … camping stuff."

"What kind of *camping stuff*?"

It hadn't occurred to her that Marshall probably didn't have any idea what to pack. Unlike her, he hadn't grown up enjoying the woods. She was out of practice, to be sure, but she had some experience. He had none. She took a step toward him.

"Let's take a look in that pack."

Marshall swung it from his shoulder, and it landed heavily on the ground, the weight of its contents anchoring it to the carpet of pine needles. Penelope lowered her pack.

"What'd you bring? The kitchen sink?"

"Should I have?"

She chuckled and he opened his pack. As he pulled out the items, Penelope named them.

"Solar charger, bug spray, water bottle." She looked at him approvingly. "So far, so good. Trail mix, sleeping bag …" She watched as Marshall wrestled with something large and smooth and glossy. "A textbook?"

Marshall pulled the book from his pack. "I'm almost done with it."

Penelope laughed. "Marshall, you brought a textbook into the woods to go camping?"

"I have two novels in there, too … for when I finish this one."

"Hardcover?"

"Yes. Paperbacks are flimsy and less durable. Harder to come by too."

"Marshall!" Penelope shook her head. "You won't have the time or light to read. It's no wonder you're so tired, lugging these heavy things all over the forest."

She helped him repack his *camping stuff* and they continued on. Marshall seemed a little refreshed by the short break.

"What's that tree?" Marshall asked, pointing.

"White oak."

"And that one?"

"Red oak."

"How do you know?" he asked.

"When you cut them down, one has wood that looks a little red and one has wood that's paler."

"But these aren't cut down. How could you tell one is white and one is red?"

"By the leaves."

"They both have green leaves."

"Yes, but the red oak has pointy leaves, see? And the white's are more rounded." She picked a fallen leaf from the ground and ran her finger along its edge. She handed it to Marshall.

"How do you know these things?"

"I just know from being in the forest as a kid. My mom taught me."

She remembered a time when people – at least some people – used to know these things. Used to know the names of the stars and their constellations. Used to pay attention to the phases of the moon. Used to know a red oak from a white oak. But that was before technology made everything essential, uninteresting or unnecessary as if the natural world was disconnected from humans. Or humans were disconnected from the natural world. As if people could simply seal themselves away inside a city's cinderblock walls, live independent from the world of trees and clouds and wild creatures.

Nature and people were not separate entities. Unlike water and oil, humans were actually mixable with nature. Some felt it was better to live inside a techno-world, claiming that absconding from nature was a way to protect and preserve it. Or what was left of it.

"If we stay out of it," they would say, "we can't destroy it."

"If we stay out of it," Penelope's mother had said, "we'll forget it's there. How can you love something you don't know? How can you protect it if you don't know how valuable it is?"

"What's that one?" Marshall asked.

"Sugar maple," Penelope replied, watching Toby relieve himself at the base of the tree. "They're gorgeous in the fall."

"What's your favorite?"

Penelope paused. She had never thought about a favorite tree before. For a moment, she wasn't sure, but then her eyes alighted on a grove of white pines a dozen or so yards ahead.

Marshall followed her gaze. "Evergreens?"

"Yeah. White pine."

"Why?"

"They never go to sleep. They stay awake through everything and never miss a day. They're always the first to sprout after a devastating event … like a forest fire or a bulldozing. They're the first to reclaim the forest, and they do it *fast*. They don't waste time. Those trees over there?" She pointed to the pines. "They're probably only four or five years old and look how tall they are." She sighed. "A forest of pines is a young forest … young and always green."

Penelope had spent most of her life in central Virginia annoyed with white pines – the way they tainted everything with their dusty, yellow pollen each spring. She often watched the stuff drift from the trees and float away in a yellow cloud before settling on the cars and sidewalks. Now, there was something more that called to her. A youthfulness, a vitality. She felt both tender toward and jealous of the little stand of trees. They would be here, taller and greener, long after she was gone.

"What was the devastating event?" Marshall asked.

"What?"

"The devastating event. What happened to let those pines sprout up?"

"I don't know."

"Oh," Marshall replied.

A strange sensation of loss and quiet dread and familiar sorrow filled Penelope's soul. She took a long look at the young pines. Taller, more mature trees, most of them deciduous, towered above them, protective, sheltering. What *had* happened to the trees that had been there before? What kind had they been? She was tempted to search for evidence of what had been, but she suppressed it – it didn't matter. The former trees were gone – the new trees had claimed their place – and beginning with them, this spot in the forest would heal. "Let's keep going," she said.

They hiked until dusk, and when they came to a clearing, the thick canopy gave way to a dome of blackness, stars scattering across it. Penelope caught her breath. It had been well over a decade since she'd been away from the city lights, and she had forgotten the immensity of the universe.

"I've never seen stars like this before." Marshall stared into a vastness that seemed to spread for miles. "Not real stars like these." He stood still and shook his head. "It's dizzying."

Penelope didn't know what to say. She herself felt like this was the first night she'd ever seen the stars. Everyone was so disconnected now – from the Earth, from themselves, from each other. *How aloof we've become from the real world,* Penelope thought. *How distant. And nobody even realizes it. Everyone just carries on with their daily chores as if nothing else matters. But everything matters.*

Her mother's wise words surfaced, and she savored the memory. "All this technology is taking us farther away from what's real."

Penelope looked over at Marshall and smiled. "I feel like I'm flying back in time." She wiped away a tear. "I'm a little girl again, camping in the forest with my mother. And I'm standing here naming all the constellations." She laughed and glanced around. "I half-expect to hear her calling me back to camp. Look up, Marshall. We're looking back in time. The stars we're seeing burnt out millions of years ago."

They died long ago, Penelope thought. *Long before I was even a thought. Before my parents were born. Before their parents were alive. And I can still see them.* She smiled at the thought. *I can still see them.* Maybe she wouldn't just evaporate after all, a faint memory, here and gone in so short a time – maybe someone would remember her fondly. Maybe she'd remain, invisible but ever present, like the stars. Bea would remember her. Maybe Marshall, too.

Marshall looked back at the way they'd just walked and pointed. "Look at that."

Above the trees, a warm, golden glow stained the black canvas, an arch of orange hovering in the distance.

Penelope smiled. "The city," she whispered. "That's why we can't see the stars from there."

After a few moments of reflection, they crossed the clearing and reentered the trees. Hiking a few yards, Penelope tripped on something hard and unforgiving. Marshall held her arm.

"You okay?"

"Yeah," she replied, feeling around with her foot in the dark. "Something's here."

It was a concrete step. If it hadn't been there, she would have walked straight into the wall only a few feet in front of her. She stepped back and looked up at a stone edifice, covered in vines. She pulled aside the ivy and revealed a four-paned window. A door, clinging to the frame by a single hinge, swayed when she touched it.

"Marshall," she whispered, "we found a house."

"You mean this was where someone used to live?" Marshall seemed genuinely surprised.

"Yes. Where some*one* used to live."

Penelope took a cautious step up and peeked inside. No roof, just the stars sparkling across the sky. One wall was missing, but the one on her left featured an elaborate mantle and fireplace. An oriental rug was in front of the hearth, decaying, half covered in moss. It crunched as she stepped on it. Old ashes still rested in a heap in the fireplace. Tattered curtains, barely clinging to the windows, gently swayed with a light breeze where the glass was missing. Under one window sat a small, round table with a chair. A second one was turned on its side with its fourth leg missing.

"Come inside," she whispered to Marshall.

Chapter 44

Marshall, 20 May 2045, Age 28, T-minus 49

Marshall stepped inside with Toby at his heels. "It's hard to believe anyone ever lived anywhere but the city."

He had read about farms and the countryside and cabins hidden in the woods, but seeing one for himself was something else altogether. It was just like what Penelope had said about the stars – they were stepping back in time.

Marshall allowed himself, for a moment, the luxury of imagining. Imagining what it would be like to live in a time when people didn't know – when *he* didn't know – how much time they'd been given, how much time they had left. What it would be like to live in a house like this with Penelope. No whirring cars. No glaring city lights to drown the stars. No countdowns or ADDEs. No *Experiment*. No enrollment. He'd never wondered about these things before he knew her. They hadn't seemed to matter.

"Let's sleep here tonight," Penelope said, sliding her pack off her shoulder. She sat it on the floor beside the hearth. "We can pretend we live here. That it's another place and time."

Marshall sat his pack beside hers. He opened it and pulled out three books. He sat them on the mantle just the way he'd seen in the local museum's paintings.

"I'll build a fire," Penelope said.

"You know how to do that?" Marshall asked as he poured dog food into a bowl for Toby.

He'd never seen anyone build a fire before. It was hard to believe that anyone knew how to do such a primitive thing.

Penelope squatted in front of the hearth. "Yeah … my mom taught me."

Small flames were soon crackling and within moments, a fire roared to life. Marshall knew from watching TV and AR what fire looked like, sounded like. But he never knew about the aroma – the glorious sweet, smoky smell.

Penelope stoked the flames as Toby crept up behind her. He sniffed and paused. He looked briefly at Marshall before snuggling in beside Penelope. His eyes stared at the fire. She tussled the soft fur between his ears.

Her loosened hair glowed, reminding him of a halo. She was an angel, a glimpse of heaven guarding the gates of hell. He thought of the flaming swords in Genesis, guarding the tree of human knowledge. And here she was, the cherubim – unenrolled, her days unnumbered, her life unencumbered by an expected end.

He took two steps and sat beside her. They sat side by side until the flames calmed. Marshall stroked Toby's back. It was warm to the touch. Toby let out a slow, satisfied sigh. Marshall now understood the romance of a crackling fire, the enchantment of the shadows off dying embers, and the sweet scent of burning wood.

Penelope used a stick to stir the fire, and the flames rekindled. As it roared and popped, Marshall watched the orange light dance across her features. He could feel the warmth on his face, his neck, his chest.

Penelope stood and unrolled their sleeping bags. She placed one on top of the other to create a single space to share. After crawling inside, she patted the empty space beside her. With the fire blazing, Marshall took his place on the other side. He felt her shiver as she pushed her body against his.

"Hold me," she whispered and rolled over, snuggling into the curve of his embrace. "I'm cold."

Tentatively, Marshall wrapped an arm around Penelope. His face buried deep into her hair. She smelled like the fire and faintly of fresh shampoo. He breathed in, the air cool against the back of his throat. The firm, round shape of her buttocks pushed against his pelvis, and his knees tucked snuggly into the back of hers. His chest pressed against her back. He gently scooched away as he felt himself swell, hoping she hadn't noticed, wouldn't notice.

He'd read about this all week, but now that he was actually here, he felt uncertain. His body touching hers – the fire warming their skin – the sleeping bags soft.

"I brought some books to read," he said, trying to distract his mind from the desires of his soul.

Penelope rolled over and faced him. The glow from the hearth created the same angel-in-the-flames image from the start of the evening.

"I know." She smiled. "That's why your pack was so heavy."

Marshall extricated himself from the sleeping bags, stood, and grabbed a book from the mantle. He sat near the hearth with his back to the fire.

Penelope propped herself up on one arm and watched.

Chapter 45

Penelope, 20 May 2045, Age 26, T-minus 1

Penelope thought she had felt the slightest pressure against her back, the first sign that perhaps Marshall was interested. But he stood and picked up a book. His fingers ran up and down the pages, his eyes glued to the words.

Clandestinely, she removed her clothes while still under the sleeping bag.

"It's Poe," he said and read, "'Ah, distinctly I remember it was in the bleak December; And each separate dying ember wrought its ghost upon the floor.'" He looked up and smiled. "Our fire reminds me of that part."

"I can see why," she said, wondering where he was going with this, and praying that he'd soon join her. "Come back under the covers."

"I love you," Marshall said.

"I love you, too." She paused, watching him watch her from the shadows. "That's why I want you to come back under the covers."

She lifted the sleeping bag, revealing her nakedness, her eyes never leaving his. Marshall scanned her body and stopped at the scar on her leg.

"What happened?" he asked.

"That accident."

"Really?"

"I was trying to save that woman's life. I found out later it was her deathday. The possibility never crossed my mind."

"And the scar?"

"The doctors could've erased it, but I wanted to keep it. The small one above my eye too." She pointed.

"Why?"

"It's part of my story. A sort of … badge of honor." She shrugged. "Why would I want to erase an experience? It happened. It's not like erasing the scar erases the memory." She paused. "No one else sees it that way. The doctor thought I was crazy."

And the truth was, now that she was enrolled, she felt vindicated. Scars were for survivors. They only form on the living. The scar was proof she wasn't dead. Not yet. No one – least of all her doctors – could understand Penelope's decision to forego the procedure to remove the scars and smooth the skin back to normal. Bea constantly gave her a hard time about it.

Marshall only whispered, "I see."

Penelope thought that maybe he *could* see. He could see the scar. He could see *her*. Maybe, he understood. "Come back to bed, Marshall."

Marshall replaced the book on the mantle and removed his shirt. Penelope's gaze traced the space from his belly button to the button on his pants. She stood, letting the sleeping bag puddle at her feet. She pressed her breasts against his chest and slowly unzipped his pants. She kissed him, long and deep. Her skin felt chilled, but she was warm at her core.

Marshall's hand ran down the back of her neck, then up to her hair.

The Raven echoed through her mind as she slid his pants down his thighs. *'Is there – is there balm in Gilead? – tell me – tell me, I implore! Quoth the Raven 'Nevermore.'*

Marshall stepped out of his pants. He placed one hand on the small of her back, and she gazed into his eyes. Her hand caressed his strong jawline as his searching eyes grew intense, a darker and deeper blue.

'Tell this soul with sorrow laden, if within the distant Aidenn, It shall clasp a sainted maiden whom the angels name Lenore –'

Marshall gently coaxed her unto the covers. She held the bag open for him and was somewhat surprised at his assertiveness. One hand on the nape of her neck, the other already between her legs, he pulled her toward him.

"I thought this was your first time," she whispered.

"Books," he replied.

She chuckled. "Of course."

He pulled her face toward his, kissing her as he slid his hand higher up her inner thighs. She reached down and felt him, hard and throbbing. The guilt she felt about him not knowing was immense – vast as the sky that seemed to spin above, stretching from horizon to horizon. But her desire was stronger. Surely, she deserved this type of love. Within this darkness lit only by a small fire, it was her moment. She was granted this time, and she wouldn't waste it letting her enrollment determine her fate. She refused to make decisions based on her deathday. She was still the master of her time, however short. Her life was hers to live. And she'd chose to spend it – the rest of it – with Marshall. She would give herself over to him entirely, body and soul. A moment that was totally theirs.

He rolled on top of her. She opened her eyes and could see Marshall, the universe blazing behind him. The black sky, the Milky Way, the spinning constellations. She spread her legs beneath him and arched her back, feeling him enter, the initial pressure followed by a sweet release as her body welcomed his presence.

Chapter 46

Marshall, 21 May 2045, Age 28, T-minus 49

When Marshall woke, the fire had already fizzled and died. A few orange embers glowed weakly from the ash. Toby was curled up at the foot of the sleeping bag. The stars hung listlessly in the sky – tired, as if they might fall at any moment. It was strangely bright. He sat up and glanced around at the ephemeral, silver luminescence. The scene reminded him of a black-and-white photo like in the local museum.

Beside him, Penelope was sleeping peacefully, the pale skin of her naked shoulder a stark ivory in the unfamiliar, white light. He gently ran his hand over her skin and watched the goosebumps rise. She stirred, rolled over to face him, and opened her sleepy eyes.

"What is this?" Marshall asked.

"What's what?"

"Where's all this light coming from?"

Penelope sat up and glanced around.

"Fire's out," he whispered. "Why isn't it pitch dark?"

Penelope smiled and pointed. "Moonlight."

Moonlight. Of course. "How magical." Marshall felt as if he were a character in one of his books. A poem by Whitman came to him as if floating down on one of the moonbeams.

'Look down, fair moon, and bathe this scene; Pour softly down night's nimbus floods –'

Marshall tried to stop his mental recitation, but the words flooded his consciousness –

'– on faces ghastly, swollen, purple; On the dead, on their backs, with their arms toss'd wide, Pour down your unstinted nimbus, sacred moon.'

He didn't like the way that poem ended.

Chapter 47

Penelope, 26 June 2045, Age 26, T-minus 1

Penelope absentmindedly brushed her teeth in front of the bathroom mirror, ignoring the chirps and beeps as an infrared laser, mounted just under the vanity light, unapologetically scanned her body. Bea had taken to calling the mirror *Dirty Old Man,* because it so thoroughly '*undressed you with its eye.*' When she glanced up, Penelope's reflection was cocooned in a basket of green lines. A grid that made it seem like she was wearing an overlay of old-school graph paper similar to what she had found in her mother's old desk. The lines followed her movements as a stream of data flowed across the top of the mirror.

It was creepy, imagining that Dirty Old Man knew more about her body than she did. She stared at the streaming data, green and glowing.

Height: 1.75 meters
Bust: 96 centimeters
Hips: 106 centimeters
Waist: 82 centimeters
Weight: 64 kilograms
Heart Rate: 75 bpm

Little arrows beside each measurement pointed either up or down to indicate an increase or a decrease. A simple dash denoted no change. Up arrows accompanied each measurement except for height.

Damn it. Why did Bea install this thing, anyway?

The mirror seemed designed to remind Penelope that her attitude toward sweets was catching up with her. What difference did it make anyway? It wasn't like she had a lot of time. She might as well enjoy as many cakes and brownies and ice cream sundaes as she could. She resumed her daily grooming, ignoring Dirty Old Man in favor of clipping her nails.

Suddenly, Dirty Old Man erupted into a series of alarms she'd never heard before. They lasted approximately five seconds and ended with Dirty Old Man declaring, "Congratulations!" in a decidedly feminine voice.

"Congratulations?" Penelope squinted at the data scrolling across the top of the mirror. "For what … still being alive?"

The word *PREGNANT* appeared in bold red letters, standing out against the indifferent green.

"Pregnant?" She fell to her knees and stared at the clippers that now rested near the tub. "Pregnant?" she whispered.

"Hey!" Bea called, her voice muffled through the door. "You almost done? I'm about to pee my pants."

"It's unlocked," Penelope stated.

The door creaked, stopping after just a few inches.

"Okay to come in?"

"Come in," Penelope whispered.

Bea, her hair in a bun, stray stands curling around her face from a night of sleep, tiptoed inside. She stepped over Penelope and dropped her pants before sitting on the toilet. "Sorry … was gonna burst."

Penelope didn't look at her. She just kept staring at the white vanity as if her answers would suddenly appear. She vaguely heard the toilet flush, but it sounded distant, as if from a different apartment.

"What are you doing on the floor?" Bea asked. "Hello? You okay?"

"No," Penelope whispered. "I'm pregnant."

"Excuse me?" Bea knelt beside her friend. "How do you know that?"

Penelope pointed at the mirror. "Dirty Old Man."

Bea's eyes widened. "He can do that?"

"She, actually."

"She?"

"Yeah, she threw a hissy fit and said *congratulations* and –"

"Dirty Old Man *talks?"*

Penelope shook her head and sighed. "Yes, Bea. Do you know anything about this mirror? You bought it. God! It beeped and chirped and lost its little, machine mind. Told me *congratulations* and displayed the word *pregnant* in bright, red letters."

"Do you think he … I mean she … do you think it's right?"

Penelope shrugged.

Bea stood and leaned against the counter. "How did this *happen*?"

Penelope sighed.

"I know *how* it happened. I meant weren't you using protection? With all the ways people are empowered to plan things, you sure find a way around 'em all."

Penelope took in a deep breath. "I'm dying … I'm sorry if birth control isn't one of my top priorities." She took in another deep breath before adding, "I stopped worrying about protection when I thought I was getting married. Everett and I wanted kids. Never thought I'd have enough time to meet someone else, let alone fall in love and find myself pregnant. We used a condom … what were the chances? How *did* this happen?"

"Does Marshall know?"

"*I* didn't know until thirty seconds ago. It's only been a few weeks since we slept together."

"Does he know about your deathday yet? Have you told him?"

Penelope looked at her hands and shook her head. Her tears fell, and she used her fingers to wipe her nose.

"You have to now."

"Why?"

Bea knelt and placed her face close to Penelope's. "Number one … he's going to be a single dad. Number two … becoming a parent changes everything." Bea took in a deeper breath. "Number three … he needs time to prepare to be a parent on his own terms. You owe him that much."

Penelope remained quiet.

"You owe your *child* that much. Jeez, Penelope, really?" Bea stood.

Penelope looked up. "People have managed for millennia to have kids without preparing. There's an inherent risk in living."

"Listen to yourself." Bea sat at the edge of the tub. She leaned over and rubbed her eyes. "Don't you *dare* leave me with this mess to clean up. I have plans of my own, plans for my life. I'm sorry you don't. But the rest of us do, and you can't leave us … me … with *your* loose ends. This is very irresponsible … not to mention selfish. Choices have consequences. You *know* you're going to die, and you know when." Bea shook her head. "Damn, Penelope, your baby is going to grow up without a mother!"

Penelope stood and grabbed a tissue. She blew her nose and wiped her eyes. "Nobody asked you to clean up my loose ends." Her voice lowered as she held back more tears that threatened to fall.

"You don't have to ask," Bea whispered. "You know I'll just do it. Marshall will need help, and you know I'll help him. I love you, Penelope." She sighed. "It's what friends do."

"*Promise* me." Penelope clenched her jaw and looked away.

Bea stood and grabbed a robe from off a hook. She gently wrapped her friend inside its warmth.

Penelope studied her friend – olive skin, chestnut brown hair, almond-shaped eyes, and a smooth button nose. Funny, smart, loyal. Why in the world hadn't she found the husband she wanted yet? Why hadn't *he* found her?

Bea and Penelope locked eyes.

"I promise," Bea whispered. She wrapped her arms around Penelope.

Relief and guilt washed over Penelope as she cried in Bea's warm embrace.

Chapter 48

Penelope, 27 June 2045, Age 26, T-minus 1

The metal of the bench pressed against her back at Shiplock Park. The place where Marshall asked her out for the first time. Funny to imagine a time when she hadn't known him. He was such a big part of her life now – what she had left of it. She took in a deep breath and looked around. The cherry blossoms were gone for the year, and it suddenly hit her that she would never see them again – this was her last spring.

Without warning, her tears dripped, trickling down her cheeks. She didn't wipe them away. The warmth felt soothing. She just let them fall. Small pearls of emotion, bearing in their wake her guilt, her loss – all with the slight flavor of salt. She would tell Marshall she was pregnant. That they were having a baby. She wanted to feel happy. And she was, but the joy was stymied by her hiding the truth from the man she loved, and by the fact that she'd never see him as a father or know their child. Her joy was now tainted by the fact that she simply didn't have time. Her baby would be the last thing she ever did – her final act.

Still – that was at least something wasn't it? She would leave behind her legacy. The *powers that be* had granted her that much.

She imagined how she would tell Marshall. Which news to deliver first – her pregnancy, her enrollment, or her T-minus age? What would he say? What would he do? It was all too much. She'd just have to say it. Thinking about it wasn't making it easier. Delaying wasn't helping.

Penelope took one last look around the park. Everything seemed serene, normal, indifferent. Despite the heaviness of her heart and the clock ticking away every second, runners still sprinted, and their jagged conversations, although mundane, tugged at something inside. She glanced over at the mothers chatting with each other. The strollers rolled along the paved trail as if tomorrow meant nothing. Cyclists whizzed by on narrow tires, and the whine creasing the air gave her reason to pause. Tomorrow, no cars would drive down the street – no music would blare from the speakers – no words would drift on a fresh summer breeze, not for Penelope.

She studied the water that lazily brushed against its banks. A few turtles were sunning themselves on a protruding log. She reached out her hands, allowing the sun's warmth to touch her soul. Another tear fell. Today was a day for ice cream and walking a dog. Tonight would be an evening for dining outside or spreading blankets on the grass.

Unless you're me.

Everyone else would go on with their lovely summer day, oblivious to her situation, much the way they would, in time, go on with their lives, oblivious to her death. No one who saw her sitting alone knew the torment wrestling inside her heart. No one who saw her sitting alone would remember her tomorrow. Everything would simply keep moving in endless cycles of seasons – lightness and darkness. She stood and began her trek down the Capital Trail, heading for Marshall's.

Chapter 49

Marshall, 27 June 2045, Age 28, T-minus 49

"Penelope." A robotic voice announced her arrival.

Toby raised his head, and his nose pointed at the door.

"That's strange, isn't it, Toby?" Marshall said.

Usually, Penelope would graph him that she was on her way, and he'd wait for her in the lobby. Sometimes, if she were walking, he'd meet her down the block. He always liked to maximize their time together. Marshall opened the door, and Penelope brushed inside.

"You should've told me you were coming," Marshall said. "I would've been more prepared." It was early, and he was still wearing his sweats from the night before. He hadn't even had his morning coffee yet.

Penelope stared at her feet, allowing her arms to dangle. Tears rolled down her cheeks.

Marshall led her to the couch and sat beside her. Toby rested his head gently on Penelope's knee. Marshall understood her crying when she left Everett. That was a sad thing. People cried at sad things. "I only meant I would've gotten ready. I didn't mean to upset you." He didn't understand crying over – well, over nothing. "Why are you crying?"

Penelope's shoulders shook with two or three sobs before she could manage, "'I have seen the eternal Footman hold my coat, and snicker, And in short,'" she paused, gulped down a breath of air, and her voice shook as she finished, "'I was afraid.'" She buried her face in Marshall's shoulder.

He could feel warm, wet tears through his shirt, the fabric sticking to his skin. Toby whined once, and readjusted his head on Penelope's leg.

"And when I'm gone, well, 'would it have been worth it, after all, After the cups, the marmalade, the tea –'"

"Stop," Marshall said. "Something's been bothering me."

Penelope sat back and looked at him with bewilderment.

"Coffee spoons," Marshall said.

"Coffee spoons?" Penelope wiped her nose on her sleeve.

"Yes. Coffee spoons. Prufrock *drinks* tea … always tea. So why does he measure out his life in coffee spoons?"

If anyone knew the answer, Penelope would. Hadn't she been the only one who understood the coffee spoons aside from himself?

"I never … I never noticed." She laughed.

Marshall sighed, sensing that somehow, everything would be okay.

Penelope snuggled into the couch, resting her cheek against the moist spot on Marshall's shirt. "I have something important to tell you. Really important. Three things, actually."

Marshall struggled to imagine what they could be, but before he had time to throw out a guess, Penelope was out with one of them.

"I'm pregnant."

Marshall took in a deep breath, trying to formulate his thoughts – so grandiose, so transcendent – into simple, human words. He had taken precautions, been responsible. And still – a baby? What were the chances? Then again, what were the chances of life on earth? The perfect distance from the sun, the perfect composition of a planetary core, and a moon to stabilize its axis. All these factors and more had to come together. And still – life.

Marshall looked out the window and stroked Penelope's blonde hair.

"All the beautiful things … I never knew what they were before. They didn't exist for me. I never noticed them." He paused, looking down at her beautiful face streaked with tears. "I notice them now. Sunrise, sunset, spring flowers, falling stars … frost on windows. You …" He sighed. "They're all the things that make life worth living."

"And they're all so temporary," she said, more to herself than to Marshall, and he wondered what she meant.

She was right, of course. Sunrise blazed into day, sunset faded into night. Blossoms wilted and died. Falling stars burned out and frost melted. But there was so much beauty and vitality while they lasted. No one ever wished they hadn't seen a falling star just because it ended.

Eager to hear more good news, Marshall asked, "What's the second really important thing?"

Penelope hardly took a breath before she spat the words, "I'm enrolled."

Marshall stiffened and his eyes widened. "What?"

Penelope lowered her gaze. "It's why Everett left me."

She was pregnant and enrolled? It was a lot all at once, and not all good. The baby, now that was good news, and he was happy about that. But the enrollment? That meant Penelope had lied to him.

"Okay. Okay," he said. "That's okay."

He nodded, trying to convince himself more than to assure Penelope. She had lied to him, but somehow, he didn't *want* to feel about it the way he did. He didn't *want* to feel betrayed. He had known all along – he told himself – that she was dying. They all were. From the day they were born, dying.

Everyone had an expiration date. He just hadn't known that Penelope knew hers. Because – she had lied to him. She had hidden it. But this didn't have to change anything, did it? It did, though. It changed a lot of things. She had *lied* – to him. And he had trusted her. He rested his head in his hands with his elbows on his knees. "How much time do you have?"

"Marshall –"

He held up a hand and closed his eyes. "How much time?"

There will be time, there will be time
Time for you –

"Nine months," she whispered.

– and time for me.

"Nine … nine *months?*" Marshall opened his eyes.

"I'm sorry."

Marshall understood. He was not ready to admit it, nor was he ready to forgive … but he understood. Penelope had been afraid … afraid of losing what she had already lost once before. But his anger at her dishonesty and selfishness felt stronger than his understanding. Stronger than his love. "I … I need you to go," he whispered.

"Marshall –"

"Please," he said without meeting her gaze.

She stood.

Toby gently moved to let her pass.

Marshall watched as she rested an apologetic hand on Toby's head and felt the slight disturbance of air as she left. He did not turn to watch her leave. He just listened as the door opened and softly closed.

Chapter 50

Penelope, 13 July 2045, Age 26, T-minus 1

"Penelope?" Bea yelled from the kitchen.

Penelope rolled over and grabbed a pillow, covering her head. She had kicked the thing off the couch to make room for her bloated belly. But now she needed it to muffle the world.

"Penelope!"

Penelope heard Bea come into the room, but she remained quiet.

"Penelope." Bea snatched the pillow and tossed it onto the floor. "I've been calling you."

"I know," Penelope replied. "I've been ignoring you."

"We're out of coffee cake. Will you bake some?"

"Don't want to," Penelope said, shoving her face into the cushions.

"Get your sorry ass off my couch!"

Penelope remained still.

"We're not doing this again." Bea pulled on the blanket, tossing it across the room.

"Give it back!" Penelope sat up.

"Get off the damn couch and get it yourself."

"No!" She sat back and hugged her knees.

"You look pathetic. A grown woman curled up on the couch halfway through the day. Hair's a mess, mismatched socks, same clothes as yesterday … and the day before that. You're acting like a baby."

"I'm *having* a baby."

"You're acting like one too. Do you really want to spend what time you have left, wallowing in self-pity? You have things to do. You don't get to lay around because you're alone. And you're not having that baby on my couch."

"You have all the time in the world."

Bea took a few steps closer. "You have time to plan and get ready for that baby. Be responsible. The whole point of enrollment is having the time to plan. And you're squandering it. What the hell? Take advantage of the choices you've made." Bea walked over and picked up the blanket and tossed it back at Penelope. "Here … how do you say it … oh yeah … you've made your bed … lie in it!" Bea stormed into the kitchen and grabbed her keys. "I'm going for coffee cake." The door slammed behind her.

Penelope sat on the couch. She stared at the blanket and pillow on her feet. Why didn't anyone understand? She *had* made plans. But that was *before* enrollment. She wanted to bake cakes and marry Everett and have children. Their life would have been simple and wonderful, unclouded by the knowledge of when it would end. Enrolling only obstructed her life, including all her plans. *What was that song? The one by Death Cab for Cutie.* She hadn't heard it in years.

Every plan is a tiny prayer to Father Time …

That was it. Something like that. Well, that kind of planning had been okay with her, because at least it allowed for some hope that Father Time might answer.

But Father Time had abandoned her. And so had Marshall. She had lied. She had hurt him. She had misled him. She was guilty.

But the baby was innocent.

What ate at Penelope wasn't just that she was going to die, but that she was going to leave her child motherless. She couldn't leave her child fatherless too. Imagining her baby being alone terrified her. She loved this child. No one else, aside from the father, could possibly love this baby more. Her baby needed a father – needed Marshall. Penelope couldn't leave, couldn't die, before knowing that Marshall would be there. Father Time hadn't answered her, but maybe Marshall would. She picked up her phone.

"Graph Marshall."

Chapter 51

Marshall, 13 July 2045, Age 28, T-minus 49

She had given him a sense of life he had never known. Knowing what he would soon lose made life seem even duller than before she'd colored it with her yellow flowers, delectable cakes, and understanding of coffee spoons. He was in love with *the most beautiful woman in the world.*

And she was dying.

He had kissed her. Discussed poetry with her. Eaten dinner with her. Admired the city at night with her. And – camped in the forest with her.

Maybe that had been more than he was entitled. Maybe he should be grateful for the brief experience. Whoever had said it was better to have loved and lost than never to have loved at all was wrong. Knowing what he was missing – now, that was worse.

"Ignorance is bliss," he said to his translucent reflection in the window, city streets crisscrossing his chest, buildings rising from his neck to his hairline. It made him think of the time Penelope had holographed him, when he could see the city through her body, like a ghost.

Toby trotted into the kitchen, tail wagging. A little too chipper for Marshall's dreary mood. Then again, he couldn't help but smile.

"Hi, Toby. Don't mind me." Marshall sat back and stared at his black coffee. His wrist hung limp, dangling the coffee spoon into his mug. He studied it.

'I have measured out my life with coffee spoons. I have seen the moment of my greatness flicker.'

"I miss Penelope."

Toby sat in front of Marshall and stared up at him.

"I missed Penelope yesterday. And the day before that, and the day before that. I've missed her all week. And I will miss her next week. When will it stop?"

Toby's tongue drooped, and he cocked his head. He stood and took a step closer before sitting back down. He rested his head on Marshall's leg.

"You wouldn't know, would you? Neither would I. It would sure be easier if I did. I can count down to my deathday, but I don't know how long I'll endure the pain of missing Penelope."

Toby whined.

A translucent, two-dimensional Penelope flickered into the room. She wore rumpled sweats and looked – exhausted, discolored, and flat. Not healthy, even for a graph.

"Toby?" Marshall stood. "She's graphing me."

Toby stepped aside as if to make room for Penelope.

"Marshall?" her voice implored.

He picked up his phone from beside his window, pointed it at the holograph, and pressed *decline*. Her image froze, quivered, and vanished. Marshall's chest tightened, and his hands shook.

One more muffled statement, "Marshall," hung in the air for only a moment before fading, and Penelope was gone.

Marshall leaned back. He wiped his forehead before staring at his hand. He sighed and took in a deep breath. "I know." Marshall whispered. "Nothing's keeping us apart. And I could've answered. Maybe I should've."

Toby whined.

It seemed easier, somehow, to remain angry. Letting anger fill the void that lost love left behind seemed less painful. The pain would help remove her from his life sooner rather than later. He had to rid himself of the delusion that they'd spend their life together before their hearts and souls became too entangled.

Spare myself some heartache. Fewer memories. Fewer ghosts.

But what if he had it all wrong? He stared into his coffee cup, now room temperature – tepid. Life sometimes resembled coffee – bitter and stagnant and black. Counting down to a deathday wasn't so bad when he was part of a couple. But now as a single, he had to reevaluate – there was more to life than just dying, for he had a purpose with Penelope. Without her, what was life except numbers?

Marshall stared at his bitter, black coffee, the same flavor and color as his mood. There was nothing he could add to sweeten it.

"Coffee spoons."

Toby tilted his head and barked.

"Why *did* Prufrock want coffee spoons? Why measure a life that way?"

Toby whined.

"The poet talked about drinking tea. Doesn't make sense."

Toby barked.

"You're right, Toby. Nothing makes sense."

Chapter 52

Marshall, 24 July 2045, Age 28, T-minus 49

Marshall stayed late at work. Many an evening he watched as his reflection grew bolder in the window across from his desk. The daylight faded, and the office lights soon overpowered the sun's sinking rays. He thought about his mother. He thought about Penelope. They had both betrayed him. He was unlucky in love. He was unlucky in general. He should have seen it coming. It was all too good to be true.

He studied his reflection where it floated at a desk hovering high above the city lights. He shook his head, and his reflection shook its head.

As the last colleague left the office for the night, he placed his hands on his desk and pushed himself out of his chair. He locked the door behind him and stepped into the stairwell. Toby trudged along beside him. Marshall started when he heard his name. Toby hadn't alerted him to anyone.

"Marshall?" a voice said from below. "Sorry, didn't mean to startle you."

Bea? Toby knew Bea. Recognized her as a positive interaction, a friend. "Ambushing me in a dark stairwell? Not startling at all."

Bea tilted her head and smiled. "Was that sarcasm coming from those lips?" She climbed the last few steps before slightly punching his arm. "Proud of you. You're getting good."

Marshall chuckled. "Thank you."

A small sense of pride flooded his gut in spite of his resolve to be cold to Bea. She must have known. Bea was an accomplice of sorts. Aiding and abetting in Penelope's deceit. He understood why she hadn't said anything. After all, she *was* Penelope's friend first.

Penelope's friend, first? Is Bea my friend?

Toby seemed to think so, failing to alert him of her presence. He had to admit that maybe Toby wasn't wrong. He did feel a certain delight at the unexpected encounter. Once he got over his initial start.

"Penelope's been trying to reach you."

Marshall nodded and pushed the door open. He took a few steps and stared up at the streetlight. "Did she send you?"

Bea sighed. "God, no. I'm *not* her *minion*. I'm her best friend. There's a difference."

Marshall shrugged and walked away.

"Damn it, Marshall. Wait up!"

Marshall slowed his pace.

"I came on my own. She'd be pissed if she knew. So don't you dare tell her."

"I won't." Marshall kept his eyes forward, secretly warming at the idea that he was sharing a secret with someone. Maybe he did have a friend in Bea. After all, she had come to see him, and Penelope hadn't put her up to it. Penelope didn't even know about it. "I don't plan on telling her anything ever again."

"Marshall, don't say that." Bea stepped forward and grabbed his arm.

Marshall stopped and stared at Bea's hand. "Why not? It's the truth."

"Penelope's in *love* with you." She squeezed his arm. "What about your baby?"

Marshall stared at Bea. He had thought about the baby. Their baby. Penelope would die soon, and what would happen to their baby?

"I have thought about the baby. I don't know what to do."

Bea's eyes shined. She bit her lip and took in a deep breath. "You're missing out on the love of your life. Every day you're wasting time." Tears formed and she tried to wipe them away. "I wish I could find someone to love me like you love Penelope. Even for just a little while. Even if it meant that I lose him. You two are lucky. Don't you see it?" She let go of Marshall's arm. "You have everything. Even if it's only for a few months. Love. A baby. Marshall, you have a *family*. Don't let it slip away. Don't waste the precious time that you and Penelope have left." She stared at him. "You'll regret it. I know you will. It'll be the biggest mistake you'll ever make. A mistake you can never fix. I came here for Penelope … yes … but also for you. Don't throw it away, Marshall. Think about your baby."

"She lied to me. And I'm trying –"

"Damn it … Penelope *loves* you!"

"Yeah, well. So did my mother."

"Exactly. Fucking exactly! They told you lies for the same damn reason."

"And what reason was that?"

"Love, you ass!" Bea took a step back and shook her head. "Penelope was trying to protect you."

"Protect me? From what?"

"From missing out on the love of your life. And now I'm trying to protect you from the same thing." She glanced away.

Bea was Penelope's friend. But she was also his friend. His heart pounded as he held back tears.

"I'm going now, Marshall. Do the right thing. If not for yourself, for your family … you know what the right thing is." She turned and took a few steps before turning back. "I love Penelope, Marshall … and … I love you too."

Marshall smiled. He had a girlfriend. He had a friend. And he was going to be a father. And maybe that was lucky, really. Maybe.

Chapter 53

Marshall, 29 July 2045, Age 28, T-minus 49

Toby whined at the end of the leash before picking up his pace and wagging his tail.

Marshall looked in the direction Toby was headed. It was Penelope. Although he didn't want to admit it, it was thrilling just seeing her. His spirts lifted in spite of himself.

"Thank you for agreeing to meet me," Penelope said, sitting on their bench in Shiplock Park.

Marshall looked at her and tried not to feel anything. Nothing made Marshall feel – but Penelope did. Colors were more vibrant. The lights glowed brighter.

He smiled. Her eyes seemed grayer than normal. Her blonde hair was pulled back in a loose bun. Several wayward strands had worked their way free and were blowing like glistening spiderwebs in the wind. She reached up and tucked a few locks behind her ear. The sunlight caught the diamonds on her bracelet, almost blinding him. He blinked several times.

The brightness had the effect of making her look like an angel. His resolve melted. He sat on the bench beside her. A blind spot prevented him from seeing her face for a few seconds. When his eyes recovered, she was smiling.

The most beautiful woman in the world was smiling at him. For a moment, he forgot the betrayal and his bruised pride. He cupped her face with his hands and kissed her gently as if she were delicate and would break. As if she would vanish into the sunlight.

"Can you forgive me?" Penelope whispered.

Toby looked up at them, panting a smile.

Marshall forced himself to take his hands from her soft, warm skin. He rested them on his knees, harder and less inviting. He sighed and looked down at the ground. "I want to."

"I tried to tell you many times," she said.

"You should have."

"You're right. I should have. But every time I tried, I was so happy with what we had … I wanted all of it … before I died. I didn't want to sabotage it. I was afraid. I was so afraid."

"Afraid of what?"

"That you would walk away like Everett did. That I would lose everything all over again. I was selfish. I was mean, and I should've told you. I'm sorry."

Marshall stared at her hand as it made a tentative move for his. He let her grab it.

"I have a brother," Penelope said. "*Had*. Kurz. He died before I was born. Dad had hinted that if he had known Kurz's life was going to be so short, he would've given him up. Said it would've spared them a lot of sorrow."

Marshall waited and listened. Her hand felt warm and moist. Under his thumb, he could feel her pulse. How many beats were left?

"My mom would never do that. She always told me how happy she was for the time she'd had with my brother. Giving him up would've meant they'd miss all that love and all those memories." Her eyes were the color of the sky just before sunrise, the palest gray and rimmed in red. "And now we're having a baby." Her eyes earnestly searched his.

She pulled back her hand, and he suddenly felt cold and empty.

"Will you think about it? And maybe we could start over? Or pick up where we left off? Or something?" She looked down at her belly and placed one hand on the tiny bump. "If not for me … for our baby?"

"I'll graph you," Marshall replied.

Penelope leaned forward and placed a kiss on his cheek. "Thank you," she whispered. She stood and walked away.

Marshall sat on the bench for a long time after Penelope left. Toby rested beneath him.

"What difference does it make, Toby?" he said. "What difference would it have made if she'd told me sooner? Would I have left her then? No. Would I have done anything different? No. Well, maybe I would have tried to steal more of Penelope's time for myself."

But their relationship had transcended beyond him or Penelope. They had created a third. The thought of the way his father had abandoned him was repugnant. His father had betrayed him. His mother had lied to him. He wanted this baby. *So much.* How could his father ever have not wanted him? How could any father ever forsake his child? The idea was preposterous, overwhelming. He pressed his fingers to his eyes and dragged his hands down his face. He didn't even know his baby yet, but he loved it. Beyond measure. An infinite number of coffee spoons couldn't contain his love for his baby – or for Penelope. She had lied to him and so had his mother. But perhaps now, he understood why. He considered what he would want his child to know if the truth were painful. What purpose had truth served in his life? It had cost him his relationship with his mother. Could he repair that relationship so his baby would have a grandmother? He knew now why his mother had protected him, understood her fierce desire to spare him pain. Would she forgive him for being so callous, so naïve? He didn't know. But he did know two things – he wanted this baby, and he never wanted his child to feel anything less than infinite love.

But Penelope would die and soon. Very, very soon.

And would it have been worth it, after all,
Would it have been worth while,
After the sunsets and the dooryards and the sprinkled streets,
After the novels …

Yes. It would be worth it. It would all be worth it. Every pang of heartache would be a reminder of the love he was honored to share with her. Every tear, proof of his courage.

So, there was his answer. If his only regret was that he hadn't properly savored his time with Penelope up to this point, that they didn't have more time, what sense did it make for him to keep pushing her away? To stack up regrets in place of memories? His world was a better place with Penelope in it, even if he didn't get to keep her very long. And Marshall was the luckiest man in the world, because she had chosen to share her time with him. However little of it there was.

Chapter 54

Penelope, 4 August 2045, Age 26, T-minus 1

Marshall sat down across from Penelope and rested his hands on the table. He kept his eyes down, and a short eternity seemed to pass before he finally looked up at her and cleared his throat. "Hello." He glanced around the little coffee shop. "Nice place."

"Thanks for graphing me," Penelope replied. "And for meeting me here."

"You're welcome."

Penelope didn't know where to start. She had stayed up all night rehearsing dozens of ways to apologize. "I'm sorry I'm dying." This apology was not one she had practiced. "And … I'm sorry I lied about it."

"You didn't lie about dying," he replied.

"I know but –"

"I'm dying too. We're all dying. It's nothing to be sorry about. You never said you weren't dying. You just said you weren't enrolled. You lied about enrollment. And you want my forgiveness for that … not for dying."

Penelope studied the orange cranberry scone resting on the plate in front of her. It stared back indifferently. Exactly how could she reply to that statement? He was right in his literalness. She had lied about being enrolled, not about dying. "You're right."

He studied her face.

She struggled to meet his gaze. This must be how Marshall felt most of his life. Afraid to meet everyone's gaze, averting his eyes, looking at something else. She blinked back her hesitance and forced an unsteady gaze.

"I think I know why you did it," he whispered. "Lied, I mean. I think I understand."

Penelope's stomach clinched. Maybe he could forgive her if he could understand.

"You didn't want to cut our time together shorter than your deathday does." He looked down and wet his lips. "Neither do I."

As if on their own, her hands landed on top of Marshall's. She nodded with tears in her eyes. "I was afraid."

"You thought I might do what Everett did. But I'm not Everett, and that's not fair."

She nodded and choked back her tears. "Nothing about what I did was fair. I was selfish." She squeezed his hand and leaned forward, closing her eyes. She felt exhausted. "But our baby ..." She swallowed and tried again. "Our baby needs you. Because I ... I won't be here to ..." The lines of the familiar poem marched through her mind in tune with her heartbeat.

There will be time, there will be time
Time for you and time for me.

But there was no time, and she couldn't bear to finish the thought. She gave in to her emotions and cried. When she felt a warm pressure against her forehead, she opened her eyes. Marshall was now sitting next to her, resting his head against hers. It was probably his way of saying that he forgave her. She tilted her head and placed a soft kiss on his cheek.

Neither of them said anything for what seemed like a very long time. Penelope glanced out the window. People were crossing the street in the rain. The drops chased each other down the glass, colliding and merging before separating again. As they splashed onto the brick sill, they shattered into smaller droplets.

"Penelope," Marshall whispered. "I've thought about what you said the last time we were together. About Kurz and about our baby. I've thought a lot about my dad, and maybe he was the one who betrayed me and not my mother." His voice choked. "I could never do to our baby what my dad did to me." Marshall placed his hands on her face and gently thumbed away the tears.

Penelope allowed her tears to fall. Her child would grow up knowing love. Even if she had to be alone for the remainder of her short time, she could leave knowing that Marshall would step in and take over. She couldn't ask for more than that.

"Will you marry me?" he whispered.

And time for yet a hundred indecisions,
And for a hundred visions and revisions.

A strange laughter bubbled up behind Penelope's tears. She smiled. "Yes."

Chapter 55

Marshall, 5 August 2045, Age 28, T-minus 49

"I don't want our vows to say, *'til death do us part*,'" Marshall said, sitting beside Penelope on Bea's yellow couch.

The moon hung heavily over the city, its light nothing more than a round puncture in the black sky. Tonight was nothing like the veil of light that had bathed the forest the night they'd camped in the decaying house. He glanced at their reflection in the window. The moon seemed suspended just above their heads. If he reached up, he could probably pluck it like a ripe apple from a tree and hand it to her.

"Agreed," Penelope said. "It's morbid."

"And untrue. I'll love you long after."

Penelope leaned her head on his shoulder. He could smell the subtle perfume of her shampoo. Marshall thought of the moonlight that had illumed the forest that night. The night he and Penelope had conceived a child. The same poem that haunted him then, haunted him now.

Look down, fair moon …
On the dead, on their backs, with their arms toss'd wide,
Pour down your unstinted nimbus, sacred moon.

In the city, the moon didn't shine on anything. Instead, its light drowned within the garish glare of the streetlamps and spotlights that illuminated the advertisements towering over I-95.

The door swung open, and Bea blew in, flinging her purse onto a chair and plunking down between Penelope and Marshall so the moon hung just above Bea's head. Marshall was growing rather fond of Bea, but he sometimes wished she was less adept at inserting herself into – everything.

Bea looked from one to the other and smiled. "Hi … what are we doing?"

"We …" – Penelope pointed to Marshall and herself, making an exaggerated arch above Bea's head – "… are talking about wedding vows."

"Geez …" Bea stood and chuckled. "No need to rub it in. I'm leaving."

Penelope grabbed a pillow and swung it gently at Bea's legs.

"I can tell when I'm not wanted." Bea held up her hands in surrender. "I'll be in the kitchen." She stopped at the threshold. "*My* kitchen! In *my* apartment!" Then she added, more to herself than to the lovebirds on the couch, "Relegated to my kitchen."

"Love you!" Penelope called.

"Ah-huh." Bea's voice echoed from near the refrigerator.

Penelope and Bea's relationship fascinated Marshall. He had always wanted a close friend. The closest thing he had, aside from Penelope, was Toby. Marshall glanced at the moon again as Bea sauntered back, sitting in the chair by the window. She draped her legs over the arm and looked at the night's sky.

"Don't mind me," she said. "Keep talking. I'll just sit here and stare into the darkness … alone … by myself …"

"Where do *you* want to have …" Penelope asked Marshall, "… the wedding?"

Bea jumped off the chair and plopped down between them again. "Oh, yes!" Her voice rose with excitement. "Where *are* we going? Where are you guys gonna take me? The girl who lives down the hall, she and her fiancé are planning an AR wedding in Tahiti. And a woman I know from yoga just got back from an AR wedding in Europe somewhere. My hairdresser –"

"The forest," Marshall stated so loudly he surprised even himself.

He wanted to marry Penelope in the old house – the place where he first discovered moonlight and starlight and a real fire. The place where, if he were being honest, he felt he'd already married her.

Bea wrinkled her nose. "The forest? Like the real one?"

Penelope looked at Marshall. She smiled and nodded.

Chapter 56

Penelope, 6 August 2045, Age 26, T-minus 1

Penelope and Marshall stood, hand-in-hand, at the edge of the forest. Or, at least, where the edge of the forest was supposed to be. Though Marshall's compass confirmed they were standing in the same physical place, the forest edge had retreated miles, leaving broken trees, charred grass, and a few tenacious birds, perched on dead branches. A temporary chain-link fence separated them from their intended pathway. Toby sat beside Marshall and whined, looking wistfully at the vast, empty space.

Penelope placed a hand on one of the fence's metal links. Above them hung a sign.

No Admittance

Penelope sighed. "Should we climb over?"

Marshall looked down at Toby and shook his head.

Penelope understood. They would not be able to heft him over the fence. "There has to be a weak spot somewhere," she said. "A place where we can peel it away and slip through."

Marshall nodded before shoving the compass into his pocket. They walked along the fence until they found a section with a small opening. Marshall knelt and with considerable effort rolled up the chains to create a gap large enough for them to crawl through.

Penelope wriggled under first, the fence catching on her hair. Toby dutifully crawled through next and waited beside her. Marshall inched through and stood. He dusted off his knees and smiled.

Now arm-in-arm, they traversed the desert of splintered trees, many not yet aware they were dead – leaves still clinging to their branches, though yellowing and crepey. They aimed for the old house. The hike was rather short without a forest or heavy backpack slowing them down.

When they reached the spot that for them had been magical, they stopped and stared. It was no longer sheltered by layers of strong, standing trees or curtained with clinging vines. Instead, it stood starkly naked and exposed. The tallest remaining wall boasting the chimney, towered over the shorter, more crumbled ones. Stones were scattered about as if they had detached themselves and tried to run away.

Penelope grabbed onto Marshall's arm and sighed. "Look ..."

A holograph flickered in the sky.

DANGER

FORCEFIELD FENCING

AREA CLOSED FOR CITY EXPANSION

As she silently read the last few words, a grinding sound echoed from the shadows. A clattering machine breached the remaining wall of the house – indifferent and efficient in its destruction.

Marshall took a defensive step, but Penelope's hand held firm. They watched, together, as the metal monster ate their home – their little piece of the past. Within a few meager minutes, the house was no more – razed to the ground, nothing but a pile of rubble. The machine meticulously collected the stones, dumping them into a large bin attached to its bed before rolling out of sight and grumbling into the distance. There was no other sound. Only the rumble of its mechanical wheels squeaking through the quiet air, breaking the silence.

No birds sang in the trees. No crickets chirped in the shade. No wind blew.

Penelope took in a deep, shuddery breath. She thought of Fitzgerald's Nick Carraway. *'You can't repeat the past.'* The line seemed reasonable and true when Nick had advised Gatsby. Now, it haunted her. She understood Gatsby's yearning. But she didn't have the luxury of his denial. Her clock was ticking, and she knew exactly how much time she had left.

"We can never go back, can we?" she whispered. "Even when we think we can, we can't."

Progress, so called, was irreversible. Steinbeck's observation in *Travels with Charley* ran through her mind. *'I wonder why progress looks so much like destruction.'*

She squeezed Marshall's hand. "This time next year … maybe sooner … you'll be standing right here in the middle of a busy intersection."

But *she* wouldn't be. She didn't have that much time left. She'd be like this old house and the forest – permanently erased.

Chapter 57

Penelope, 15 August 2045, Age 26, T-minus 1

Bea delicately patted Penelope's forehead with a sponge covered in liquid foundation. She dabbed her skin here and there. Bea wasn't wearing much makeup. She didn't need it. Her smooth, olive complexion lent itself to nudity, and her long eyelashes, uniformly thick, lined her almond-shaped eyes better than any eye pencil ever could. Bea had coated her lips in a natural-looking gloss that emphasized fullness more than color.

So where *was* Bea's Mr. Right? Most would have considered Penelope pretty, but she always felt as if her looks paled in comparison to Bea's natural, flawless loveliness. What did Marshall … anyone … see in her that they didn't see in Bea?

"You're really beautiful," Penelope said.

"Shhhh … don't move your face. You'll mess it up. Quiet while I'm working." Bea gently gripped Penelope's jaw. "Hold still."

"Sorry," Penelope whispered, trying not to move her lips. She waited for Bea's hand to rest at her side. "You really are."

"No, I'm not. You just think so 'cuz you're my friend. If I were pretty, I'd make some sort of effort to look prettier. But it doesn't matter, 'cuz I always look like this."

"You *always* look gorgeous. You don't have to try."

"I don't have to *bother* trying. Waste of time. What you see is what you get."

Penelope nodded. What she had that Bea lacked was confidence. Where Penelope was self-assured and comfortable in her own skin, Bea had always been needy, insecure. Bea was hungry for attention and eager to fall in love. People could sense that, and no matter how attractive the physical package was, it was easily tainted by the air of desperation. How big a part did Bea's enrollment play in all that? Would she be so preoccupied with finding a husband if she weren't counting down to her deathday? If that stupid *Life Planner* app weren't always reminding her the time to perfect her plan was waning with each passing day? Maybe. Maybe not.

"Anyway," Bea whispered. "If I were half as pretty as you, I'd be married by now."

"There's more to marriage than being pretty."

"Easy for you to say."

"Pretty didn't make a difference to Everett," Penelope replied.

"Yeah and good thing too, 'cuz now you have Marshall."

Bea was onto something. If she hadn't enrolled or if Everett hadn't dumped her, she'd still be planning a wedding, creeping ever closer to death, living the wrong life. She was surprised to discover how repulsive a thought that was. She'd be naively baking cakes at The Cakery, never knowing how selfish and shallow that man really was.

"Bea … do you ever stop to think about it from the other side? You're too caught up in searching for Mr. Right. Stop looking for him. Let *him* find you." She paused. "Go find yourself."

Bea dropped her hands to her side. "Two men have wanted to marry you. Two. In a really short amount of time."

"I don't think Everett counts."

"He's an asshole … so what? He *still* wanted to marry you."

"Not badly enough."

"Lucky for you."

"True."

Bea sighed. "Two for you and I can't find just one."

"I already told you, it's because you're looking too hard. Stop trying. Stop planning. Just let things happen."

"I don't have time for that …"

Bea paused and Penelope wondered if Bea realized she might've struck a nerve. After all, Bea had a lot more time than she did. Why was she in such a hurry?

"Sorry," Bea added. "It's your wedding, and I'm happy for you."

Penelope smiled. "I know."

"It's just that … I want you there … with *me* on *my* wedding day. Just like this. And if I don't hurry up and find someone, I know you won't be there."

Penelope sniffed, holding back tears that were threatening to fall. As one tear escaped, she sighed.

"Now look at what I've done …" Bea pulled out a tissue. "You'll ruin your makeup." She gently wiped the tear off her friend's face.

Penelope held Bea's wrist. "I love you. I'm glad you're here."

"Yeah," Bea whispered. "Me too."

Penelope stood in front of the podium, Bea on her left, Marshall on her right. Toby sat between them. The revised wedding plan was a small, intimate affair at city hall. No fanfare. No AR. Just simple and quiet.

The magistrate stood on the other side of the podium and recited the lines. Penelope, absorbed in her own thoughts, hardly heard a word. Here she stood, promising Marshall what was left of her life, which wasn't much. How short this marriage was going to be, how abbreviated the family life she'd dreamed of.

She felt like a fraud, making promises about forever as her time ticked consistently away. Standing tall and making the most of it, Penelope was maximizing what she'd been allotted – camping in the forest, revisiting the stars, falling in love, getting married, having a baby. Perhaps going out with a bang would allow her life to continue until the candle burned all the way down. At least she wouldn't linger the way some did, feeling overdue in heaven. She didn't know what happened after this, but here, at least for now, she was going to make things good. She looked at Marshall. He smiled and blinked away the tears welling in his eyes. Maybe now he finally understood how it felt to cry joyful tears. She had at least given him that.

The Master of Marital Relations cleared his throat. Penelope's eyes met Marshall's. He slipped the simple, gold band onto her finger. The touch felt real and warm.

"I now pronounce you man and wife." The Master of Marital Relations lifted his hands above his head. "You may now kiss the bride."

Bea squealed and threw her arms around the newly married couple.

Toby whined as he gazed up. His tail wagged as if he understood.

Marshall kissed Penelope.

And in that moment, she felt as if she just might live forever.

Chapter 58

Penelope, 10 September 2045, Age 26, T-minus 1

"I don't know why you guys have to be so weird," Bea said.

They stood on the front porch of Marshall and Penelope's new-old house, overlooking a large front yard. Sprawling greenery spread out, dotted with tall trees and large boulders. In the distance, the city skyline protruded into the horizon. The buildings resembled fingers reaching up to the sky.

Heaven is waiting, they seemed to say, pointing to the exact location. *Right up there, just above those clouds.*

"We're not weird," Penelope replied.

"Old-fashioned then."

"I've always been old-fashioned."

"I know, I don't know *why*. Do you know how hard it was for my car to find this place? It's practically off the grid. Besides, I feel naked way out here. Totally exposed." Bea shivered.

Penelope leaned on the railing and savored a long inhale. The aroma of approaching fall was sweet and crisp. "I don't. I feel free. Besides … it's not *that* far. We can still *see* the city." She pointed.

"I can't believe places like this exist. Look at all that green stuff."

"It's called grass." Penelope was astounded at their good fortune. Almost no free-standing homes were available anymore, and the ones that were, were often neglected and uninhabitable. "And we got it so *cheap.*"

"Of course you did. Nobody wants these anymore. Who's gonna buy this place besides you? It's out in the middle of nowhere, far away from anything except the forest. No one around. Too quiet."

"Exactly." Penelope hugged herself and smiled.

Heaven couldn't be waiting. Surely, she was already there. This house and yard and trees were her heaven. The farmhouse with the wraparound porch and rolling fields and huge kitchen and – how unexpected – a working *fireplace.* She placed a hand on her belly and relished the sounds of Marshall and Toby moving around inside the house. She looked over at her friend.

"This is heaven."

And if that were true – then what *would* come after? She looked out over the property as if her answer might lie there, somewhere. The leaves wore that pre-autumn hue – not quite yellow but no longer green. They were in purgatory, hovering between two seasons, unwilling to let go of their summer leaves, but hurried on to fall by cooler nights and northerly breezes. It was only a matter of time before the trees were powerless to fight against it. She wondered if anyone else noticed the subtle change from fresh, summer green to golden, vintage tint. Probably not. She felt like the trees – stuck between two ages instead of two seasons – unwilling to let go of her youthful vigor yet rushed toward death by – by what? Not by age. By time? Fate? Nature, even? She rested her hands on her baby bump.

"And Marshall's gonna live here all alone … by himself after you …" Bea closed her eyes.

"After I die?"

Bea stared down at the porch. "Yes … sorry."

Penelope shrugged. "He won't be alone. He'll have Toby and Eden and you. You'll come visit … a lot, I hope."

"You know I will." Bea wiped her eyes.

"I know you will." Penelope sighed. "Maybe you'll even learn to like it out here."

"No, I won't."

"Yeah," Penelope said. "You're right. You won't." She sat on the top step and patted the plank beside her.

"It is pretty up here," Bea said, sitting next to Penelope. "I'll admit that much. I wouldn't want to live here, but it's the kind of place I could maybe learn to like visiting."

Penelope laughed. "That's the kind of thing my mom used to say about cities. 'I could never live there, but I sure like to visit.'"

"Yeah, well, your mom also liked camping."

"So do I."

"I know. I won't hold it against you."

"You'll help Marshall, won't you? And Eden?" Penelope looked down at her belly. She ran her hand along the curve, holding back her tears.

Bea scooted closer.

Penelope smiled as she felt a warm touch on her shoulder.

"You know I will," Bea whispered. "You don't have to ask. But I'm not excited about having to trek all the way out here to do it."

Penelope nodded. "It's just … I'm trying to make sure that everything … everyone is ready." She forced a smile. "You know … planning like you told me to."

"Yeah. Like I told you to." Bea's voice sounded hollow as she cleared her throat.

Penelope looked across the yard. The sun was beginning to set behind the city. The chill of night was running close to the heels of a warm day – a harbinger of winter.

"You know," Bea said, "even with all this planning, none of us will be ready to let you go. Even though we know it's coming. Planning ahead just makes *things* easier … arrangements, logistics, expenses. It doesn't actually make *it* easier … the not-having-you-here. I won't have a friend anymore."

"You'll have Marshall." Penelope sniffled.

She turned her back to the sunset and leaned against the railing. Marshall was inside with Toby, unpacking … arranging … nesting. She closed her eyes and took in a deep breath. How many sunsets did she have left? "Do you think Marshall will find someone after I'm gone?"

"Do you think I will?"

Penelope didn't know the answer to either of those questions. There were a lot of things she would never know. Things and people she once enjoyed believing she *would* know. Like a future Mr. Bea. She once believed she'd get to know him and Bea's children. Even her *own* child.

"Probably not," Bea said, answering her own question. "It won't be long before I'll be an old spinster."

Penelope laughed. "An old spinster? Now who's old-fashioned?"

"Seriously, why hasn't anyone loved me enough to want to spend their time with me? Why hasn't anybody ever wanted to marry me?"

"Bea …" Penelope turned serious. "Have *you* met anyone *you* wanted to marry?"

Bea was quiet for a moment. "No. But do you think I will? And what if I do, and he doesn't feel the same way? I'll just be Eden's old spinster aunt … no family of my own, no best friend."

"You'll have so much freedom. And you have so much *time*. You'll find someone."

"You think so?"

"If effort has anything to do with it … yes."

Penelope glanced back at the setting sun. The rays were just touching the rooftops. Only a pale, thin line separated heaven from Earth. That's where she was right now – that pale, thin line. One foot on solid, familiar ground, the other reaching into the unknown, no matter how much she wanted to stay put, toward a future growing ever shorter. One day, not long from now, she'd feel the abyss with the tip of her toes.

Chapter 59

Marshall's Annual Deathday Diary Entry

Date: October 10, 2045

Entry No. 11

Ken's trying to sell me on this new countdown app – unimaginatively called Countdown. Swears by it. He's constantly popping his head into my office, wasting time by telling me how much time he has left. And he always seems really happy about it too, which defies all reason and logic. He must realize the numbers are getting smaller. I'm constantly trying to forget how little time I have left with Penelope, and Ken is joyously counting down his days. Anyway, as he was eating my deathday cake, and I watched little particles of crumbs accumulate on the corners of his mouth and launch into the air at each plosive, he explained all about how my deathday is the perfect day to start using Countdown.

"It's got down-to-the-minute accurate timing, Marshall! Down to the fucking minute! That's new, yah know." Then he laughed again.

But I don't know what was so funny, and he simply shoved another bite of cake in his mouth. Anyway, I did know that there's 'down-to-the-fucking-minute accurate timing.' I might rather have liked not to know exactly what time I am going to die, in addition to exactly what day, but the notification came through my Enrollment app, and there's no unseeing it. My time? 11:58 p.m. I will get most of my last day. Sunrise. Sunset. All three meals. I let Penelope know about the update as soon as I found out. She turned her notifications off.

To be frank, her deathday (Penelope's) is on my mind a lot more these days than my own, even today. I have so many more deathdays. So many more days than she does, and so many are going to be without her. The difference between the number of days is actually quite stark. I've got 17,534 days to her 114. That's 17,420 days without Penelope. This is my last deathday with Penelope. This is the last ADDE I'll write while Penelope is still here, but I have a feeling I won't be done writing about her for a long, long time. I have a feeling I'll be counting down the days until I get to see her again, provided that's what happens. I hope it is, but no one really knows, do they? All this talk about heaven waiting and expected ends. It's just talk. Just hope. What does it say about us that our hopes are pinned on something completely unknown and unknowable?

Lately, I've been wondering why I enrolled at all. It's not like I was ever particularly curious about when I'd die. I wasn't scared, either. I was indifferent, I suppose. Dying was a paradoxical fact of life. An abstract thing I knew would happen someday, but that didn't seem immediate enough to be relevant. I think I've figured it out. If I enrolled, I thought I would be more like everyone else. I would fit in. I would have something to talk about. We would have something in common. I thought it would be nice to know what that felt like, to have something in common with someone, with lots of someones. So I enrolled. But the truth is, I'm still different. I just know exactly how long I'll be different, in this life, on this planet. It doesn't matter that I enrolled. It probably wouldn't even matter if I pretended like I was happy I enrolled. Ken would still make fun of me (at least, I think he's making fun of me) most of the time. He might stop, might think I was more like him, if I bought into all that Deathday Celebration stuff the way everyone else does. Do Something Deadly and all that. His deathday, Ken's, was a couple weeks ago. He was in my office when his Life Planner app went off.

"What does it say?" I asked.

He smiled, looking down at his phone. "'It's your deathday: Do something deadly.'"

That must be a thing now, because just a few hours ago, my app went off and advised the same thing. 'It's your deathday: Do Something Deadly.' It's like a whole movement now. This idea that we should all take a big risk every year on our deathday. Silly, though. Everyone knows there's no such thing as risk, not anymore. Not really -- not real risks. Anything you do that might've killed you even ten years ago is just a thrill ride now, with more automated safety features than I care to count. Or, more often, it's just AR. I guess Ken's wife was ahead of the game. She sort of had that idea when she took him bungee … fucking … jumping on his deathday last year. Anyway, I didn't do anything deadly today. Not on purpose. I got in a car at one point this afternoon, and a decade or two ago that could've been fatal. So that was my celebration.

Anyway, what I really want to say is this. Today, I ate deathday cake. Penelope made it for me. And she won't get to make me another one. Next time I write an ADDE, Penelope will be gone.

Signed: Marshall Milton, Participant No. MM10102093

Chapter 60

Marshall, 4 November 2045, Age 28, T-minus 45

"Stop it!" Penelope laughed, wiping away the icing Marshall had just playfully dabbed on her nose. "This is serious."

"Sorry," Marshall replied. It was hard for him to resist the temptation to do it again. He liked hearing her laugh – that surprised, uninhibited laugh she often had when something caught her off guard.

"I don't think you are." Penelope smiled.

Marshall tried not to smile. "I'm not."

His grin broke through his stony façade. He wasn't sorry. He wanted to hear her laugh as many times as he could before the sound existed only in his memory. Penelope had offered to record a memorial graph, if he wanted her to – maybe Eden would want to see it someday – but it felt a little too much like leaving a ghost behind. Marshall was glad she had decided against it. A memorial graph would have been too painful. Too much like having her with him without actually having her here. A memory was better. It offered no illusion of presence. In fact, a memory was proof of the past, and that was healthy. Because it was true – or would be in a very short time. He should work on accepting her fate, since there was no changing it, no stopping it.

"Well as I was saying." Penelope's tone was didactic. "You don't want to use an electric mixer for this part … the old-fashioned way works much better. Your arm'll get tired and that's when you'll know you're done mixing … unless there're still lumps. Then you'll have to do better. Mix the batter more."

"And what if my arm is too tired but there're still lumps?"

Penelope dipped in her finger and tasted it. She smiled. "You have two arms." She waved her hand in the air. "Switch arms."

"Oh." That was simple enough. Marshall just might get the hang of this. Weren't people always saying easy things were a piece of cake?

"People like to say *easy as pie* or *piece of cake*," Penelope said as if reading his mind. "But they're talking about eating the pie or cake, not baking it."

Marshall's heart sank. He liked to cook. He was good at it. But cooking and baking were not the same. Would he get the hang of it before Penelope was gone? He wanted to bake birthday cakes for their daughter. He wanted to teach her how to bake when she was old enough. It was a way to keep Penelope alive in their lives.

Keep Penelope alive …

It hit him all at once that when Eden celebrated her birthdays, Penelope, her mother, wouldn't be there. When Eden learned to bake, Penelope, her mother, wouldn't be there. Penelope wouldn't be there for any of it.

He had accepted this on an intellectual level, of course, but the gravity of the knowledge hadn't settled on his awareness until this moment.

"I don't want to do this without you," Marshall whispered. The words escaped before he was aware of saying them.

"What? Bake a cake?" Penelope kept stirring, her eyes glued to the bowl.

"Bake a cake. Raise a child." Marshall sighed. "Live."

Penelope stopped stirring and allowed the spoon to clink against the side of the bowl. "Marshall." She looked serious. "You have to. You have no choice. Your deathday is decades away. Our daughter needs you." She took a step closer and grabbed his hand. "You *have* to." She took a deep breath. "For me … for Eden. Take her camping, please. Take a few risks. Live and *love* living. Teach her everything. You have the time … I don't. You can't use what time you have left wishing that I were still here … that wouldn't be healthy for you or Eden. You two can do so much … see so much … and love and live *so* much. Please, Marshall, live for our child … live for us. You'll get to meet her. Hug her and kiss her and teach her. You're so lucky."

Had she just told him he was lucky? Him, a man who fell madly in love with a woman he wanted to spend the rest of his life with, only to discover the rest of *her* life amounted to mere months?

Marshall stared at Penelope without saying anything. Her hair was pulled back and mostly hidden beneath a pink bandana with a white, paisley pattern. Her sleeves were rolled up to her elbows, which was a good thing for her shirt, because her arms were speckled with flour and flecks of cake batter. Her stomach bulged beneath her apron. She would forever be the most beautiful woman he had ever seen.

"You're beautiful," he whispered.

Penelope rubbed her cheek with the back of her hand. "Ah, stop it."

Chapter 61

Penelope, 2 January 2046, Age 27, T-minus 1

The tree was still up, though Penelope's last Christmas had come and gone. Ken had made sure to commemorate the occasion with an *Our Last Christmas Together* ornament. Never mind that this was also their *first* Christmas together. No one had bought them an ornament for that. Ken's gift remained in the original box, shoved into a corner of the attic to be forgotten.

"It would," Marshall had vowed, "never grace the bough of a Christmas tree in my house."

Penelope sighed and looked out the window. She was trying to translate her most private thoughts into coherent sentences. Snowflakes drifted through the air, reminding her oddly of spring. She had always loved the way the white grace of pear blossoms drifted through the sunlight on a warm day. When she died, she would drift out of this world like a snowflake or a wayward petal, just as her daughter drifted in.

She looked down at the blank paper, full of potential. Who knew how her daughter's life would read, what experiences would fill the pages of her existence. Penelope would never know. The start of the new year marked the last month of her life. She would not see the calendar flip to February. Today was her birthday, cozied-up in the same month as her deathday. The dates actually resided in the same column on the damn calendar – the first Tuesday, and four squares downs, the last Tuesday.

Dearest Eden,

What's going to kill me?

… was her daughter the reason this would be her last birthday? Until enrollment, she'd always believed there'd be about fifty more. She'd had no idea this was her last. She always dreaded turning thirty. A little afraid the decade would make her feel old. Now, she was jealous that she'd never turn thirty or forty.

Perhaps a deathday was actually a celebration of how much life was waiting, not so different from a birthday. The day wasn't to celebrate a beginning, but then again, was it to celebrate an end? What if a deathday was to honor that a person was alive, and the end was years away?

What difference does it make?

Since enrollment, her life had been a series of finalities. Her firsts were also her lasts. Her first and last Christmas with Marshall. Her first and last New Year's Eve with Marshall. Her first and last birthday with Marshall.

Bittersweet – knowing there was more would have made each second sweeter. But for Penelope, the knowing only made each occasion depressing.

This is Mommy's handwriting. My paper, saved from school. My pencil too. All *from my school days. keep these little things close. My hand held this page. I*

Mommy. It felt strange to write it in plain English when she'd never get to hear her daughter say it. Penelope set down the pencil and glanced out the window. Snowflakes still drifted through the air. Time was moving too fast, her days falling away. She wished she could slow it down, or better yet, stop it.

Chapter 62

Penelope, 28 January 2046, Age 27, T-minus 1

Penelope stood next to Bea and Marshall on the precisely coordinated corner of Broad Street and 21st. They watched together as the precisely choreographed traffic whizzed by. Toby sat at their feet. Penelope felt Marshall's gaze on her belly – on their baby. She absent-mindedly ran her hand over the curve of her stomach. They didn't have much time left. Penelope wouldn't allow herself to wonder if her daughter would be her cause of death. If somehow the pregnancy or delivery that would bring their daughter to them would also take her away. The thought tugged at her mind frequently. She was forever working to keep it at bay, at the edge of her consciousness. She was engaged in this mental battle when the panicked voices of fellow pedestrians shook her back to the corner of Broad and 21st. Toby was on his feet, ears alert.

"Somebody do something!" a woman yelled. "Slow down."

A man's voice was next. "Stop it! Stop it!"

Penelope heard a familiar but unplaceable sound. A sort of roar or rumble. She had heard it before, somewhere, sometime. From her peripheral vision, she noticed the movement. It was to her left. A red blur. She turned and watched as an antique car, an older model with a fallible, human driver, sped toward the intersection. The driverless cars, their sensors alert to the danger, parted like the Red Sea to save their own passengers, zipping up the void behind the red car. Marshall moved to push Penelope out of the way, but the angry grill of the red car met her body before his hands could. The screeching of tires and the grinding of metal assailed her with blinding volume. Several people screamed. Bea grabbed Toby's leash and darted to the side. Penelope's eyes widened as the grill of the red car closed in.

Her body catapulted several feet into the street. The red car hissed, its front end crumpled against the pole where she had just been standing. Marshall knelt beside her, taking her hand in his.

"Penelope," he whispered.

She took in a deep breath, and pain radiated up through her back, striking her head. Searching for Marshall's face, all she could see was blackness. She tried to talk, and a warm liquid filled her mouth. "Eden," she managed, gulping. Never had talking been so hard. She felt like she was drowning on dry land.

Her foot, the one so recently on this side of existence, bridged the gap between this life and the next as she stepped across that pale, thin line separating ground from sky, Earth from heaven. She saw herself as a green light drifting across the dark water, peeling away from land and sailing out to sea. Both feet were now planted on the same side of that great divide. There was a weightlessness, a release, a relief. A beginning. And an end.

Chapter 63

Marshall, 30 January 2046, Age 29, T-minus 48

They had emptied her body of the baby. *She* – the baby – would survive, though *she* would need an e-womb for a while. Marshall had struggled to understand how the clear, impersonal, pill-shaped e-womb would provide a more nurturing place to prepare for the world than the warm, dark confines of Penelope's womb. But when he saw his wife just laying there, so still, so lifeless in that hospital bed, he understood. The e-womb was the baby's best chance.

"I'll wait with you," he whispered to Penelope. "I'll sit here. I won't leave." He held her hand, so cool and soft. He rested his head between her neck and shoulder, breathing in the familiar scent of her shampoo. Strands of her hair tickled his nose.

It was early morning when a doctor entered and stood near Eden's e-womb.

"What are you doing for her?" Marshall asked, his face still tucked into Penelope's neck.

"Checking vitals … checking temperature … adjusting IVs."

Marshall looked up and saw the doctor adjusting knobs and wires on the e-womb. "No," Marshall said. "I meant for my wife."

The doctor frowned. "Mr. Milton, there's nothing more we can do –"

"Just a few more hours. Maybe she'll wake up and see our daughter."

The doctor shook his head. "Mr. Milton, your wife will not wake up." He sighed. "I'm sorry, but your wife is brain dead. There's been no neural activity since she arrived. Her body is alive, but that won't last." The doctor placed his hand on Marshall's shoulder. "Maybe this is for the best. She feels no pain … no fear."

Marshall nodded and bowed his head.

He wasn't sure when the doctor left or when Bea arrived. Perhaps he had fallen asleep. Bea was now snoozing in a chair across the room with her head against the wall. He stood and glanced down at his wife. He sighed – her chest was still rising and falling. She was still alive. He counted her breaths – one, two, three, four –

Bea stirred.

"How's Toby?" Marshall asked.

"Confused and lonely."

"Thanks for taking him home."

"Of course." Bea pulled her chair over next to Marshall and rested her head on the armrest. "I was surprised you didn't want him here."

"I do," Marshall whispered. "Want him here, I mean. But I don't want him to see me so … sad." Marshall sighed – that wasn't the right word. *Sad* was not deep enough or heavy enough or hollow enough. What word was? *Empty? Distraught?*

There wasn't a single word that encompassed how he felt. He felt like the whole world was caving in on itself. Like there was nothing but a black hole. Toby wasn't trained to fix black holes.

Marshall kept talking just to fill the void. "It would make him feel like he wasn't doing his job. And he's such a good boy. I don't want him to feel like he's not doing his job. He does a good job."

Bea nodded. "He does," she whispered. "He's a good dog."

Marshall stared down at Penelope as she took in a long, raspy breath. Her eyes were closed, and her body seemed to be working hard just to breathe. One breath and then another and then another. And then … nothing.

Penelope's chest remained still.

Bea stood.

Marshall felt the weight of Bea's warm hand on his shoulder. He waited. He watched Penelope's chest for any signs of a breath. He placed a hand just below her nose, silently pleading for a soft, warm exhale. Nothing. Quietness. Stillness. A darkened hospital room with a lonely husband hovering over his wife's body, and their tiny baby encapsulated in some *thing*. He waited.

Breathe, Penelope, please.

Nothing.

"I'll get somebody," Bea whispered.

He felt her hand lift, heard the soft footsteps that carried her to the door. A click and Marshall knew he was alone. He sat beside his wife's bed and listened to his own breathing. What he wouldn't give to hear hers.

The moment had passed too quickly, and Marshall found himself wishing for just one more second, even of that hellish purgatory, that excruciating wait for her to breathe. At least she was there. At least she was with him. At least her hand was warm in his. At least he had hope.

But now, she was gone.

And he was alone.

Chapter 64

Marshall, 7 February 2046, Age 29, T-minus 48

The service was over. Everyone had left. Even Bea had finished saying her goodbyes.

"It was just like her," Bea had said, "to die in an accident. Who dies in an accident anymore? Or gets *buried?* Old-fashioned to the end."

Toby and Marshall remained. They stood at the edge, looking down at the greedy ground, so eager to claim Penelope as its own. The gravedigger hummed complacently behind them, waiting for its sensors to indicate all living, biological organisms had cleared the area, so it could begin its indifferent and efficient replacing of the earth.

Bleary-eyed, Marshall stared into the vacuous hole. Toby growled and Marshall thought he saw a few yellow petals drift down into the blackness, landing on the lid of the coffin. He held his daughter in the crook of one arm, used the opposite hand to rub his eyes, and looked again. Several small, yellow petals now rested delicately on the lid. Marshall glanced up, and there, standing on the other side of the grave, was Everett, a bouquet of forsythia plumes in his hand. "They're about to be in season."

Everett blew his nose. His eyes were red. The two men looked at each other from across the gaping hole.

Marshall felt like the gravedigger had dug a hole in his heart, instead of the ground – hollowed it right out. "I know," Marshall said.

"Can I leave them here? For her?"

Marshall nodded.

"I honestly didn't think it would be so painful when she …" Everett rested the forsythias on the headstone at the edge of the grave. "Is that Penelope's baby?"

Marshall glanced at his daughter, then down at the casket now cocooning his wife. He nodded.

"Can I see her?" Everett's voice sounded like the rustling of dry leaves skittering across pavement … raspy, hoarse.

Marshall walked around the rectangular hole and stood next to Everett.

Toby didn't follow.

Everett gasped. "What's her name?"

"Eden."

Everett mouthed the name. "Penelope didn't want to enroll. I encouraged her." He paused. "Pressured her. Then I left her." He shook his head and chuckled a sad laugh. He looked at the baby again. "I wanted someone with more time."

Marshall didn't respond. He knew it was his turn to say something, but he didn't know what to say.

"Was it worth it?" Everett asked. "The pain you're in now … was the love worth it?"

"Yes," Marshall replied without hesitation. He smiled at the baby tucked in his arm.

"You're a better man than I am, Marshall," Everett said after a few moments.

Marshall thought so too, but somehow understood that he shouldn't say it.

Everett took a shuddery breath, offered a weak laugh laden with regret. He turned and quietly made his way across the vast, green lawn, the wind blowing his jacket behind him.

Marshall watched him walk away. The forsythias made a slight rustling sound as the wind blew.

The gravedigger hummed.

The forsythias slid down the headstone, coming to rest, prone, in the grass. Marshall aimed for the parking lot. As he topped the hill and spotted his car, he heard the gravedigger whiz to life, and felt the first thud of earth land atop Penelope's casket.

Chapter 65

Bea, 1 September 2046, Age 27, T-minus 29

Bea scanned the crowded bar for a man named *Sully.* She had found him on *Together Forever.* After searching each face for the likeness posted on the screen, her eyes landed on a man who was also scanning the crowd. She smiled. It was him, and he seemed to recognize her. His face brightened and he waved.

"Nice to see a familiar face in a sea of strangers," she said.

He laughed. "Nice to see *you* in person."

They found an empty table and sat.

Sully was handsome in his crewneck sweater, which was appropriate for the crisp night air. His brown hair was unkempt, but clean, and he wore a wholesome smile.

Cute.

Bea could definitely look at this guy every day. His appearance didn't stray far from the graphs and photos he'd used on the app. A bit shorter than she'd imagined, maybe, but that was forgivable.

"I hope you don't mind … I ordered us drinks," he said.

"Oh, thank you." The drink was not her concern.

The waitress placed the glasses on the table and scanned Sully's phone. He added funds, and she smiled as she walked away.

Bea placed the drink to her lips, and Sully touched her hand.

"Wait," he said, tilting his glass toward her. "To us!"

To us? Bea raised a brow. Hadn't they just met? What was this … *to us* … stuff? Was that supposed to sound seductive? Was this another guy whose goal was to tally up one-night stands? Her last date had been only twenty years old and T-minus 3. It hadn't taken her long to realize that *he'd* just wanted to sleep with as many women as possible before his deathday. What a waste of a perfectly good evening. Her *Life Planner* app was on her case, but wasn't *to us* just a little premature?

She wasn't sure what to say, so she didn't say anything. She tipped her glass and her head. The golden lady slid down the back of her throat. The warmth spread across her chest and into her arms.

"You know what appealed to me when I first came across your profile?"

Bea sat back, ready for her ego to be stroked, wondering if he would say it had been her eyes or her smile – those were the two most popular. She didn't believe it most of the time, not really, but hearing it never got old.

"Your deathday," Sully said, leaning back.

"My …" – Bea sat up a little straighter – "… what?"

"Your deathday," he repeated. He leaned forward.

Bea could smell his spicy cologne.

"You're my chosen one, Bea."

"Chosen one for what?" Bea asked, placing her hands on the edge of the table.

"Fate? God?" He chuckled. "The universe?" Sully reached across the table and clasped her hands. He gently pulled them to the center of the table.

Bea was too shocked to snatch them away.

"Heaven is waiting," he whispered.

Bea cringed.

"And I've been waiting too. I've been looking *so* long for the right girl to go with me."

"Go with you where?"

He winked. "To heaven."

His grin made something crawl up her back and she shivered. "To heaven? And … why does that make *me* your chosen one?"

She hid her hands under the table.

Sully laughed and the echo screeched through her ears. "We have the *same* deathday! The exact same deathday. We can spend our time here together, and then we'll depart together, and then arrive in heaven together. It's perfect. It was meant to be. We'll never be apart. We'll be *together forever,* just like the app says."

Why were all the handsome ones always so weird? Bea rubbed her nose and sniffed. She glanced around and shook her head. Whatever happened to a drink and a couple of dances? C*hosen one?* Was he nuts*?*

Her date a few weeks ago hadn't been much better. He was thirty-five, T-minus 10, and *super* morbid. *He'd* wanted to build an entire romance around death. "We can find our burial plots together," he had said. "Write each other's requiems and epitaphs and obituaries instead of wedding vows." And he was obsessed with Poe – like wanted to *be* Poe.

Bea glared at Sully. She thought about the Poe-wannabe and the horny T-minus-3-year-old. She glanced at her phone and frowned at the *Together Forever* app, which was blinking at her. The people in the bar seemed happy. But were they happy … any of 'em? Did knowing make their lives any better? Did it make *hers* any better?

"Excuse me," she said, standing. She draped her purse over her shoulder and smiled. "Ladies room." She raised her brows and left the table.

The restrooms were near the front of the bar. So was the exit. Bea glanced back briefly as she stepped onto the crowded sidewalk. She took in a deep breath and allowed the damp air to caress her face. A few driverless cars sped by.

At Marshall's it was probably quiet. Here in the city, things were unnaturally alive and awake, heedless of the Earth's rotation or the difference between sunlight and moonlight.

God, I sound like Penelope.

She looked around at the automated city – driverless cars in sync with their perfectly choreographed dance. Graphs, translucent and insubstantial, popped up here and there, waving for only a moment before vanishing once a conversation had ended. Music from the bar echoed between the buildings. Right now, she would have preferred crickets. Were there crickets in the city? Probably not.

She pulled her device from her purse, opened the *Together Forever* app, and scrolled through a few photos. So many faces of all ages and colors. Her thoughts flew to Penelope. Her finger hovered over the screen. And then she did something Penelope never would have believed. She deleted the app.

"Bea?"

She turned and frowned.

"Are you okay?" Sully asked.

"Sorry, I –"

"I thought you had to use the ladies room. It's, uh … inside." Sully gestured to the door.

He seemed good-natured, but Bea's heart rested somewhere else. "I know," she replied. "But I have to go."

Sully shook his head and laughed. "I think I got the message … back in there." His eyes lowered, and his smile disappeared.

His features were handsome, and the look they wore so pitiful that she almost wanted to stay just to be nice. But then she remembered that the most attractive thing about her to him was when she was going to die.

"Thanks for the drink." She walked down the street and summoned her car. When it pulled up, she sat on the operator side. "Penelope's," she stated.

Bea pulled out her key and unlocked the door. The house was quiet and dark. She tiptoed up the stairs to Eden's room and peeked in. Marshall was reading to the sleepy baby he held in his arms. Bea inched her way in and sat on the floor.

"*Goodnight Moon,*" she whispered. "I love this story." She rested her head against Eden's crib.

Marshall continued reading. He finished and smiled at his sleeping daughter.

Bea stood, placing a plush lamb in the crib.

Marshall gently laid the sleeping Eden near the toy. He smiled at Bea.

She smiled back, now seeing what Penelope must've seen the whole time – a *real* family. Bea had been looking for it in all the wrong people, all the wrong places. Marshall and Eden – they were her family now. Penelope had given them to her. It wasn't Bea's plan. It was better. It was Penelope's.

Epilogue

Marshall, 30 January 2051, Age 34, T-minus 42

Marshall and Bea worked long and hard on the cake, though they both knew it could never compete with one of Penelope's culinary masterpieces.

Toby waited patiently for them to spill something and seemed disappointed when they didn't.

"We should've started practicing weeks ago," Bea said. "What the hell were we thinking? Today's her birthday. Coupla' dummies if you ask me." She leaned against the counter, looking defeated.

Marshall frowned at the lopsided cake now drooping to the right. "It'll still taste good." He smiled a half-grin. "I hope."

"Will it?" Bea pushed herself away from the counter. She pinched off a piece.

"You'll ruin it!" Marshall said, playfully slapping away her hand.

"Ruin it?" She chuckled. "Are you for real? Are we looking at the same thing? We ruined it a long time ago." She popped the pinch of cake into her mouth and hummed. "Yum. It's actually not half bad … now, where's the recipe for the meatloaf? I want to get started on it."

"Here …" Marshall pulled Penelope's cookbook from the shelf to expose his copy of *Joy of Cooking*. A piece of paper drifted to the floor, and Bea picked it up.

"Is this the recipe?" she asked, unfolding it. She read the first few lines before handing it to Marshall.

"This is not." Marshall stared at the letter. "What is this?"

Dearest Eden,
This is Mommy's handwriting. My paper, saved from school. My pencil too. All

Marshall sat at the kitchen table where Bea had placed the cake adorned with five candles. He stared at the lopsided thing and sighed. He gently smoothed out the creased letter.

So much of life is beautiful, my baby. Moonlight and love and friendship and learning. Even when things feel less than beautiful, when you feel sick or afraid or guilty or confused, don't despair. These things are all living, too. They mean you're alive. I loved living. And I loved your father

Marshall felt the familiar sting building behind his eyes, the warmth threatening to spill over the brim of his lids. He pulled in a deep breath, steeling himself against his emotions. Penelope was alive once and not that long ago. He could sense her in the tender words. He could almost touch her vitality seeping from her fingers through the pencil. He could smell her in the air that hovered in the kitchen. The aroma of chocolate – a familiarity and warmth that he missed.

your heart. I wish I could meet you. How strange that you have grown inside me, that we have never for an instant been apart, and yet, I will never hold you. I wish you could know me. The hands that would have braided your hair, buttoned your jacket, held your own little hand.

Marshall glanced over at Bea and for a moment, he thought he could see Penelope standing next to her. Her hair was pulled back and tucked under that pink bandana, her arms coated in flour. She was smiling. Her ghost seemed to be alive – everywhere.

"What's it say?" Bea stepped up to the table.

Marshall read, "'My biggest regret is that I will leave as you arrive.'" Marshall set the letter on the table.

Bea held it, and her eyes filled with tears. "She left a letter?" she whispered, reading.

on this page. I hope you will forgive me for not being there with you. My biggest regret is that I will leave as you arrive. It was never my intention. I feel selfish sometimes. That is one thing always to remember, Eden: People do selfish and foolish and sometimes bad things. Forgive them, okay? They are not really selfish or foolish or bad. They are human. You are too. I will love you forever and ever.

Marshall nodded.

Bea wiped her eyes. "Will you let Eden read it?"

"When she's older."

"Birthday!" Eden yelled, running into the kitchen, her grandmother right behind her. Eden's eyes landed on the hideously deformed cake. "Yum!" She climbed onto her chair and placed her hands on the table. Her grandma tucked a napkin into Eden's shirt collar.

"Thanks, Mom," Marshall said, lighting the candles as they sang.

Eden giggled.

His mother smiled.

"Birthday girl gets the first bite," Marshall said, slicing off a generous piece and placing it in front of her. "How does it feel to be so old?"

"Five is nothing to joke about," Bea said, wiping away another tear and sniffling.

"You have to take the first bite, Eden," her grandma said, handing a plate to Bea. "No one can eat any cake until you do, birthday girl."

Eden took a bite and crumbs tumbled down both sides of her mouth. "Mmmm." She hummed.

Her grandma tousled her hair.

Marshall smiled across the table at Bea.

After the cake and the balloons and the presents, the day faded into evening, and Eden was a year older. Another year without Penelope. Marshall stood at his daughter's bedroom window and stared at the night sky. He listened to the sound of Eden sleeping and looked up at the moon. The high, wispy clouds looked like the feathery-frost Old Man Winter had painted when Marshall slept on wintry nights as a boy. He would wake and trace the delicate ice crystals on the other side of the pane with his finger, and his mother would tell him to try to memorize the way it looked – winter's artwork – because it would melt as soon as the sun found the glass, no matter how cold it was outside. And Marshall thought of Penelope and all the beautiful and temporary things that made life worth living – flower blossoms and icicles and sunrises.

Marshall looked at his daughter, sleeping soundly in her new, big-girl bed. He looked up at Bea, rocking in a chair across the room, and at Toby, graying now, asleep on a rug at the foot of the bed. He had stopped counting down his days. He had stopped counting time. From Penelope, he had learned to start living. And he knew that Penelope was not dead – not really. He had read somewhere that time could be measured according to the good that unfolded – the good one achieved. With time, it was quality that mattered, not quantity. If that were true, Penelope would live forever – her good timeless, her time limitless.

She lived on in this little girl. The little girl who wore her mother's blonde curls and smiled her mother's warm smile and delighted in things Marshall never would have taken notice of before – the plushness of a certain soft blanket, the number of airplanes streaking their white tails across a blue sky, the yellow of the forsythias in the garden outside.

The breeze rustled the barren branches of the cherry tree keeping vigil outside Eden's window. In just a few months, its branches would be lush with delicate, pale pink petals. Petals that would drop and float away, replaced with summer's green leaves.

Eden stirred. "Read to me, Daddy?" she whispered. "Mama's favorite poem. Please?"

Marshall sat on Eden's bed. He opened the book and took in a long, deep breath. "'Let us go then, you and I, when the evening is spread out against the sky …'"

A little breath of a breeze disturbed the cherry tree again, and a pale, yellow petal drifted down from the ceiling, landing on the page. Marshall and Bea looked up wonderingly.

Toby thumped his tail gently against the floor.

Eden smiled.

AUTHOR'S NOTES

Readers will likely notice the pervasive presence of literary references throughout this work, especially to classic American and British writers. It is safe to say that much of the literature I have studied and taught influences my writing in a myriad of ways.

Joy of Cooking

My Grandma Stuart presented me with the *Joy of Cooking* as a wedding gift. On the inside cover, I found a note written in her pretty, cursive handwriting. The first meal I ever made was in her kitchen in Michigan. To be honest, I find very little joy in cooking today. But I do love to eat.

Tess of the d'Urbervilles Thomas Hardy *(1840 - 1928)*

Tess of the d'Urbervilles, published in 1891, was considered graphic and initially censored. Today, it is one of the oldest classics in the civilized world. I recently stumbled across the passage that is referenced in this book. It perfectly expresses my wonderment at the phenomena of life and death. Tess's fear of death can be compared to Penelope's. Angel Clare deserts Tess because of her past. And Everett deserts Penelope because of her future or lack thereof. With this thought, we must ask ourselves how often our lives are directed by another, our happiness dependent on another, another who can turn the tides of our existence from bliss to tragedy in a single heartbeat.

Paradise Lost John Milton *(1608 - 1674)*

It's no coincidence that Marshall shares his last name with this poet. John Milton explores man's first disobedience, as when Adam tastes the forbidden fruit from the Tree of Knowledge. Penelope was happy and living a blissful existence when she was given the unholy knowledge of her deathday. It is only then that her journey through hell begins and life as she knew it ends. Is knowledge a power or a curse? Is ignorance bliss? When is it better simply not to know? These are some of the concepts I explore throughout my novel.

My junior year was a tumultuous one. At the start of the school term, my family moved from Pennsylvania to Virginia. Perhaps for that reason, much of what I read during that time has remained fresh in my mind. It occurred to me that perhaps that is also why I enjoy teaching high school English, particularly American literature.

The Love Song of J. Alfred Prufrock T.S. Eliot *(1888 - 1965)*

Written in 1911, the poem was published in 1915 and again in 1917. T.S. Eliot's speaker explores his anxieties, insecurities, and inner life. The refrain *"there will be time"* stresses his romantic hesitation and early regrets. How often do we assume we have all the time in the world to prepare for our future? We have time to fall in love. Time to finish college. Time to have children. Then one day, we awake and discover that time has escaped us. That time is behind us. Time has completely forsaken Penelope, and she feels cheated and robbed.

The Crucible Arthur Miller *(1915 - 2005)*

Many writings in American literature portray yellow as synonymous with decay and corruption. *The Crucible*, published in 1953, describes the horrors of the Salem witch trials during the 1690's as a way to explore the perils and fallout of McCarthyism. During the trials, more than two hundred were accused. Of the thirty convicted, nineteen were hanged. Arthur Miller wrote *The Crucible* to advocate for tolerance and warn against mass hysteria. The symbolic significance of the yellow bird Abigail claims is Mary Warren's spirit sent to torment those in the courtroom represents how corrupt and decayed the court has become. The color yellow is significant to Penelope for different reasons. The color follows her throughout the novel and becomes her safe haven as she is threatened by the dark shadows, which Penelope associates with the Grim Reaper.

The Great Gatsby F. Scott Fitzgerald *(1896 - 1940)*

Fitzgerald's description of Myrtle's smoldering energy and the idea that we can't live forever stuck with me. The notion that *we should take our chances while we have them* is pivotal throughout my story. Yellow plays a significant symbolic role in Fitzgerald's novel … Gatsby's yellow car, the yellow yolk inside an egg's gleaming, white shell, the yellow center of a daisy amid its pure, white petals … all symbols of a hidden corruption. For Penelope, the color yellow means something different. The yellow forsythias she loves so dearly are harbingers of spring, signaling a renewal and rebirth, ideas that appeal to Penelope as the end of her life grows ever closer.

The Yellow Wallpaper Charlotte Perkins Gilman *(1860 - 1935)*

In 1892, Charlotte Gilman used her story to reveal how easily our world and society's expectations can imprison us. How everyday life can morph into something threatening, something that punishes. In the yellow wallpaper of her room, an unnamed narrator finds hidden patterns, describing them as hideous and revolting. She believes a woman is trapped behind this suffocating design. This hidden figure represents the narrator's inner self, urging her to be free and escape her societally and medically imposed prison. In many respects, Penelope is trying to escape her own prison, the one she entered the day she enrolled. She never wanted to enroll, fearing what knowing would bring. Why do we step into situations even when we know we should run in the other direction?

The Raven Edgar Allan Poe *(1809-1849)*

Poe wrote *The Raven* while his wife was suffering with tuberculosis. Poe knew she was dying. His speaker in *The Raven* grieves the death of his lost love, Lenore. Marshall's life becomes dreary with the loss of Penelope. The poem foreshadows Marshall's loss of his first and only love. In many ways, Marshall and Penelope grieved her death together while they waited for their daughter to arrive. Throughout this book, the concept of life over death rings vividly with one overarching question … *is it worth knowing the hour of our death?*

Since my early days, I have been smitten with the ethereal quality of moonlight. I once spent an evening near a lake, staring at the moon and studying its reflection on the water. I searched for the darkest fields just to see them bathed in moonlight without the interference of city lights. Until they crossed the rainbow bridge, I enjoyed years of pre-dawn, moonlit walks with my dogs, Jack and Sadie, watching our shadows follow us along the street. As our time together ebbed and I became aware that our walks were numbered, those precious moments seemed even more so, flavored with the bittersweet knowledge that any walk could be our last.

Look Down, Fair Moon Walt Whitman *(1819 - 1892)*

The moon is a powerful symbol in religion, literature, and art. From the beginning of man to the end, the moon will always carry a divine power of mysticism and awe. Marshall's first real experience with moonlight is one of wonder and amazement. And it is something that he found with Penelope. Through his love for the most beautiful woman in the world, Marshall experiences everything as if it were new and perfect.

The first two lines of this poem express this awe and seem innocuous, promising even, as if each word evokes an image of peace, beauty. But before the end of the second line, readers realize the scene is not beautiful but gruesome, peaceful only in that the violence has ended. All that remains is the gore. This juxtaposition speaks of Marshall's experience – everything with Penelope feels so perfect and right – but a grim revelation is brewing. When this poem occurs to him, Marshall almost senses the truth, but he pushes it away; he resists. He doesn't want to see. He doesn't want to know. He doesn't like the way the poem ends.

Travels with Charley: In Search of America John Steinbeck (1902 - 1968)

Steinbeck's paradoxical observation about progress and destruction in America profoundly awakens even the most wary reader. What society deems as progress may not always be. Penelope and Marshall stand together and stare at progress – a leveled forest. Ancient ruins that are only partially standing were once glorified as something wonderful, something to be proud of. What we create today will be gone tomorrow. Are today's achievements always tomorrow's ruins?

Maybe we should take a step back, slow down and enjoy the buzzing of a bee, the whisper of a breeze, the march of puffy clouds. Must we know everything?

Amanda Sue Creasey

Amanda is a high school English teacher, freelance writer, and doting dog mom of two. She's a member of James River Writers, the Poetry Society of Virginia, and the Virginia Outdoor Writers Association. She spent five years volunteering at Richmond Animal League. When she's not teaching or writing, you can find Amanda walking, hiking, or paddleboarding with her dogs, running, or traveling the country.

Amanda has written since she could hold a pencil with about forty journals and diaries to her name. *An Expected End* is her debut novel. Her work has appeared in *Chicken Soup for the Soul*, and her poetry, outdoor journalism, and nature photography have earned recognition from the Poetry Society of Virginia and Virginia Outdoor Writers Association.

She earned an undergraduate degree in German, English, and secondary education from Michigan State University. She holds a graduate degree in creative writing from the University of Denver.

You can sign up for her newsletter online.

https://amandasuecreasey.com
https://amandasuecreasey.substack.com
Instagram @Amanda_Sue_Creasey

Amanda Sue Creasey

The Love Song of J. Alfred Prufrock

T.S. Eliot, published by The Egoist Ltd, 1917

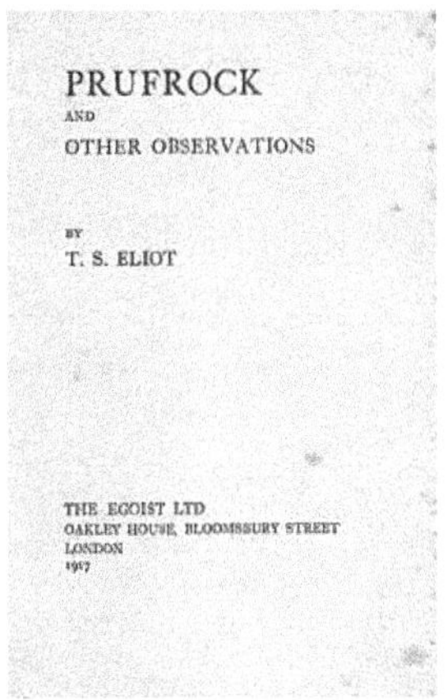

Title page of the collection of T. S. Eliot's poems entitled Prufrock and other observations, published by The Egoist Ltd, 1917

S'io credesse che mia risposta fosse
A persona che mai tornasse al mondo,
Questa flame staria senza piu scosse.
Ma perciocche giammai di questo fondo
Non torno vivo alcun, s'i'odo il vero,
Senza tema d'infamia ti rispondo.

Let us go then, you and I,
When the evening is spread out against the sky
Like a patient etherized upon a table;
Let us go, through certain half-deserted streets,
The muttering retreats
Of restless nights in one-night cheap hotels
And sawdust restaurants with oyster-shells:
Streets that follow like a tedious argument
Of insidious intent
To lead you to an overwhelming question…
Oh, do not ask, "What is it?"
Let us go and make our visit.

In the room the women come and go
Talking of Michelangelo.

The yellow fog that rubs its back upon the window-panes,
The yellow smoke that rubs its muzzle on the window-panes

An Expected End

Licked its tongue into the corners of the evening,
Lingered upon the pools that stand in drains,
Let fall upon its back the soot that falls from chimneys,
Slipped by the terrace, made a sudden leap,
And seeing that it was a soft October night,
Curled once about the house, and fell asleep.
And indeed there will be time
For the yellow smoke that slides along the street,
Rubbing its back upon the window-panes;
There will be time, there will be time
To prepare a face to meet the faces that you meet;
There will be time to murder and create,
And time for all the works and days of hands
That lift and drop a question on your plate;
Time for you and time for me,
And time yet for a hundred indecisions,
And for a hundred visions and revisions,
Before the taking of a toast and tea.

In the room the women come and go
Talking of Michelangelo.

And indeed there will be time
To wonder, "Do I dare?" and, "Do I dare?"
Time to turn back and descend the stair,
With a bald spot in the middle of my hair –
[They will say: "How his hair is growing thin!"]
My morning coat, my collar mounting firmly to the chin,
My necktie rich and modest, but asserted by a simple pin –
[They will say: "But how his arms and legs are thin!"]
Do I dare
Disturb the universe?
In a minute there is time
For decisions and revisions which a minute will reverse.

Amanda Sue Creasey

For I have known them all already, known them all –
Have known the evenings, mornings, afternoons,
I have measured out my life with coffee spoons;
I know the voices dying with a dying fall
Beneath the music from a farther room.
    So how should I presume?

And I have known the eyes already, known them all –
The eyes that fix you in a formulated phrase,
And when I am formulated, sprawling on a pin,
When I am pinned and wriggling on the wall,
Then how should I begin
To spit out all the butt-ends of my days and ways?
    And how should I presume?

And I have known the arms already, known them all –
Arms that are braceleted and white and bare
[But in the lamplight, downed with light brown hair!]
Is it perfume from a dress
That makes me so digress?
Arms that lie along a table, or wrap about a shawl.
    And should I then presume?
    And how should I begin?

. . . . .

Shall I say, I have gone at dusk through narrow streets
And watched the smoke that rises from the pipes
Of lonely men in shirt-sleeves, leaning out of windows? …

I should have been a pair of ragged claws
Scuttling across the floors of silent seas.

. . . . .

And the afternoon, the evening, sleeps so peacefully!
Smoothed by long fingers,
Asleep… tired… or it malingers,
Stretched on the floor, here beside you and me.

An Expected End

Should I, after tea and cakes and ices,
Have the strength to force the moment to its crisis?
But though I have wept and fasted, wept and prayed,
Though I have seen my head [grown slightly bald] brought in upon a platter,
I am no prophet – and here's no great matter;
I have seen the moment of my greatness flicker,
And I have seen the eternal Footman hold my coat, and snicker,
And in short, I was afraid.

And would it have been worth it, after all,
After the cups, the marmalade, the tea,
Among the porcelain, among some talk of you and me,
Would it have been worth while,
To have bitten off the matter with a smile,
To have squeezed the universe into a ball
To roll it toward some overwhelming question,
To say: "I am Lazarus, come from the dead,
Come back to tell you all, I shall tell you all" –
If one, settling a pillow by her head,
    Should say: "That is not what I meant at all.
    That is not it, at all."
And would it have been worth it, after all,
Would it have been worth while,
After the sunsets and the dooryards and the sprinkled streets,
After the novels, after the teacups, after the skirts that trail along the floor –
And this, and so much more? –
It is impossible to say just what I mean!
But as if a magic lantern threw the nerves in patterns on a screen:
Would it have been worth while
If one, settling a pillow or throwing off a shawl,
And turning toward the window, should say:
    "That is not it at all,
    That is not what I meant, at all."

. . . . .

Amanda Sue Creasey

No! I am not Prince Hamlet, nor was meant to be;
Am an attendant lord, one that will do
To swell a progress, start a scene or two,
Advise the prince; no doubt, an easy tool,
Deferential, glad to be of use,
Politic, cautious, and meticulous;
Full of high sentence, but a bit obtuse;
At times, indeed, almost ridiculous –
Almost, at times, the Fool.

I grow old… I grow old…
I shall wear the bottoms of my trousers rolled.

Shall I part my hair behind? Do I dare to eat a peach?
I shall wear white flannel trousers, and walk upon the beach.
I have heard the mermaids singing, each to each.

I do not think that they will sing to me.

I have seen them riding seaward on the waves
Combing the white hair of the waves blown back
When the wind blows the water white and black.

We have lingered in the chambers of the sea
By sea-girls wreathed with seaweed red and brown
Till human voices wake us, and we drown.

Leaves of Grass. Boston: Thayer and Eldridge, year 85 of the States. [1860-61] [Title page].

Look Down Fair Moon

Walt Whitman (1819-1892)

Look down fair moon and bathe this scene,
Pour softly down night's nimbus floods
on faces ghastly, swollen, purple;
On the dead on their backs with arms toss'd wide,
Pour down your unstinted nimbus sacred moon.

Acknowledgements

My gratitude goes out to Indignor House Publishing, Lynn Moon and Shannon Pearson, for investing in my story. Lynn endured hours-long phone conversations with me every week for over a year. Both drove hundreds of miles to my book contract party only for it to be canceled just minutes before it was scheduled to take place due to several positive Covid tests among those who planned to attend.

I extend a heartfelt "thank you" to Brew Craft Bar and Kitchen in Chester, Virginia, for their grace and understanding when said last-second Covid cancellation occurred.

My friends and family deserve my gratitude for their support and encouragement. Many of them, including (but not limited to) my grandparents, parents, and sister Anne, read various drafts in addition to outlines, synopses, and query letters. Anne even adorned her guest bathroom with forsythia blooms once in anticipation of my visit. My cousin, Tommy Stuart, helped me with the math involved in figuring out dates, ages, birthdays, and deathdays, a process in which I often lost myself (and my mind). Many colleagues also played important roles in the completion of this project, and to them, I am grateful. In particular, Kathleen White, Sonya Lee, and Tabitha Strickler were all supportive, helpful, and encouraging. Fellow writers like Lesley St. James and Nikki Forman acted as sounding boards.

The influence of four children permeates much of this book – Annabelle, Charlie, Louise, and Margaux. They helped me gain a sense of what motherhood means, and in their own ways inspired my vision of Eden, as well as Penelope, Bea, and Marshall's love for her. Many things they've noticed or loved or delighted in peppered the pages, reminding me of what makes life beautiful.

A warm, little hand that wants to hold mine.

A baby reaching for me.

The weight of a child on my lap and a book in my hands.

Birthday parties.

Bedtime stories.

The plushness of a certain soft blanket.

Airplanes streaking their white tails across a blue sky.

The color yellow.

Thank you to my first dogs, Jack and Sadie, whose companionship cheered me during my early drafts. I must thank them for their tolerance of my weekly drives to VisArts when I would leave them to participate in a novel-writing class.

And to my current dogs, Nacho and Soda. I thank them for their companionship during the querying and publishing process – and for getting up with me (sometimes getting me up) for my four a.m. writing and revising sessions.

From all four of these dogs, I understand better what a mother feels for her children and was able to imagine how Penelope would feel about leaving Eden motherless.

I owe much to James River Writers, an invaluable community, where I learned about the Visual Arts Center of Richmond novel-writing class, taught at the time by author Matt Cricchio, whose encouragement and guidance were essential. I also owe a debt to the women of that workshop for their feedback, ideas, and enthusiasm.

Thank you, Sara Davis, Rick Ridpath, and Tracey Ridpath, for acting as sensitivity readers. I am particularly grateful to Rick for his consistent encouragement and faith.

Thank you, Stephanie Bourbon, for believing in my story and me when I was starting not to.

Mike Zaweski has my gratitude for his one-of-a-kind original cover art and the effort and time he put into creating it. No AI could have done better.

I am also grateful to my friend and talented photographer, Jamie Wulfekuhle-Zaweski, for my beautiful and dog-inclusive author photos.

Printed in the USA
CPSIA information can be obtained
at www.ICGtesting.com
LVHW090234131023
760742LV00026B/33/J